THE
POISON
APPLES

THE POISON APPLES

LILY ARCHER

Feiwel and Friends
New York

A FEIWEL AND FRIENDS BOOK
An Imprint of Holtzbrinck Publishers

Library of Congress Cataloging-in-Publication Data Available

ISBN-13: 978-0-312-36762-6
ISBN-10: 0-312-36762-7

First Edition: September 2007

10 9 8 7 6 5 4 3 2 1

www.feiwelandfriends.com

For my mother,
who is also my best friend
And for my best friends,
who are also my family

THE POISON APPLES

Prologue

Dear Stepmothers of the World:

As you probably know, more than 50 percent of marriages in America end in divorce. And more than 75 percent of divorced men end up remarrying. That means there are thousands—millions!—of stepmothers out there. Stepmothers in North Dakota. Stepmothers in Florida. Thin stepmothers and fat stepmothers. Rich stepmothers and poor stepmothers. Beautiful stepmothers and ugly stepmothers. Good stepmothers and bad stepmothers.

This book is not about the good stepmothers.

We're not saying good stepmothers don't exist. We know they do. We have faith. We know somewhere out there are stepmothers who love and care about their stepdaughters, stepmothers who give good advice and make goofy jokes and play Monopoly and rent slapstick comedies and take their stepdaughters out for Ethiopian food. In fact, there are probably *thousands* of girls out there with *really stellar* stepmothers.

Those girls are welcome to write a book about how great their stepmothers are.

We are not those girls.

We are the Poison Apples.

We all happen to have Incredibly Evil Stepmothers.

So. To any stepmothers who may feel that the stepmother population is unfairly represented in our book: We don't know what to say to you. Sorry? Honestly we have no idea why we ended up with such horrible stepmothers. Fate? Karma? Bad luck? In any case, we had enough good fate/karma/luck to meet one another at boarding school and form a family. Because the existence of the Poison Apples helped us realize something: You have to take your fate/karma/luck into your own hands. You cannot let the evil stepmother win.

This is our story.

To the good stepmothers: Keep on keepin' on. We hope to meet you someday.

To the bad stepmothers: You have been warned.

Signed,
The Poison Apples

PART
ONE

ONE

Alice Bingley-Beckerman

R. seemed okay at first. She invited me and Dad over for dinner at her apartment on the Upper West Side, and we spent most of the evening just standing around and watching her cook. R. was mesmerizing: she swept around the kitchen in her silk robe and purple eye shadow, stirring bubbling pots of marinara sauce and bending down every few seconds to kiss Godot, her Yorkshire terrier. I could tell Dad was charmed by her. She was beautiful and funny and she kept singing lines from different musicals. Dad would say, "*The Pajama Game*, right?" and she'd shriek, "YES! EXACTLY!" and then he'd sip his beer in this pleased-with-himself way. And it was nice she'd invited me. I guess it was like their first date, so it was a pretty cool move for her to say, "Why don't you bring your daughter?" It made her seem easygoing, sweet, kid-loving. Not at all like a crazy, jealous psychopath, right?

Wrong.

Dad and I were so innocent and unsuspecting. Probably because it was the first date Dad had been on since Mom died. We had no idea that R. Klausenhook—Tony Award–winning actress and darling of the New York theater scene—would turn out to be a bona fide Evil Person. Actually I think Dad still has no idea that R. is a bona fide Evil Person.

Hence the tragedy of my story.

The whole never-ending suckfest (that's what my friend Reena calls it—you'll hear about her later) started two years before, when I was thirteen and my mom died. She had cancer. It was pretty much the worst year of my life. Afterward I had to deal with all my classmates saying: "Oh my God, I'm so sorry. My great-grandmother died last year and it was really hard for me. I totally know what you're going through." I'd want to scream, *Your great-grandmother was ninety-five and living in a nursing home and you saw her three times a year, how could you possibly know what I'm going through—my MOTHER died, you idiot,* but instead I'd smile and nod. Because I make a point of not picking fights with people. I'm Alice. I'm the quiet girl in the funky clothes. Everyone likes me. Kind of. I'm everyone's third-best friend. This is what the entire school wrote in my junior high yearbook: "It was great knowing you! You are the sweetest!" Or: "You seem really really sweet! Have a great summer!" Or: "Thanks for being so sweet! You go, girl!" Eventually I realized that "sweet" meant no one knew me, and that (so far) I hadn't done anything to tick off anybody.

I did have it pretty good for my first thirteen years. I was an only child and I lived in this awesome brownstone in Brooklyn with my mom and dad. They were both writers. Pretty famous writers, actually. My dad is Nelson Bingley and my mom is (was) Susan Beckerman. Maybe you've heard of them. They both wrote novels that got a lot of attention before I was born. Once I tried to read one of my mother's books, but it was way too weird. The first sentence had like three words in it that I didn't even know existed. But having two writers as my parents was really nice. They were at home a lot, typing away in their studies, and they always had these bizarro friends staying with us, like famous painters and musicians and movie directors. I still have this real glass eye that an Italian sculptor gave me as a birthday present. Other kids would come over to my house, shake their heads enviously, and say things like: "Your parents are the coolest." Yup, I was that kid. I had the cool parents.

But then one day I just had one cool parent.

It was rough for a while. Our house felt really big and empty, and there was a lot of me and Dad sitting silently in our dark living room every night and watching stupid TV programs that Mom would have hated. It also took me a whole year to stop myself from thinking, *Wait till Mom hears this*, whenever something interesting or cool happened. But then the day I stopped thinking, *Wait till Mom hears this*, was pretty horrible, too. Because there's forgetting your mother is dead, and then there's realizing that you're used to your mother being dead. The second feeling is actually worse.

Things went on like this for about a year and a half, until Dad wrote a play. It was his first play, and it was about a woman dying of cancer. Big surprise, right? But everyone *loved* it. Dad's agent called in the middle of the night and said she couldn't finish reading it because she was crying so hard. Three weeks later a Broadway theater picked it up and R. Klausenhook—the best actress in the city, the actress who guaranteed sold-out houses and Tony Awards—wanted to star in it. Six weeks after that, it opened and *The New York Times* gave it a rave review, and Dad was smiling in a way he hadn't smiled since, well, since Mom, and three weeks after that, R. Klausenhook invited us over to her apartment for dinner. And I was happy for Dad. I truly was. I thought that maybe if he stopped being so sad all the time, I would stop being so sad all the time.

Dumb theory.

Anyway, R. really laid on the charm that first night. And the woman was an incredible cook. She made endive salad and garlic-roasted hen and baked eggs with tomato and basil sauce and this amazing raspberry tart sprinkled with fudge. Dad and I totally pigged out.

"Mmrf," Dad said, wiping his mouth with a napkin. "This is the best meal I've had in I don't know how long. Alice and I usually just microwave frozen fish sticks for dinner."

Now this is true. Dad and I did eat a lot of fish sticks. But somehow Dad's saying this to R. Klausenhook made me feel just a wee bit defensive. We were trying, you know? We were doing okay for ourselves.

"Oh no," said R. "That's awful. Food is unbelievably important to me. I believe that every meal should be its own sensual experience."

I didn't really know what she was talking about, but Dad listened intently and nodded his head like three times in a row.

R. reached across the table and placed her bejeweled fingers over mine. "What about you, Alice?" she asked. "What are your passions?"

"Um . . . ," I said. I looked to Dad for help. He just smiled blankly at me.

"You know," said R. "My passions are acting and food. And sex, of course. What are yours?"

I almost choked on my mouthful of baked eggs. "Uh . . ."

Dad jumped in. "Alice really loves snowboarding. Don't you, Alice?"

I nodded, relieved. "Yeah. Sure. I like snowboarding."

The truth was, I'd snowboarded about twice in my entire life. But okay. You could call it my passion. Whatever. I would have *liked* sex to be one of my passions, but I hadn't been given the opportunity to have it yet. I'd made out once with Keaton Church (this jerko senior) at a party on the Lower East Side during my freshman year, but he was just using me to make his ex-girlfriend jealous (they got back together the next day). That was the range of my experience. The only person who seemed interested in me was my second-cousin Joey Wasserman. Joey lived in Philadelphia and had a beard and smoked like six joints a day and tried to mack on me every Thanksgiving.

As Reena would say, my life was a real suckfest. I was fifteen, my mom had been dead for almost two years, and I'd never even had a boyfriend.

But things were about to get a lot worse.

Dad and I took a cab home that night after dinner at R.'s place, and he couldn't stop smiling. We didn't say anything for a while as we cruised down Madison Avenue, past all those fancy stores with their glowing storefronts. I breathed on the cab window and then absentmindedly drew a little *R* in the fogged-up glass.

"What does R. stand for?" I asked.

"Rachel," Dad said, this moony grin still plastered across his face.

7

"Then why doesn't she just call herself Rachel?"

He put his arm around me and kissed the top of my head. "I really like this woman, Alice. In addition to being wonderfully talented, she's very sweet and giving. She's not crazy like most of the actresses I meet."

I nodded. There was an awkward pause. Dad cleared his throat.

"Did you like her?" he asked.

Looking back on that evening, it probably wouldn't have made any difference if I'd said, "No, Dad, I didn't." Things probably would have turned out the same. But I still think about it a lot. Because back then I just wanted Dad to be happy, and not miserable like he'd been since Mom died, and I wanted to be a good daughter, and R. seemed nice enough, even if she was a little . . . eccentric.

So I looked Dad in the eye and said: "She was fantastic."

And, to tell you the truth, he looked so thrilled and relieved that I felt like it would have been cruel to say anything else.

Before long the two of them were Officially Dating. It started with Dad coming home late a couple of times a week with red wine on his breath, humming songs from different musicals. Then one Saturday morning I stumbled out of bed, walked into our kitchen, and there was R. in a purple satin bathrobe, flipping pancakes on the stove.

"Hello, darling!" she sang out, and gave me a perfumed kiss on the cheek.

Let me remind you that the last woman who'd stood at our kitchen stove flipping pancakes was my mother, Susan Beckerman. And Susan Beckerman is—was—not the type of woman who wore satin bathrobes and called people "darling." Mom liked sweatpants and her nickname for me was "Crinkle." Her nickname for Dad was "Gherkin."

Dad walked into the kitchen and sat down at the table in his pajamas, smiling bashfully. All of a sudden it seemed like the three of us were a *family*. And the truth was, I didn't know R. at all. I just knew that her passions were food, acting, and sex, and that she played a cancer patient in my father's Broadway show. Also she wore a lot of perfume in the morning. But what was I going to do? Things were out of my control.

"Those pancakes smell great," I said, and sat down at the table. Dad reached over and squeezed my hand.

A couple of months went by. It was the spring of my freshman year. I wanted a boyfriend, and I didn't get one, and I wanted a best friend, and I didn't get one (I only had *kind-of* best friends, girls who considered me their *second-* or *third*-best friend after their *real* best friend), and I wasn't chosen to sing a solo in our school's April Chorale Concert. Dad and R. kept seeing more of each other, and I was invited along less and less. Sometimes R. would come over and cook us dinner, but more often I'd come home from school and there'd be a note stuck to the microwave saying: "*Went to movie with R. Back before 11.*" Sometimes I heard them giggling in Dad's bedroom at night. Once I even heard bedsprings squeak, at which point I shoved my fingers in my ears, covered my head with five different pillows, and hummed the national anthem. Still, Dad was happy, and I was glad he was happy.

Then came the Announcement.

One afternoon I came home from school and there was a bottle of champagne on the coffee table in the living room.

R. danced out of the kitchen and embraced me even more enthusiastically than usual.

"HELLO MY DARLING," she bellowed.

"Hey, R.," I said. "What's the champagne for?"

She widened her eyes, her spiky eyelashes almost reaching her eyebrows, and put a finger to her lips. "Wait until your father comes in," she whispered.

A second later, Dad came in from the kitchen. "Hey, baby," he said.

"Hi," I said. Then I realized he was talking to R.

"Hey, baby," she murmured, and they put their arms around each other and kissed. I didn't even bother to look away. In the beginning I would turn around when they kissed in an attempt to seem respectful (also it was gross to watch), but eventually I realized that they didn't even care. Or notice. Finally Dad broke away from R.'s embrace.

"Hi, Alice," he said. "We have a very exciting announcement."

I tried to smile. This little voice inside my head piped up: *What if they get married?* but I quickly told it to shut up, that was absurd, they'd only been dating for three months.

Dad and R. sat down on the couch and held hands. "Alice," said Dad, "R. and I are getting married."

I blinked. I swallowed. I pinched the inside of my palm to make sure I wasn't dreaming.

"What do you think?" asked R. "Are you happy?"

That was an interesting question. Am. I. Happy? I didn't even know how to begin to form an answer. No, R., I'm not happy. My mom is dead, and you're sleeping with my father and filling the house with your perfume, and the longer you're around the less interested you seem in me, and you've only been around three months.

"You've only been around three months!" I blurted out.

The smiles on their faces kind of wobbled and disappeared. I could tell they were shocked. Why? Because I'm Alice. I'd been nothing but *sweet* and *nice*. I'd been nothing but *supportive* and *wonderful*. But no. Not anymore. Marriage? After three months? That was crazy. Mom and Dad had dated for six years before they got married.

"Alice," said Dad, "try to sound at least a little excited."

"I'm not excited," I said. "I'm infuriated and irate." (I'd been studying vocabulary words for the PSATs.)

"Why?" asked R. "It's very hurtful of you to say that, Alice. Your father and I are in love."

"I DON'T EVEN KNOW YOU!" I yelled.

Then I burst into tears and ran upstairs.

Okay, I admit it. Not the most mature response. But I'd reached the end of my rope. Where had being nice gotten me? I threw myself onto my bed, sobbed into my pillow, and waited for Dad to come upstairs to talk to me. I would reason with him. I would say: "Dad, I'm not saying break up with her, I'm just saying give it a little more time. What's the rush to get married?" We'd hug and he'd stroke my hair.

I kept crying into my pillow. A few minutes went by. I cried a little louder. More time went by. I wailed. I beat the wall with my fists. I looked at my clock. I tiptoed down the staircase and peeked into the living room.

They were gone. Their coats were missing from the foyer. I couldn't believe it. They hadn't even left a note.

I felt pretty bad for myself that afternoon.

But I didn't even know that things were about to get much, much worse.

Have you ever had a nightmare where someone in your life like turns on you? When I was really little, I had these recurring dreams about my mom and dad turning into evil ogres who wanted to eat me. Whenever I woke up I'd feel this flood of relief, like: *Thank God. It was all a dream. My parents are actually not evil ogres who want to eat me.*

After I failed to be Ultra-Supportive and Excited about Dad and R.'s upcoming wedding, R. basically turned into an evil ogre who wanted to eat me.

And I never got to wake up.

It's hard to describe. But the woman hated me. *Hated* me. You could see it in her eyes. Maybe she'd hated me the whole time, but in that case my little tantrum gave her permission to hate me openly. I tried to apologize the next day over breakfast ("Um? You guys? Sorry for freaking out yesterday. . . ."), but she totally ignored me and started babbling at Dad about wedding plans. Dad thanked me with his eyes, but the two of them just talked about chocolate versus lemon wedding cakes until they left the table.

I thought maybe R. would only be mad at me for a couple of days, but instead it only seemed to get worse. She'd walk right by me in the living room without saying hello. She refused to make eye contact at meals. Dad would try to initiate conversation between us, but it never really worked. Sometimes it just made things even more horrible.

"I've been thinking about what kind of bridesmaid dress you'd like to wear at the wedding, Alice," Dad said over dinner one night, smiling at me across the table.

Before I could even answer, R. shot Dad a death glare. "Alice isn't going to be a bridesmaid, Nelson," she said sharply.

"She isn't?" Dad asked.

"No. Ruth and Pammy are my bridesmaids. Remember? I want Alice to be the flower girl."

I looked up in shock. "Wait, what? Isn't the flower girl supposed to be, like, a child?" The second after I said it I regretted it.

"You are a child," R. said, looking directly at me for the first time in, like, a week. But this time it was an uncomfortable, creepy, piercing stare.

"I'm fifteen."

"That doesn't sound very old to me. And it's not like you've exhibited the most mature behavior in the world, have you?" She smiled at me triumphantly over her wineglass.

I opened my mouth. I looked to Dad for help. He was staring down at his plate. Coward.

"I just don't know why I can't be a bridesmaid, too," I finally said.

"Because my sister and my best friend are going to be my bridesmaids," R. said calmly, "and I need a flower girl."

I closed my eyes. It wasn't so much the bridesmaid thing as the fact that R. now obviously hated my guts and was totally happy to let me know just how much she hated my guts in whatever way possible. So sitting there at the table, silently, with my eyes closed, I did something I'd never really done before. I prayed.

To whom or what, I'm not sure. My mom? God? I prayed that something would save me from this situation. I prayed that this wasn't actually my life. I prayed the same prayer as that girl at the beginning of *Forrest Gump* (okay, I didn't have a lot of prayer references to draw from. My parents were never that religious): *Let me be a bird and fly far, far away from here.*

That prayer was another bad idea. Where was I going to fly?

The answer turned out to be rural Massachusetts.

Because a few weeks later there was another Announcement.

I was sitting on the couch after school, reading a celebrity gossip magazine (Dad disapproved of all celebrity gossip magazines). It was early June. The wedding was scheduled for early July. Our house had been overrun with florists and caterers and planners, all displaying photo albums and ribbon cuttings and bouquets for R. to choose from. I usually skulked around the background, waiting for someone to ask my opinion.

No one ever did.

Anyway, this was a particularly quiet afternoon. R. was out tasting hors d'oeuvres at some catering place in Manhattan. I'd taken the opportunity to sprawl out on the couch and just . . . vegetate. To my surprise, Dad came out of his study, walked into the living room, and sat down next to me.

"Hey, kiddo," he said, putting his arm around me.

"Hey, Dad," I said, and got this nice warm feeling all over my body. It felt like the old days. The old depressing Mom-is-dead days, but at least not the terrifying, nightmarish, Mom-is-dead-and-R.-is-going-to-become-my-stepmother days.

"What're you reading?" Dad asked.

"Nothing," I said, grinning, and tucked the celeb mag into the couch pillows.

"I want to talk to you about something," Dad said tentatively.

I sighed, relieved. Maybe we were going to figure something out. Maybe R. didn't hate me after all. Or maybe they were going to postpone the wedding for a while. Or maybe— at the very least—they'd decided I didn't have to be flower girl.

"Go ahead," I said.

"Well," Dad said. "This is kind of interesting. I didn't think this was going to happen, but R. feels very strongly about it, and . . . it might be for the best."

The warm feeling was slowly melting away from my body. Was this *more* bad news? Was more bad news possible? I actually couldn't even come up with a worst-case scenario in my head.

I sat up very straight and looked at Dad. "Okay," I said. "What is it?"

"We're going to move," he said.

"Out of this house?"

"Yes."

My body went numb. Okay. Right. The house I grew up in. The living room with the chocolate milk stain on the carpet. The kitchen with the sun coming in through the ivy plants. Mom's shabby study with all her old books. The red staircase with the creaky step. My bedroom with the little stained- glass window. The glow-in-the-dark stars on my ceiling. Our front stoop. Our backyard. The Fernandez family across the street. Images of my life were flashing in front of my eyes like memories, even though I was still sitting in the middle of the living room.

I breathed deeply. *Act mature*, I told myself. "Okay," I said. "Where are we moving? Are we staying in Brooklyn?"

"Uh, no," Dad said. He seemed to be having a hard time getting the words out. "We're moving to Manhattan."

Okay. Right. No more Brooklyn. More images flashed before my eyes. No more brownstones and cute little streets. No more Brooklyn Heights. No more Park Slope. No more Phil's Diner. No more walking along the East River. No more sledding in Prospect Park. No more Junior's cheesecake. No more living five blocks away from school. Wait. School. I'd been going to the same Brooklyn Heights Montessori school for my entire life. I knew everyone there. I didn't *love* everyone, but I knew everyone. I was supposed to graduate in three years. We'd already started raising money for our senior class trip.

"I can still go to Montessori, right?" I asked Dad, trying to stop my voice from trembling. "It'll just be a longer commute, right? Where are we going to live in Manhattan? Will we be close?"

"Well, that's the thing," Dad said. He turned away and stared out the window. "That's the thing, Alice. We're moving into R.'s apartment."

"But that's on the Upper West Side. That's really far away from school."

"I know."

"R.'s apartment is also really small."

"Yes. It is."

I reached out and shakily grabbed hold of Dad's shoulder. He winced.

"Dad?" I asked. *Act mature act mature act mature act mature.* "Um. I . . . where am I going to sleep if we live in R.'s apartment?"

Dad finally turned to face me. His eyes were red. He looked guilty and scared. He looked like he'd just done something really bad. Like murdered a kitten.

"It's okay, Dad," I said weakly. "It's gonna be okay. I'll be okay sleeping in the living room. Or the study. Doesn't she have a study? If I can fit my bed in then I can—"

"Alice," Dad said suddenly. "You're not going to live with me and R. It doesn't make sense. There's not enough room, and you'd have to switch schools, anyway. In the fall you're going to attend a boarding school in Massachusetts."

There was a long, excruciating pause. I tried to think of everything I could say to Dad. I tried to think of what might make him change his mind. *I don't want to go. I refuse to go. I love New York City. I don't want to go to Massachusetts. I don't want to go boarding school. I'll be good. I'll live in R.'s bathroom. I'll sleep in a tent. I'll live with friends. I'll live with the Fernandez family. I'll be a bag lady in Central Park.* Anything.

"It's actually an incredible opportunity," Dad said. "I showed them your transcript and they were very impressed. They were willing to let you in even though the admissions deadline had passed. You'll get a great education. And it has a beautiful campus."

Massachusetts. Wasn't Massachusetts supposed to be cold? And boring? I remembered driving through Massachusetts on our way to a vacation house in Maine when I was little. It had lots of pine trees and gray highways. And fruit stands. And weird farmers with missing teeth.

I stared into Dad's eyes. *Dad,* I tried to silently implore him. *I don't want to freak out right now. I don't want to give R. another reason to hate me. I don't want you to think I'm a bad daughter. Just. Please. Don't. Make. Me. Go.*

The weird thing was, I could tell that Dad was also trying to tell me something with his eyes. He was silently begging me to be okay with this. To not make him guilty. To not make him feel like he was marrying a psychopath who wanted him to send his daughter away to boarding school.

Although he actually was marrying a psychopath who wanted him to send his daughter away to boarding school.

"Well?" Dad said, his voice cracking. "That's the plan. How does it sound to you?"

I broke away from his gaze and stared into the kitchen. I looked at the little crystal hanging in the window above the sink. Mom had bought that crystal when I was in elementary school, and we'd strung it up together in the window with dental floss.

"It sounds . . ." I said. I took a deep breath. "It sounds fantastic."

The New Y

Klausenhook/Bingley

Renowned stage actress Rachel Klausenhook was married yesterday to writer Nelson Bingley at Cipriani 42nd Street before a crowd of more than five hundred guests. The ceremony culminated in musical performances by some of Broadway's brightest stars. An interfaith minister officiated.

The bride is best known for her Tony Award–winning portrayal of Masha in Andre Blackmun's 1987 revival of *The Three Sisters*, and her original star-making turn as Debbie in the original cast for the 1975 hit musical *Say Yes*.

The bridegroom is an acclaimed novelist and two-time winner of the National Book Award. He was previously married (wife deceased), and has a fifteen-year-old daughter, Alice.

The couple met during rehearsals for Bingley's first-produced Broadway drama, *School of Luminism*.

"I knew right away," Klausenhook confided during the reception, radiant in a crimson Donna Karan gown and elbow-length white gloves. "Nelson walked into the rehearsal room, and I thought: 'That's the one.'"

Roses seemed to be the wedding's theme—red roses lined the walls and banquet tables, and each guest received a pink damask rose inside a glass box. The flower girl, Bingley's daughter, Alice (dressed in all black), threw white rose petals across the aisle just before Klausenhook made her way toward the altar.

The bride is keeping her name.

TWO

Reena Paruchuri

I hate yoga. I've always hated yoga. I mean, come on. Who wants to stand still for ten minutes with one leg lifted in the air? Who wants to lie on the ground twisted up like a pretzel while some lady in velvet stirrup pants tells you to "relax"?

White chicks, I guess.

Apparently yoga was originally an Indian thing. Ha. That's hilarious. I'm Indian, and everyone in my family is Indian, and if you asked any of us to get into a downward dog or child's pose position, we'd laugh in your face. And whenever I drive by a yoga studio (there are like ten billion here in Beverly Hills) and look through the windows at the crowds of skinny young women in short-shorts, contorting themselves into freaky positions, they're all white. White as white can be. Lily white. Wonder Bread white. Snow white.

Hmm. Speaking of Snow White. Actually, wait. More about how I hate yoga first.

I really, really, really hate yoga.

Don't get me wrong. Exercise is cool. I love running. I love dancing. I love *moving*. I'm just not interested in staying still, or relaxing, or being aware of my breath. Why relax? There are Things to Do! There are People to Meet! There are Plans to Make!

My older brother Pradeep says I sometimes remind him of a small, hyperactive dog.

He is such a jerk.

Anyway. I should probably be honest with myself and admit that maybe a teensy-weensy part of the reason I hate yoga so much is Shanti Shruti.

Shanti Shruti is a yoga teacher at the Beverly Hills Integrated Living Iyengar Yoga Body Arts Center. She is white, skinny, blond, blue eyed, and twenty-five years old.

She is also my stepmother.

Let's do some math. Shanti Shruti is twenty-five. I, Reena Paruchuri, am fifteen. My father, the distinguished heart surgeon Rashul Paruchuri, is fifty-three. Shanti Shruti is ten years older than me, and twenty-eight years younger than my dad. I'm not exactly sure what that means (that *I* should marry Shanti Shruti?), but I know that it's not a good thing. Trust me.

You may be thinking: Shanti Shruti! What an interesting name! Is it Hindi? Was Shanti Shruti born in India? Is she from Bangalore? Bombay?

Um, no. Shanti Shruti was born in Skokie, Illinois, and she was raised outside of San Francisco. And oh yeah: her name isn't really Shanti Shruti. It's Amanda Weed. She was raised by Charles and Mary Weed, inheritors of the Weed Breez-ee Air Conditioner fortune. Amanda Weed only became Shanti Shruti after she studied abroad in India during college and decided that even though on the surface she appears to be the

21

Whitest Chick in the World, she is, deep in her soul, an Indian woman. An Indian woman who wears skin-tight, pink T-shirts with the word *Om* stenciled across the boobs.

I first met Shanti Shruti a year and a half ago. In yoga class.

At that point I didn't know I hated yoga. I'd never done it before. My best friend Katie persuaded me to go with her. She was all, like, "It's so relaxing," and "It tones your butt." (My best friend Katie is a white chick. So, you know. You can't blame her for liking yoga. It's just a weakness that all white chicks have.)

So I went with her. Once. To try it.

And therefore, as Pradeep is fond of telling me, I am entirely to blame for our parents' divorce.

"Shruti," Shanti Shruti explained to us that first day of class, facing the mirror while neatly folding herself into the lotus position, "means 'what is heard' in Sanskrit. It represents divine knowledge. Shanti means 'tranquility,' or 'inner peace.'"

I glanced at Katie and pretended to strangle myself. Katie giggled. Shanti Shruti looked at us in the mirror and blinked her big blue eyes disapprovingly. Then she twisted herself out of the lotus position and shimmied upward into a standing pose. She stretched her arms out parallel to the floor and tucked her right foot behind her left thigh.

"Imagine yourself," she whispered, "as an ancient tree. You have deep roots. You have branches that stretch out into the sky. You are grounded. But you also can fly."

The twenty white chicks in the class and I attempted to

imitate the pose. A bunch of them balanced perfectly and did kind of look like trees. I took a deep breath. I put my right foot behind my left knee. I started to wobble. I steadied myself. And wobbled again. And then steadied myself. And then wobbled again. I concentrated hard and finally steadied myself. For a good ten seconds. Until I toppled over and crashed to the floor.

"Oh my God!" Katie shrieked.

Shanti Shruti rushed over and helped me up.

"I'm okay," I said. "It's fine."

"Take a deep breath," she instructed me. "Find your center."

"I'm fine," I said loudly.

She backed off.

I spent the rest of the class counting the minutes until I could get out of there. The hour seemed to stretch on forever. We lay on our backs with our legs in the air (painfulpainfulpainful) while Shanti Shruti told us to think about "nothing." Instead I thought about (in the following order): Peanut M&M's, Katie's mysterious dislike of Peanut M&M's, thong underwear (pros and cons), the third Harry Potter movie, the fifth Harry Potter book, geometry proofs, my dead grandfather, how visible the faint mustache above my lip is when I'm standing in the sun, how visible the faint mustache above my lip is when I'm not standing in the sun, whether I should return the cardigan I just bought at Nordstrom, and, finally, whether James Yonus-Good, the most gorgeous and inaccessible senior at Beverly Hills High, had maybe—just maybe— glanced at me the other day while buying Ring Dings in the cafeteria.

And then class was over.

"Stay calm," Shanti Shruti told us as we rolled up our sticky mats. "Don't forget to let yourself blossom."

I was going to blossom my way out of there and never come back.

My father was waiting for me and Katie, leaning in the door frame in the yoga studio, hands in his pockets, looking amused. I made a beeline for him.

"Get us out of here, Dad," I whispered.

"This is interesting," he said, grinning. "You like this yoga?"

I started to say, "Are you kidding me?" when Katie nudged me and tilted her head toward Shanti Shruti, who was standing behind us, getting ready to leave. Shanti smiled sweetly at all three of us.

"Is this your daughter?" she asked my father.

"This is my Reena," he said, putting a hand on my shoulder.

"She's a wonderful student," said Shanti.

I was probably the worst student she'd ever had.

"Reena is good at everything she does," my father said proudly.

Also a lie.

"Where are you from? Originally?" Shanti asked him.

I rolled my eyes at Katie. My father has a really obvious accent, and people are constantly asking him Where He's From. It's the first thing they say when they meet him, and it always drives him crazy. He'll be in the middle of open-heart surgery and one of the nurses will say: "What an interesting accent. Where are you from?"

I looked at my father to see how annoyed he was. But the weird thing was, he actually looked kind of pleased. And . . . nervous? No. Impossible.

"I'm from a university town in northern India," he said. "It's called Santiniketan. The poet Tagore founded a famous school there."

Shanti gasped. "I love Tagore!" she said. "He's my favorite poet ever!"

"You know Tagore?" asked my father.

"Of course," said Shanti, nodding solemnly.

"It's rare I meet an American woman who knows about Tagore," he said.

"I use him in class all the time," Shanti said. "You know what my favorite Tagore line is? 'Everything comes to us that belongs to us, if we create the capacity to receive it.'"

There was a long pause.

"Beautiful," my father said softly. "I had forgotten about that poem."

"Oookay," I said. "We should probably drive Katie home now."

"Yes, of course," he said, shaking his head as if to clear his thoughts. "Of course."

And so we bid Shanti Shruti good-bye (forever, I thought), piled into Dad's car, and drove away.

It was a long time before I thought about yoga—or Shanti Shruti—again.

Almost a year later, I walked into our house on a sunny Saturday afternoon and found my mother lying on the kitchen floor in a heap, sobbing and yelling incomprehensibly.

"Did someone die?" I asked. It was the first thing that came into my mind.

She looked up at me, her eyes bloodshot.

"Worse," she whispered. "Your father is leaving me."

"That's not worse than someone dying," I said. (Okay. Not the most supportive thing to say. But I'd gone totally numb with shock.)

My mother burst into a new round of sobs. "I'm *going to die*," she moaned.

"No, Mom," I said. I was trying my best not to start screaming and crying myself. I knelt down on the floor and put my arms around her. She wept into my shoulder. "You're not going to die. You're not going to die. You're going to be okay."

But what I was really thinking was: She is *so* not going to be okay.

My mom and dad got married in India when they were eighteen. They were one of those couples where you couldn't imagine one without the other. It's not like they had the same personality (my dad is kind of quiet and serious and critical of everyone, and my mom is loud and hilarious and accepting of everyone), but it was as if they each had the personality they did because of the other person. Does that make sense?

Everyone always said: "Your mom and dad are just so perfect for each other." They were one of those Great Couples. Parmita and Rashul. And they'd moved to America together, and my mom had raised us and worked as a waitress while my father went to medical school, and she was by his side when he got his first job as a surgeon, and together they'd moved out of our tiny apartment in the Valley and into our big beautiful white mansion with the big green lawn in Beverly Hills. If it weren't for my mom, my father would never have achieved everything he'd achieved. And if it weren't for my father, my mother would never have been able to finally relax and live in a beautiful house in a beautiful neighborhood after all the hard work she'd done.

Back to my mom sobbing on the floor:

"This must be some kind of misunderstanding," I said. "Where's Dad?"

"Gone!" she shrieked. "Gone!"

At this point Pradeep came in through the back door. He froze in his tracks and stared at the two of us crying on the kitchen floor.

"I'm assuming this is girl stuff," he said. "Am I allowed to leave?"

"Yes, leave!" my mother screamed, collapsing into my arms again. "Leave! Like father, like son! Abandon me! Abandon me forever!"

My brother looked aghast.

"Don't leave," I mouthed to him over my mother's shoulder. He nodded, his face drained of its color.

Eventually my mom calmed down enough to show Pradeep and me the e-mail (that's right, e-mail) that she'd just received from my father an hour before:

from: Rashul Paruchuri rparuch@ucmedcenter.com
to: Parmita Paruchuri parmeepatch@hotmail.com

Hello, Par:

Please do not forget to buy the soy milk for Reena when you go shopping this afternoon as I am quite concerned about her lactose intolerance and she is so stubborn about taking care of it herself.

Also I would like to let you know that I have fallen in love with someone else. It would be very difficult for me to tell you this in person. You have a terrible temper and I have various problems with confrontation as you know.

From tonight on I will be staying at a hotel or a different place of my choosing. Please tell Reenie and Pradeep that I will be contacting them shortly to explain in full.

I have a great deal of affection for you but think that it will be best to end our marriage in as civil a fashion as possible.

With regards,
Rashul Paruchuri, MD

It was finally starting to sink in.

My father was leaving my mother.

"I hate him," Pradeep whispered, the printed-out e-mail trembling in his hands. "I hate Dad."

"Don't say that," I said, and immediately started to cry.

My mother sat down on the floor again, her head in her hands. "I have no heart," she announced. "My heart is extinct."

"I don't think you mean 'extinct,' Mom," I said. My mother's English is pretty good, but sometimes she'll come up with these weird words and phrases that don't really make sense. "I think maybe you mean 'broken.'"

"Stop picking on her," Pradeep said.

"I'm not picking on her!" I said.

"My heart is extinct," said my mother again.

"Your heart can't be extinct," I said. "That's impossible. Wooly mammoths are extinct."

"Stop it, Reen," Pradeep said.

"YOU STOP IT!" I shouted. "GO SCREW YOURSELF!"

There was a long pause.

"If either of you see or speak to your father after today," my mother said softly, "I will never forgive you."

Dad smiled nervously and tucked his napkin into his lap.

"Well," he said.

Pradeep and I were silent. I looked around at the faces of all the other people in the restaurant. What were they thinking? Were their lives falling apart, too?

"Are you two going to say anything?" Dad asked.

Pradeep glowered into his plate. I bit my lip.

"Well, you should at least order some food," Dad said. "This is a very nice restaurant. Only the best for my children." He reached over and attempted to pat Pradeep's hand. Pradeep snatched it away.

"What's her name?" Pradeep demanded.

"Now, now," Dad said.

"Tell us her name," said Pradeep, "or we'll leave the restaurant."

I glanced at Pradeep, impressed. It was exactly a week since the e-mail and Mom's breakdown. We'd agreed to go out to dinner with Dad because . . . well, he was our dad, after all. He had the last word. He was like our boss. If he said he was taking us out to dinner, he was taking us out to dinner. Even if it did make Mom threaten to disown us (and she was always making threats she couldn't stick to). But now Pradeep was acting differently than I'd ever seen him act before. He was acting like, well, like his *own* boss.

"Her name," said Dad, clearing his throat after a long pause, "is Shanti Shruti."

The lump that had already been in my throat for the past week transformed itself into a giant boulder.

Pradeep frowned. "Is she Indian?"

"Well," Dad began.

"No," I croaked. "She's not."

Pradeep turned to me. "How would you know?"

"She's . . . she's . . . she's like my age," I whispered.

Dad slammed his fist down on the table, making the plates clatter. "She is NOT your age, Reena. Have some respect."

"I have no idea what's going on," Pradeep said. "Would somebody please tell me what's going on?"

I turned to my brother. "She's a white chick. She was my yoga teacher. She's half Dad's age. Happy?"

Pradeep opened his mouth and then closed it again.

"Dad," I said, looking my father in the eyes, "I don't think you understand what you're doing. Do you understand what you're doing?"

"Don't talk to me like a child, Reena," he said.

Tears sprang to my eyes. "Mom is a mess," I told him. "You've ruined her life."

"Your mother is going to be okay."

"You're wrong."

My father sighed. "Reena," he said. "I'm in love. What do you want me to do about it?"

Pradeep, still speechless, buried his face in his hands.

"I don't understand how you even got to know Shankee Shmooti," I said.

"It's Shanti Shruti," Dad said, giving me a withering look. "And we were friends at first. Then we eventually realized that our feelings had grown stronger and we had to—"

"ENOUGH," Pradeep shrieked.

The restaurant fell silent. You could hear the sound of a single spoon scraping against a dessert plate.

Dad cleared his throat. "Pradeep—"

"I ACTUALLY DON'T WANT TO HEAR ABOUT IT," Pradeep yelled. A tear rolled down his cheek and into the corner of his mouth. "I'M NOT INTERESTED."

"Okay," Dad said quietly. "Okay."

No one said anything for a little while.

"Listen," Dad said finally. "I want to make you both an offer."

We looked up.

"Things are going to become very difficult," he said, "between your mother and myself. We are both hiring lawyers. There is some question as to who will get the house, and—"

"Mom should get it," Pradeep interrupted. "Mom isn't having an affair with a yoga teacher."

Dad sighed. "These things are complicated."

"Where's Mom going to live if you get the house?" I asked.

"Let me finish my thought," Dad said. "Things will be messy. There is also the question of alimony. It is my suggestion—and this is only if you wish to go, of course—that you both leave LA and attend boarding school this fall. That way you will not have to be around such difficulties."

"You're trying to get rid of us," I said.

"That is not true," my father said. "I'm trying to give you another option. That is all. We all know how unstable your mother can be in times of conflict. But it is your choice."

He pulled a glossy brochure out of his pocket and put it on the table in front of us. Pradeep and I stared at it. There was a picture of a hillside covered in snow with a brick cathedral on top of it. The words *Putnam Mount McKinsey* were written across the top of the brochure.

"It's in Massachusetts," Dad said. "It's one of the best schools in the country. Shanti actually went there. Think about it. I know you're both angry with me, but trust me. It is a gift."

Pradeep and I looked at each other. Then we looked back at Dad.

"Mom needs us," I said. "You have a white chick yoga teacher. But she has nobody."

"Well, think about it," said Dad.

We all sat there in silence.

"Oh, and Reena?" Dad said after a while. "Please do not refer to Shanti as a 'white chick yoga teacher.' You and Pradeep are very important to me, but you're going to have to accept the woman I love. That woman is Shanti Shruti."

"Do you have the long underwear we bought?" my mom asked, wringing her hands.

I nodded.

"Which suitcase?" she said.

I shrugged.

"Probably suitcase number eleven," Pradeep said, chortling. "Or maybe twelve."

"Shut up," I said. It was true. I had no idea I owned so much stuff until I tried to pack it all into a single pink luggage set. Turned out I actually needed three pink luggage sets.

The three of us were sitting on plastic airport chairs, holding hands. A woman announced over the loudspeaker that our flight was going to board in five minutes. My mother quietly started to cry. Tears streamed down her face and onto her light green sari.

"We don't have to go," I told her.

"Go, go," she said. "I'll be all right. I will. Pria will take care of me."

Pria is my mother's older sister. She never married—she isn't the easiest woman in the world to get along with—but the second she found out my parents were getting a divorce, she insisted that my mother move in with her. "Don't stay in that house," she told my mother. "That house is poisoned." Pria had a nice—but small—bungalow in West LA. With only one extra bedroom. As the summer progressed, it became obvious that if Pradeep and I left for boarding school it would probably be the best thing for everyone. We didn't want to live with my dad and Shanti Shruti, but we knew that living with my mother would mean she'd have to support us, at least until the alimony was settled. And my mother didn't have a source of income. Her job, after all, had been raising us.

Also, to tell you the truth, Pradeep and I had been fantasizing about going to an East Coast boarding school since we were little kids. Boarding school just always seemed so . . . magical. Skiing. Sledding. Pine trees. Cute boys in earmuffs. We'd tried to convince our mom and dad to send us to boarding school when I was in seventh grade and Pradeep was in eighth, but they'd refused. No, at the time it was really important to them that Family stick together, and that Pradeep and I pass our teenage years spending quality time with the Family. So it was pretty ironic that boarding school was now the place they sent us when the Family completely fell apart.

And in a weird way I was happy to leave Los Angeles. I'd felt sort of numb ever since the afternoon I walked in and saw Mom crying on the kitchen floor. Kind of like I was living in a dream. Sometimes I'd even wake up in the morning and genuinely believe it *was* all a dream for a good twenty seconds. My life just didn't seem like my life anymore. All summer I hung out with my friends, and cracked jokes, and went shopping, and lay on the beach talking about cute guys, and anyone watching me would have said that I was Doing Just Fine, Considering. But it felt like the real Reena Paruchuri had been replaced by an identical robot version of Reena Paruchuri who didn't have any actual thoughts and feelings.

"Flight 1191 to Boston boarding now," a woman intoned on the loud speaker. "Flight 1191 to Boston boarding now."

My mother stood up and smiled bravely at us, the corners of her mouth trembling.

"Make me proud," she said.

"You're going to be okay, Mom," I said.

She shrugged, tears brimming out of her eyes.

"Dad is a jerk," Pradeep said loudly. "Don't waste time thinking about him."

"Pradeep," I warned.

"He is," said Pradeep.

"Go," Mom said. "Just go."

She put her hands on our backs and pushed us gently toward the gate. My heart skipped a beat. For a second, the real Reena Paruchuri flooded back into my body. And the last thing she wanted to do was get on that plane. The real Reena Paruchuri wanted to curl up like a baby, bury her face in her mother's lap, and cry forever. But it was too late. I took a deep breath, shouldered my duffel bag, and followed my brother into the buzzing white tunnel that led to our plane.

I didn't look back.

Los Angeles Ti

JULY 10,

Shruti/Paruchuri

When twenty-five-year-old yoga instructor Shanti Shruti told her friends she was dating a much older man, initially they were concerned.

"I thought, 'Oh no, there goes Shanti again, pursuing someone totally wrong for her,'" said Cindy Kallo, a close friend of Ms. Shruti's. "But then she introduced me to Rashul and it all made sense. Both of them are such calm, spiritual people. It's a match made in the stars."

Rashul Paruchuri, 53, is no ordinary "older gentleman." He is one of Los Angeles's most well-respected heart surgeons, and a warm, friendly man with a distinctive halo of gray hair. Also—despite the fact that he hails from northern India—he is not a practicing Hindu.

What, then, did guests make of the three-day-long traditional Indian celebration that took place this past weekend in Malibu, complete with *pithi*, a ceremony in which the bride and groom are covered in yellow paste the day before the wedding and rubbed down in order to "produce a healthy glow"?

"It's all Shanti," Kallo said. "She's always dreamed of an Indian wedding."

One might not immediately expect that from Shruti, a tall, lanky blonde. But the bride looked radiant in her traditional garb and headdress, and the happy couple performed their final vows on a cliff above the beach, standing in front of a "sacred fire," which they circled four times, signaling the four basic human goals of dharma, artha, kama, and moksha.

"I've never been very interested in traditional ceremonies," said the groom, who has been married once before. "But whatever makes Shanti happy makes me happy."

After the couple was showered with rice and rose petals, a *Saubhagyavati* ritual concluded the ceremony.

Normally seven married friends of the bride are asked to whisper blessings in her ear, but since none of Shruti's friends are married (some of them are still in college), Paruchuri's two children by his first marriage, Reena and Pradeep, were brought forward to administer the blessings.

"Have fun on your honeymoon," said Pradeep, the elder sibling, who was wearing a decidedly un-traditional tuxedo.

"Don't get food poisoning," added Reena, decked out in sixties-style minidress.

Then the happy couple exited—on horseback—and rode down a rocky beach path to a long white limousine that was waiting to take them back to Paruchuri's spacious Beverly Hills mansion.

The bride is keeping her name, although, Kallo confided, "It's not the one she was born with."

THREE

Molly Miller

"You are not taking the entire Oxford English Dictionary to boarding school," Candy Lamb said. She stood in the driveway, hands on her hips, squinting at me in the late summer sunlight. She wore an oversized sweatshirt that said, I'M NOT FAT, I'M PREGNANT WITH ICE CREAM'S BABY.

"Um," I said, "yes, I am."

"Everyone will make fun of you."

"I don't care."

"You'll seem like a big nerd."

I smiled pleasantly at her. "I am a big nerd," I said, and lifted Volume VI, P–Q, into the trunk of my father's station wagon. Then I started walking back toward the house, my feet crunching on the gravel. Only fourteen more volumes to go.

"You're not gonna wear that skirt, are you?" Candy hollered after me from the bottom of the driveway.

I ignored her.

Candy Lamb is my stepmother. She has short, bleached,

spiky hair. She has capped white teeth. She has a fondness for paisley leggings and blue mascara and gigantic sweat-shirts with abrasive comments written across the front. She never tires of reminding me that she was BOTH prom queen and homecoming queen BOTH junior and senior year at North Forest High School. She feels that this makes her an author-ity on two extremely important subjects: Fashion and General Coolness.

When it comes to these subjects, I am a huge disappoint-ment to her.

My name is Molly Miller. My father is Herb Miller, owner of Herb's Diner, the only restaurant in our hometown of North Forest, Massachusetts. My mother is Patsy Miller, asso-ciate manager of Shear Bliss, the only hair salon in North For-est. My little sister is Spencer Miller, the youngest North Forest baton twirler ever to win a blue ribbon at the Chester-ton County Fair.

Something that's important to know about me: I'm not re-ally that interested in Fashion and General Coolness. Or baton twirling, for that matter.

I am, however, interested in the Oxford English Dictionary.

People don't spend enough time talking about the OED. It is amazing. It's like a normal dictionary (it gives you a defini-tion of every word in the English language), but then it goes way beyond the call of duty and gives you like the complete history of the word you're looking up. Where it originated, what country and language it's taken from, who first wrote it down, and how the word has changed over time. Each word gets its own little section of quotes that demonstrate all the different ways it can be used, and the quotes are from famous books and authors, and . . .

Yeah. You're already bored. I can tell. That's okay. Everyone thinks it's boring. I'm probably the only person in the world who thinks the Oxford English Dictionary is the greatest thing since sliced bread. But I do. And I plan to work there someday. The head offices of the OED are in Oxford, England. I've never been to England, but I know I'd love it. After all, everyone there speaks with an English accent. And I love English accents. I also imagine that everyone in England reads books and drinks tea and quotes poetry and goes apple picking. Oh, they also all own horses. And walk with little white umbrellas. And play croquet.

I guess I imagine England to be the polar opposite of North Forest. Because if you're someone who enjoys reading the dictionary and you also happen to be nearsighted and have frizzy hair and weirdly pale white legs that never change color no matter how long you lie out in your backyard every summer (they turn blotchy red for like twelve hours, and then go back to pale white), and you don't really like parties or baton twirling or prom queens or homecoming queens or outdoor sports or television, North Forest is a really, really, really terrible place to live. Especially if your ten-year-old sister is gorgeous, mysteriously tan, and adored by the entire town population (2,333 people, to be exact).

I've lived in North Forest my entire life.

So have my parents. So has Candy Lamb.

For some reason they all seem to think it's great.

Sometimes I pretend that I was actually born to a bespectacled, pale-legged, croquet-playing British couple, and that I was accidentally switched at birth with the real elder daughter of Herb and Patsy Miller. But then I realize: What in God's name would a bespectacled, pale-legged, croquet-playing British couple be doing at the local hospital in North Forest, Massachusetts?

North Forest is basically one diner (my dad's), one hair salon (my mom's), one general store, one gas station, one post office, and one really terrible and underfunded public school, North Forest High. Oh, and a whole lot of maple trees.

The most important annual event in North Forest is the Fourth of July pork roast. The second most important annual event is the high school's February pancake breakfast. In the months between the pork roast and the pancake breakfast, people spend their leisure time watching television, drinking beer, shoveling the snow off their front walk and then watching a new coat of snow fall on it two hours later, playing poker, gossiping, watching more television, and drinking more beer. What else? North Forest is incredibly cold in the winter and incredibly hot in the summer. In the late spring all the trees get infested with gypsy moths, and everyone freaks out and congregates in the general store to try to come up with a solution (they never do). In the autumn everyone rakes their leaves to the curb and puts them in orange jack-o'-lantern trash bags, and if you forget to rake your leaves to the curb and put them in an orange jack-o'-lantern trash bag, you receive a very sad and betrayed-sounding note from the postman in your mailbox. (This happened to our family once, and it was my fault, and my mother never forgave me for it.)

Candy Lamb says I have a bad attitude when it comes to North Forest. She says that North Forest is an amazing place in which to grow up. Everyone knows everyone, and it's like one big family, and there's barely any crime (if you don't count the shaving cream felonies committed by the senior class every June), and the surrounding nature is so beautiful, and on a clear day you can see, off in the distance, the glorious peak of Mount McKinsey. . . .

The thing is, until very recently, just the mention of Mount McKinsey made weird, resentful chills run up and down my spine. Why? Because in the shadow of Mount McKinsey, just twenty miles away from boring, claustrophobic North Forest, lies paradise.

Perfect, unattainable, even-better-than-England paradise.

While I was growing up, sometimes, seemingly out of nowhere, a group of incredibly attractive, well-dressed teenagers would appear in the center of North Forest, buying penny candy from the general store or squeezing into a booth at my dad's diner and gigglingly ordering ice cream floats.

"Who are those people?" I would whisper, breathless, peeping out from behind the diner counter.

And my father would roll his eyes and say: "Probably Putnam Mount McKinsey students. Spoiled brats."

I wasn't sure what he meant. But I remember gazing at one of them, a gorgeous boy in a pink shirt who was gobbling down his sundae and making all the girls at his table laugh, and I remember thinking: *What I wouldn't give to be a spoiled brat.* Then, later, when their little group got up to leave, I noticed a paperback book sticking out of the boy's back pocket, and managed to catch a glimpse of its title just before his perfect denim-coated bottom sashayed out of my father's diner. The title was *The Collected Poems of Emily Dickinson.*

I'd never seen a guy that handsome walking around with a volume of poetry in his pocket. And I'd certainly never seen a guy that handsome who had read—or had even heard of—Emily Dickinson. I adored Emily Dickinson. I'd found a book of her poems at a thrift store when I was eight and had fallen

41

in love with her. She was this reclusive Massachusetts poet from the nineteenth century who never married and stayed in her little room all day and wrote poems about death and loneliness and . . .

Okay. You're bored again. Sorry. The point is, I suddenly realized that there was a school within twenty miles of my house where handsome boys in pink shirts walked around with books of Emily Dickinson poems sticking out of their back pockets. It seemed impossible. But I'd *seen* one of them. I'd seen him with my own eyes. So I casually attempted to ask my father one night over dinner how a person could go about attending this school he'd mentioned, this "Putnam Mount McKinsey."

He coughed on his food, shook his head, took a gulp of his beer, and sighed. "How do you think, Mol?"

"Uh . . . I don't know. That's why I am asking."

"You know how much it costs for one year of school at Putnam Mount McKinsey?"

"It costs money?" I was surprised. I was twelve at the time. I'd attended public school my entire life. It had never occurred to me that other people paid to go to school.

My father looked at me sadly. "Mol, I'd send you there in a second if I could. God knows you're smart enough. But the place costs thirty thousand dollars a year."

I gaped at him. "You're kidding."

"It's a school full of rich kids, honey. Brats from New York City and Beverly Hills. Kids with private jets and boats who spend their summers doing nothing in Europe. You wouldn't want to be friends with them anyway. They're probably all little jerks."

I tried to nod and look like I understood. But all I could

think was *jerks from New York City and Beverly Hills with private jets and boats who READ EMILY DICKINSON.*

From that moment on, the existence of Putnam Mount McKinsey tormented me. I mean, I'd never been crazy about the North Forest school system. The teachers weren't great (my sixth grade teacher was fond of saying I was "too smart for my own good") and everyone called me Nerd and Brown Noser and Goody Two-Shoes. Oh, and Four Eyes. And Rabbit Teeth. And Big Mouth. And Molly Miller the Puppy Killer (I could never figure that one out. I used to weep and yell, "BUT I'VE NEVER KILLED A PUPPY!" and for some reason that just made everyone laugh harder). Still, I always thought that school was like that for everyone. But now I knew that within a half-an-hour drive of my house there was a school so wonderful that people paid to attend it. And my family just didn't have the money to send me there. Actually they didn't have a fraction of a fraction of the money to send me there. And it wasn't because my parents didn't work hard. It was because life—I was starting to realize—was Totally and Utterly Unfair.

Then high school started, and Candy Lamb entered our lives, and I decided that life was not only Totally and Utterly Unfair, it was also Cruel, Sadistic, Stupid, and Pointless.

Candy Lamb was one of the waitresses at my father's diner. I'd known her for years. She was always extra-friendly and extra-sweet whenever Spencer and I came in, and she'd sneak us free slices of key lime pie when my parents weren't looking. She always seemed a little fake, like maybe she was trying too hard to make people like her, but I didn't care. She was just part of the Herb's Diner staff. There were way weirder people who worked at the diner, like Gus, the prep cook, who had one eye and claimed to be a former pirate.

But then something strange happened. One day, out of nowhere, my parents stopped fighting.

This was actually much more surreal than it sounds. The background noise of my childhood was either Spencer, tutu-clad, screeching "The Star-Spangled Banner" into a plastic toy microphone, or my parents screaming at each other in the kitchen. Actually sometimes they would scream at each other in our driveway. Or our living room. Or the upstairs hallway. They were usually screaming at each other about money. Sometimes they were screaming at each other about how my father watched too much television. Or how my mother spent too much time talking to her friends on the phone. I would hear one of them threaten divorce, and then the other would climb into the car and screech out of the driveway, but eventually, by dinnertime, we were all sitting around the table and acting normal again. I guess I trusted that no matter how bad things got, they'd never split up. Even though it sometimes seemed like they hated each other, I always assumed that that was what marriage was like for everyone. Sort of like how I'd once assumed all schools were like the crappy public schools in North Forest.

Anyway, on this particular day I was lying on the couch reading the OED entry for *punctilious* (it originally comes from the Latin for "to prick," if you're interested) and I suddenly realized that it had been more than a week since I'd heard my parents screaming at each other. I put down the OED and looked around our living room. Both of them were home. My mother was peeling potatoes in the kitchen and my father was repairing our bathroom cabinet. Spencer was at Lassie League practice. So why weren't they yelling? I started to feel nervous. I'd always hated their fighting. But now its absence was eerie. Foreboding. Like what they say about the silence before a storm.

That night at dinner, my mother—with exquisite politeness—asked my father if he would please pass her the potatoes. My father said that he would be delighted to. And would she be willing to pour him another glass of water? My mother said it would be her pleasure.

I was starting to feel ill. I tried to make eye contact with Spencer, but she was too focused on building a castle out of her mashed potatoes and humming a song under her breath.

We all finished eating and I cleared the dishes off the table and brought them into the kitchen. I came back into the dining room and sat down. My mother and father smiled pleasantly at us.

"What's going on?" I asked.

My mother's smile got wider. And creepier. Her eyes were glittering like they were behind a mask.

Spencer finally stopped humming and looked up. *"What?"* she asked, as if we were all waiting for her to do something.

My father cleared his throat. "Your mother and I are separating," he said.

There was a stunned silence. My mother's face looked like it was going to fall off.

"Why?" I asked.

"We don't love each other anymore," my mother said. She was still smiling.

"You *don't*?" Spencer squealed.

"We haven't loved each other for a long time," said my father.

"Oh," said Spencer. Her voice sounded so small that I almost didn't recognize it.

"I'm moving in with Candy Lamb," my father said. "You remember Candy."

Spencer shot me a pleading you're-the-older-sister-do-something! look.

But I had no idea what I was supposed to do.

"Candy is a very nice woman," my mother added.

My father nodded. I could hear the clock ticking in the other room.

"Well," I said, "I think this is dumb. I think the two of you are really dumb."

"It has nothing to do with you guys," my mother said. "You know that, right? It has nothing to do with you."

There was a long silence.

"I'm going to go do my homework," I announced. I pushed my chair back and stood up.

"Do you want to talk about anything, Mol?" my mother asked. Her eyes were still gleaming desperately.

"No," I said. "I just think you're both stupid jerks."

I walked out of the room, up the stairs, and into my bedroom. I sat down at my desk and pulled out my English textbook. A single tear dropped out of my eye and onto the page. It landed on the word *until* and made the black letters blur on the white page.

I stared at the textbook for a long time, not reading, just letting my eyes pass over the same sentences over and over again. I felt like my entire chest had been hollowed out. But the same thought kept running through my brain, over and over again. Eventually I said it out loud.

"Got to get out of this stupid, stupid town," I whispered.

Downstairs I could hear the sounds of my mother and father washing the dishes and cleaning up the kitchen. They weren't saying anything. Then I heard Spencer stomp up the staircase and slam her bedroom door. Outside my window, the crickets seemed to be chirping louder than they'd ever chirped before.

I didn't tell anyone that I was applying to Putnam Mount McKinsey, except for the two teachers I needed to ask for recommendations. While I was filling out application forms, I just checked yes when the school asked if I wanted to be considered for financial aid. I got a copy of my transcript from the principal's office. I forged my mother's signature. I put the entire application into a large manila envelope and put it in the mailbox downtown. Then I made a conscious decision to forget that I'd ever applied at all. After all, if they let me in— and why would they?—we'd never be able to afford it, even if they did give me some financial aid. It was unclear why I'd applied at all. But I just felt like I had to.

It was my first year at North Forest High. I'd never gotten along with my classmates, but somehow things got even worse once we all entered ninth grade. The last of my fellow awkward female students grew into themselves and got contacts and straightened their hair and started wearing pink workout pants and refused to do their homework. Suddenly everyone was only interested in talking about cheerleading tryouts and the homecoming game. Girls I'd known for years were suddenly dating red-faced senior boys with bulging muscles. Boys I'd known for years were wearing white baseball caps and studiously ignoring me when I tried to say hello to them in the hallways. I was used to being teased and laughed at, but I wasn't used to . . . not existing. I mean, it's hard not to exist in a small town.

And yet somehow I managed it.

Meanwhile, my father had moved out of our house and in with Candy Lamb, who lived on the edge of town in a tiny house with her seven-year-old twin daughters, Randie and Sandie. I barely ever saw him. Since Spencer was always off doing a thousand extracurricular activities (one, she confessed to me late one night, was kissing boys) . . . there is nothing more humiliating than having your younger sibling kiss someone for the first time before you do . . . I spent most of my time home alone with my mother, who had undergone such a significant personality change since the separation that some days I barely recognized her. For most of my life, my mother had been a huge presence in North Forest. She was loud and social and constantly chatting with her friends on the phone or organizing huge poker parties for all the women who worked at Shear Bliss. Now she was more interested in watching television or cooking by herself in the kitchen. The phone would ring and she'd refuse to answer it. Our dinner conversations consisted mostly of silence. I'd ask her how she was doing and she'd say, "Fine, honey, just great," but then I'd see that same glittering desperate look in her eyes. Our house started to get really messy. I left a bunch of dirty dishes in the sink as an experiment (my mother always *hated* dirty dishes) and she never scolded me or even reminded me that they were there.

One afternoon I came home from school and my father was sitting on our couch. I hadn't seen him in weeks.

"Hi, Mol," he said.

"Hi, Dad," I said. I put on my best fake smile. "How are Sandie and Randie?"

He sighed. "Fine."

"Where's Mom?" I asked.

"Your mom," he said, and then paused. "Your mom is having a hard time, Molly."

"What does that mean?"

"She, uh . . . she checked in to Silverwood this morning. She, uh, called me and asked me to drive her there."

Silverwood was a small complex of white wooden buildings off the highway about two towns away. I'd always pressed my face to the car window and gaped at it when we drove by on our family trips. It was, for lack of a better phrase, a mental hospital.

I stared at my father. *There's a point,* I thought, *where life gets so unfair that you stop even caring.*

"You and Spence are gonna come stay with me and Candy for a while," he said. "Okay?"

"Stupid," I said. The word just came out of my mouth.

My father gazed at me. "What's stupid?" he asked.

"Everything."

He smiled sadly. "You say the word *stupid* a lot, Mol. You've been saying it for years. But I'm never exactly sure what you mean."

"I mean stupid," I said. "I mean dumb. I mean idiotic."

He sighed. "Why don't you go up to your room and start packing up your stuff? I'm going to go pick Spencer up at her dance class and then we'll all drive to my place."

I turned and started walking toward the staircase.

"Oh," my father said, "one more thing."

I turned around. He held out a thick white envelope.

"This came for you," he said. "But I think they might have the wrong person. It's from Putnam Mount McKinsey."

I heaved the last volume of the OED into the trunk of the car, took a step back, and checked my watch. We were leaving in ten minutes. Ten minutes until I embarked on the road to paradise.

I felt a small hand tugging at my skirt. It was Sandie. I looked down at her and was reminded once again of how she resembled a tiny vampire.

"Hi, Sandie," I said.

"Are you happy to leave us?" she asked. Her mouth and cheeks were streaked with red Popsicle stains.

I smiled down at her. *No,* I thought, *of course not! Why would I be happy to leave a stupid town, a stupid high school, a stupid absent mother, a stupid emotionless father, a stupid stepmother who openly states that she wishes I were "prettier," two tiny stupid stepsisters who just spent the summer short-sheeting my bed, and a stupid traitorous younger sister who actually seems to* like *our new life on the edge of town with Candy and Randie and Sandie? Who actually seems to get along with them and enjoy their company?*

"No, Sandie," I said. "Of course I'm not happy to leave. But they gave me a full scholarship and stipend. It'll save us money if I go."

She squinted at me suspiciously.

"I'll come back to visit all the time," I reassured her, and crossed my fingers behind my back.

Candy Lamb came out of the house, banging the front door behind her. Randie followed close behind, clutching a bedraggled Barbie doll.

"You sure you don't want to change that skirt?" Candy asked.

I grinned at her. Nothing could make me feel bad now. Nothing.

"I'm sure," I said.

"HERB!" Candy shrieked.

My father emerged from the backyard, brushing the dirt off his pants. "Yep?" he asked.

"Don't you think Molly looks like a librarian in that skirt?"

He gazed at me. "Huh," he said. "I don't know. What does a librarian look like?"

Candy sighed. "Just go," she told me. "I don't care if you make a bad first impression."

"Where's Spencer?" I asked.

"SPENCER!" Candy bellowed. I winced. Candy's favorite activity seemed to be screaming the names of her new family members at the top of her lungs.

The screen door creaked open, and Spencer's blond head peeped out.

"Aren't you gonna give me a hug good-bye?" I said.

She reluctantly stepped outside and made her way toward me, teetering in a pair of enormous high heels.

"What are you doing in those ridiculous shoes?" I demanded.

Spencer's bright blue eyes flickered in Candy's direction. "Candy let me try them on."

I turned to Candy. "You're letting her traipse around in a pair of trashy high heels?"

"Excuse me, young lady," Candy snapped, "they are not trashy. And what business is it of yours if—"

"Let's just go, Dad," I said, shaking my head.

My father obediently took out his keys, and the two of us squeezed into the front seat, wedging ourselves between the piles of books I'd stacked on the floor. My father turned on the car. Just the sound of the engine purring filled my heart with excitement. Candy and Spencer and Sandie and Randie stood in the yard and watched us pull out of the driveway. Randie waved her Barbie back and forth. Sandie did a little dance. Candy still looked angry about my skirt. Spencer stared at the ground, her arms folded.

I rolled down the window. "If Mom calls, you'll give her my new number?" I called out.

"Okay," said Candy. "Yeah."

"I LOVE YOU!" Sandie yelled.

I looked at her in surprise. Neither she nor Randie had ever said anything like that before.

"I love you, too," I said slowly.

Sandie nodded and wiped her nose, smearing more red Popsicle juice across her face.

"Ready?" my father asked me.

"Ready," I said, and he put his foot on the gas.

It was nearly a half an hour later—when we were just a few minutes from my new home—when I remembered that I'd forgotten to hug Spencer good-bye.

NORTH FORE

Section C2

Miller/Lamb

Longtime North Forest residents Herbert A. Miller and Candy P. Lamb were married this Saturday at the Moody Street Church of Christ.

The couple has known each other since high school, when the bride was North Forest High's head cheerleader and the groom was the football team's star quarterback. Still, it's taken Herb and Candy more than twenty-five years and a marriage to other people to finally, as Candy puts it, "get our act together."

Candy is known throughout North Forest for her sunny personality and commanding presence at PTA and town hall meetings. Herb, a quieter but equally beloved figure in the community, is the owner and manager of the North Forest institution Herb's Diner.

The ring bearers were Candy's adorable twin girls, Randie and Sandie Lamb, and the flower girl was Herb's beaming daughter Spencer (recently awarded a blue ribbon for her baton twirling at the Chesterton County Fair). His older daughter, Molly, was the maid of honor.

The couple plans to honeymoon "somewhere in Florida."

The bride will be taking Miller's name.

FOUR

Alice

There are a lot of graveyards in western Massachusetts. Our van passed by dozens of them on its way to Putnam Mount McKinsey. There were old shady graveyards with paper-thin tombstones covered in ivy. There were new graveyards with the sun beating down and little American flags whipping in the wind. There were graveyards on the sides of mountains. There were graveyards in the center of each tiny town.

"I guess people in Massachusetts die a lot," I said to the boy sitting on my right. He ignored me.

I was smushed into a big, weird-smelling van with ten other kids who had also flown into Boston from New York. They were all returning students who already knew one another (there had been about twenty minutes of squealing and hugging at the airport), except for the one guy on my right. When we piled into the van, he'd reluctantly introduced himself to me as "Judah Lipston the Third." Then he proceeded to bury his face in a comic book for the rest of the drive.

So I had nothing to do but stare out the window at grave-yards for the next two hours.

At first we were driving through the suburbs of Boston. Then we were driving through medium-size towns. Then we were driving through small towns. Then we were driving through tiny towns. Then we were driving through places that weren't towns at all, just expanses of farmland with the occasional dot of a house off in the distance, followed by a graveyard, followed by another expanse of farmland, followed by another tiny house dot.

At this point someone yelled: "There's Mount McKinsey!"

I squinted into the distance and saw the outline of some-thing jagged and gray in the sky.

"I cannot *wait* until Mount McKinsey weekend," one girl murmured. She wiggled her eyebrows, and everyone laughed.

"The Essence Game," another girl said. "We have to re-member to play the Essence Game."

"You are sooo sadistic!" shrieked her friend.

It was like they were speaking a foreign language. I glanced at Judah Lipston the Third for help, but he was staring fixedly into his comic book at a picture of a purple alien with boobs getting blown to pieces by a small boy.

We eventually turned onto a gravel road, and then a dirt road, and then we drove past a carved red-and-gold sign that said PUTNAM MOUNT MCKINSEY. Everyone cheered. I mut-tered a halfhearted "yay."

Then, suddenly, I absorbed the fact that we were *there*. This would be the setting for the next three years of my life. (That summer I had gotten in the weird habit of thinking about my life as if it were a movie. Every time R. scowled at me, or Dad ignored me, or I had to say a final good-bye to a friend or neighbor, I would just pretend I was watching a sad movie about girl named Alice. I would even imagine the musical score—when there would be cheerful trumpets, when there would be sad strings. It was kind of sick. But I couldn't stop.)

I stared out the window. The new set for *Alice the Depressing Movie* was . . .

Unbelievably beautiful.

First of all, the campus was the greenest place I'd ever seen. I didn't know a place could be that green. There were dark green swaying pines and bright green maples and light green grass and old brick buildings with green-shingled roofs. And then there was the *light*. It was magical. The late summer sun was starting to set, and it was like the air was filled with shimmering gold. Gold light fell in patterns across the pavement in front of the buildings. Gold light shone through the branches of the trees. Gold light filled our van and made the faces of my gossiping, makeup-y future classmates look positively . . . angelic.

"This is the most beautiful place in the world," I whispered.

Judah Lipston the Third briefly glanced up from his comic book.

"Middleton Dorm," the van driver bellowed, and we came to a stop.

I took a crumpled slip of paper out of my pocket and looked at it. It said: Alice Bingley-Beckerman, Transfer Sophomore, Middleton Dorm, Room 201.

"That's me," I said, and started gathering my bags.

"Ooh," someone said, giggling. "She got the bad dorm."

I swallowed, pretended not to hear, and squeezed out of the van. It drove away and left me standing in the middle of a gravel path, surrounded by my suitcases.

I looked up at my future home.

It was, for lack of a better way to put it, a huge zit on the otherwise perfect face of Putnam Mount McKinsey.

Whereas every other building we'd driven by had been made out of beautiful, vine-covered brick, this building was made out of beige stucco. Whereas every other building we'd driven by looked like it was built in 1870, this building looked like it was built in 1970. It was dirty. It was rectangular. The windows were thin slits. It kind of looked like a prison.

It was obviously the dorm for the new students who didn't know any better.

A paper banner sagged in front of the main entrance. It said: WELCOME ALL. A bored-looking girl sat on the steps, smoking a cigarette. Filled with dread, I limped up the gravel path toward her, weighed down by my suitcases. The girl gazed at me apathetically. She had bright pink hair tied up in a ponytail on top of her head. She wore a T-shirt that was slashed open across the shoulder. She had a lip ring. She had about twelve bracelets on each arm. Most impressively, she had a long silver chain that connected a stud in her left nostril to a stud in her left ear.

I stood in front of her and tried to smile.

"Hi," she said.

"Hi," I said.

"I'm Agnes," she said.

"I'm Alice," I said.

She nodded tiredly, and stood up.

"I'm your RA," she informed me, and then she picked up one of my suitcases and started trudging into the dorm.

"Cool!" I said, and immediately hated myself for saying the

word. Somehow saying "cool" in front of someone so much cooler than me felt degrading.

I followed her inside, through a dank, carpeted lobby lined with empty bulletin boards, past some kind of lounge filled with orange furniture, and up a dark stairwell.

"You're the first one here," she said as we clomped up the stairs, "which sucks for you."

"That's okay," I said, even though my heart was sinking in my chest, "I can just hang out."

Agnes stopped abruptly in the middle of the stairs, turned around, and stared at me. "You're not going to be, like, clingy, are you?" she asked.

"What?" I said. "Clingy? I . . . no."

"Good," she said. "I'm your RA, but I'm not like your mom or anything."

"Of course," I said. Just the word *mom* made the back of my eyeballs prick with tears. I prayed she couldn't tell.

"Don't come crying to me or anything."

I nodded.

She cocked her head to one side and looked me up and down. "You're wearing all black," she commented. "That's kind of weird."

I nodded. I *was* wearing all black (I was even wearing black underwear, but Agnes didn't know that). I'd always been a pretty creative dresser, but ever since my dad and R.'s wedding that summer, the only color that appealed to me was black. So I was letting myself wear black. Every day. Why not? I was in mourning, after all. Not only for my mother, but also for the loss of my old, carefree, idyllic life.

"Why?" Agnes asked, her eyes narrowed. "Are you, like, goth? Because you don't seem goth."

"Um," I said, "No, I guess I'm not goth. I'm just—"

"Whatever," Agnes interrupted, already bored with whatever explanation I was going to give. "We're all good."

Then she turned around and started walking up the stairs again.

I had been lying facedown on my new bed for three hours when my roommate finally arrived. I heard the knob rattle, then the door open, and then all of a sudden a beautiful Indian girl was inside my room, dragging a pink suitcase behind her and screeching into her cell phone.

"It's so *dirty!*" she exclaimed.

I could hear the muffled voice of the person on the other end of the phone responding.

"Like *really* dirty," the beautiful girl shouted. "There's this, like, gray carpeting? And fluorescent lighting?"

I sat up in bed and looked at her, hoping that my face didn't look too bloated and tear streaked. The girl shot me a brief but blinding smile, and then kept talking into the phone.

"Yeah," she said, nodding and chomping on her gum. "Yeah. Totally."

Still nodding, she lugged another pink suitcase into the room. And then another. And then another. I eventually ended up counting more than ten. Still on the phone, she began to unpack them. I watched her in disbelief. Was she even going to introduce herself to me?

"No, totally," she murmured into the phone while she dragged what looked like a sequined ball gown out of one suitcase. "Totally, totally. I know. I feel the same way. Yeah. It's totally lame."

I studied her. She was wearing short-shorts, a tube top, and a pair of tiny blue high heels. A pair of sunglasses rested on top of her head. Her shiny jet-black hair curled perfectly around her shoulders. Although she and Agnes the RA couldn't have looked more different, I had a hard time deciding who was more terrifying.

The girl took a shoe box out of one bag and opened it. It was full of magazine cutouts.

"Mm-hm," she said. "Mm-hm. Blond. Mm-hm."

Was she talking about me?

"Of course not!" she shrieked into the phone. "I would never!"

She carefully unfolded a picture of a muscled male model in a tiny red swimsuit and tacked it onto the wall, wedging the cell phone between her shoulder and chin. Then she unfolded another picture of a tanned, half-naked male model. Then another one. Then another one. They all grinned at me across the room, flashing their white teeth.

I wondered if this girl was going to talk on her phone for the rest of the school year. I decided it was a strong possibility. I sat there and waited a few more minutes while she "uh-huh"-ed and "mm"-ed. Then I gave up and lay back down, pressing my face into the pillow.

"Katie," the girl said, "I gotta go. Yeah. You, too. You are such a lame ass. Yes. You. Okay. I love you. Swizzle sticks. Bye."

There was a small beeping sound as she hung up the phone. Then there was a long silence. I could hear the birds chirping outside our window.

"Hey," the girl said.

"Mmrf," I said into my pillow.

"I'm Reena."

I was suddenly terrified that if I lifted my face up and exposed it to my new roommate, I would start crying. So I attempted to speak without moving at all.

"I'm Alice," I said muffledly.

"Where are you from?"

"Brooklyn."

"Brooklyn? Like New York City Brooklyn?"

"Mm hm."

There was a long pause.

"I'm from Los Angeles," she said finally.

"Cool," I said. That *word* again. I had to stop saying that word. I also had to stop constantly being on the verge of crying. People could probably sense it in my voice. They could sense I was lonely and pathetic and nervous and scared.

"Want a Blow Pop?" Reena asked after a horrible pause. "I have cherry, and uh ... grape?"

"No, thanks," I mumbled, and then turned my face to the wall.

After a minute I heard her start unpacking again, and the two of us didn't speak until Agnes knocked on our door and told us to head down to the lounge for orientation.

The expectant faces of thirty teenage girls turned in my direction.

"My name is Alice," I said slowly, "and I like ... um, apples."

"Someone already said apples," said the girl sitting across from me.

Everyone giggled.

"Oh," I said. "Okay. Um. My name is Alice and I like ..."

My mind was going blank. I liked eggplant. I liked chocolate. I liked peanut butter. I liked raspberries. Were the any words in existence that began with *A* besides *apple*?

"I like..." My mouth was dry. I blinked. I swallowed. A wave of laughter made its way around the circle.

"Do you like artichokes?" whispered the girl on my right. I looked at her, surprised. She was tiny, with thick glasses and a smattering of pimples across her nose. She looked about twelve. I exhaled, relieved.

"My name is Alice and I like artichokes," I announced to the group.

That was a big lie. I hated artichokes. But I would have said I liked eating dog to get through my turn.

Then it was time for Reena to speak. She was sitting to my left. The two of us had been conscientiously ignoring each other ever since we left our dorm room.

I couldn't believe that my new roommate already hated me. And that I hated her.

But I only hated her because she so obviously hated me.

"My name is Reena," Reena said, with enough apathy in her voice to make it clear to everyone that she thought the game was dumb, "and I like radicchio."

"What's radicchio?" asked the bespectacled girl on my right.

Reena gasped. "You don't know what *radicchio* is?"

The girl shrugged.

"It's like this really, really delicious vegetable that they put in salads."

"Oh," said the girl with the glasses. "I guess I've never had it."

"Well, they serve it in all the best restaurants."

"Oookay," said Agnes, who was sitting in the middle of the circle. "I think that's everyone. Do you all know each other's names now?"

I looked around the circle at the faces of the other girls in my dorm. I couldn't remember any of them. They all looked the same: high ponytail, tank top, flip-flops, and sunglasses on top of their heads. They also all looked way more confident than I felt.

Except for the tiny girl with glasses on my right who didn't know what radicchio was.

She just seemed kind of ... pathetic.

"All right," yawned Agnes. "What's next?"

She took a piece of paper out of her pocket and inspected it.

"Dinnertime," she announced.

And then, like a dam had broke, everyone rose to their feet and streamed out of the room. I was left sitting on the dirty orange rug all by myself.

Why, I wondered, am I *this* person? What's wrong with me? Why am I invisible? Why am I the one who never gets swept up in the crowd? And why does my own roommate already think that I'm totally boring and lame?

Is it because I actually *am* boring and lame?

Or is it because everyone thinks I'm goth?

I shakily got to my feet and walked out of the lounge and into the cafeteria.

It was chaos.

My fellow new students had already been absorbed into what seemed like a crowd of hundreds. Everyone was squeezed around a table and talking, or yelling across the room to one another, or standing in line, or circling the salad bar and chatting. I scanned the room for one girl, just one girl, who looked alone and out of place. But everyone had already found someone. Everyone had already found *five* other someones. Even the tiny girl with glasses and zits was cheerfully conversing with a cafeteria lady.

I stood in the middle of the dinner hall, my head throbbing. *Someone come talk to me,* I prayed.

I waited around ten seconds and was suddenly jostled by a beautiful girl with red hair, holding a cafeteria tray.

"Excuse me," she said. Her violet eyes sparkled while she looked me up and down.

"Sorry," I said. "Um . . ."

Say something, I told myself. *Say something.*

I could barely choke the words out. "Um, my name is . . ."

But someone was already whispering in the beautiful girl's ear, and the beautiful girl was already staring at me and giggling.

"Reena," she exclaimed to the person next to her. "You are *so bad!*"

Then the two of them walked away, arms linked and heads bowed together, their shoulders shaking with laughter.

I held my tears back just long enough to grab a handful of croutons from the salad bar, sprint up the stairs to my room, and fall face-first onto my pillow.

FIVE

Reena

Okay, so boarding school wasn't exactly what I expected.

Is it wrong that I hoped my dorm room would have wood floors? and a fireplace? and maybe the stuffed head of a mountain lion hanging over the mantelpiece?

Instead I got dirty gray carpeting, streaky walls, a buzzing fluorescent light, and not much else.

And is it wrong that I hoped my roommate might be a nice, normal, friendly person with whom I could hold an actual conversation? Maybe even a cool East Coast girl who could teach me how to roast chestnuts and make really good hot chocolate?

Instead I got a sulky blond chick wearing all black who looked exactly like a younger version of Shanti Shruti. And even that would have been okay, if she had deigned to talk to me. Instead Miss Cooler Than Thou lay on her bed and ignored me for hours while I unpacked. Well, fine. I didn't need her. I could make friends on my own while she sat around and looked down her nose at everybody. And it made total sense when she said she was from New York City. New York City kids—I'd always imagined—were ten times more sophisticated than everyone else. But Alice Bingley-Beckerman was sophisticated in a bad way. I could tell that she thought I was immature and dumb.

Point is, I already had one snotty blond woman in my life making me feel bad. I didn't need another.

Which is not to say I wasn't seized by terror when I walked into the cafeteria that first night and realized that I was going to have find someone else to talk to. And somewhere to sit.

I picked up a plastic tray and made my way toward the hot food line. I waited as the line moved forward, trying to keep a nonchalant expression on my face. *Show no weakness, Reenie,* my father had told me on my first day of school in Beverly Hills, right after we'd saved up enough money to move there. *The key is to never let anyone know you feel bad.*

I stared over the heads of my new classmates so it looked like I was spacing out and thinking about something incredibly important.

"Ew," someone behind me in line said.

I turned around. The someone was a frighteningly perfect-looking girl with shiny red hair and porcelain skin. She was wearing a purple minidress and purple eyeliner. Her pink lip gloss was flawlessly applied. Was she talking to me?

"What *is* that smell?" she asked, her lips pursed in distaste. Our eyes connected. Okay. She was talking to me. I had to say something witty in return. Something cool. Something disaffected. I assumed she was talking about the smell in the hot food line, which, to be honest, was not as bad as it could have been. But there was something else my father liked to say to me: *Pick your battles, Reenie. Pick your battles.*

"It smells kind of like homeless man," I said thoughtfully. "Combined with old cheese. And nail polish. And my grandmother's sweat."

The girl shrieked with pleasure. "That is, like, the grossest thing I've ever heard!"

I grinned. "You haven't heard anything yet." It was true. I was famous at my high school for my disgusting sense of humor.

"I'm Kristen," the girl said. She held out her hand. I shook it.

"I'm Reena," I said.

"Reena? What is that?"

I wasn't sure exactly what she meant. "Um. It's Indian?"

"Oh. Cool." Her eyes flickered up and down my face, then up and down my body. "I like your shoes."

"Thanks."

"Are you new here?"

I rolled my eyes. "Unfortunately, yes."

"Me, too."

"Where are you from?"

Kristen tugged on the edge of her purple dress. For a split second, it looked like she felt uncomfortable. Then the look evaporated. I wasn't sure what had happened. She tossed her shiny red hair behind her shoulder.

"Westport, Connecticut," she said.

"Oh. Cool." I'd never even heard of it, but it sounded nice. Connecticut. I pictured thousands of red-haired Kristen clones, all living in perfect white houses with perfect green yards.

"Where are you from?" Kristen asked.

"Los Angeles."

"Agggh!" she yelled. "I hate you! That's where I want to move when I grow up!"

"Oh. Yeah. It's okay."

"*Okay?*" she said while cafeteria ladies spooned shapeless lumps of chicken and sauce onto our plates. "I want more information. Do you, like, know any movie stars?"

"Nah," I said, as we moved out of line into the dining hall. "I mean, except for the fact that some of them work out at my gym."

"You're kidding me."

"Uh, no. But that's not a big deal or anything. I mean, you see celebrities all the time. On the street and stuff. It's really not that exciting."

Kristen sighed. "I *totally* hate you."

We were standing in the middle of the dining hall, balancing our dinner trays on our palms. I cleared my throat nervously.

"We might as well sit together," Kristen said after a long pause.

"Yeah," I said. "Might as well."

I could have kissed her.

We made our way through the crowd, looking for an empty table. Suddenly I saw Alice Bingley-Beckerman. She was standing alone in her black skirt and T-shirt, looking around the cafeteria with an expression of utter terror on her face. For a second, I felt bad for her. But then I realized that what looked to me like fear was probably classic New Yorker disdain. She was just thinking about how uncool all her fellow classmates were.

Another nugget of gold from Rashul Paruchuri: *Be nice, Reenie. Just not too nice.*

Kristen and Alice bumped right into each other, and I saw Alice's face light up. *Oh no,* I thought. *I'm not cool enough for her, but Kristen is!* Before either of them could say anything, I leaned over to Kristen and whispered the first thing that popped into mind.

"I have to get out of here and smoke a cigarette," I hissed.

Kristen stared at me, delighted.

"You are so bad!" she shrieked, and the two of us headed off toward the exit, leaving Alice Bingley-Beckerman in our wake.

At first I felt a wave of relief. Then, slowly, I started to realize what I'd just said, and my stomach dropped.

I have this terrible habit of . . . well, you wouldn't call it pathologically *lying*, because I never mean to *lie*, but I have this habit of sometimes just saying things that, well, In No Way Correspond to Reality.

For example: My father once threw this party for all the surgeons at his hospital, and we were all standing around and mingling with champagne glasses when this one old guy said to me: "You know, I actually attended Woodstock in 1969." And, without even thinking about it, I nodded enthusiastically and said: "That's so funny! So did I!"

I was born decades after Woodstock.

The problem is, I can't control it. I don't even know that I've lied—I mean, said something that's not exactly true—until after I've already said it.

So when I leaned over and told Kristen that I needed to go outside and have a cigarette, I didn't anticipate that I'd actually have to go outside and . . . have a cigarette. I mean, I don't smoke. I took one puff at a party in seventh grade and almost hacked up a lung.

But all of a sudden Kristen was leading me out of the building and over to a shady tree next to our dorm.

"We can eat here while you smoke," she said cheerfully, and plunked her tray down onto the grass.

I patted my pockets. I think I was half-praying that a pack of cigarettes would mysteriously appear inside of them.

"Aw geez," I said, "I'm out. I'm out of cigarettes."

"Oh no!" she said, a concerned look on her face.

"Yeah. It's okay. I can survive."

"Well, you must be *dying* for one."

"Um, well—"

"I mean, you must be, like, totally addicted, right?"

I nodded, my stomach churning. "Yeah. I guess I am."

She stared at me.

"Um," I said. I looked around the lawn. Agnes, my extremely weird Residential Advisor, was lying on the grass about twenty feet away, chatting with a guy wearing leather pants. I peered over at them. The guy was holding something small and white in his hands.

"Hold on a minute," I said to Kristen, and marched purposefully across the lawn toward them.

"Hi, Agnes," I said.

Agnes squinted up at me in the sunlight, her arms crossed behind her head. A slice of her stomach was exposed, and I saw that the skin below her bellybutton was pierced with a small silver barbell.

"Hey, Nina," she said.

"It's Reena."

"Right. Reena."

70

I swallowed and smiled at Agnes and her leather pants–wearing friend. "Um, I was just wondering...do you...do either of you have a cigarette?"

The guy raised his eyebrows at Agnes. Agnes sat up.

"You smoke?" she asked, staring at me.

"Uh, yeah."

"No," she said. "No way. Not you." Her eyes seemed to penetrate into my very soul.

"Oh, yes," I said.

Agnes sighed and turned to her male companion. "God. Smoking doesn't mean anything anymore, does it?"

I had no idea what she was talking about. Neither did he apparently. He shrugged, withdrew a red pack of cigarettes from his pocket, and held them out to me. I took one, tentatively held it between my thumb and forefinger, and stared at it. One end was light brown. The other end was white. Which part did you put in your mouth?

"Cool, thanks," I said to the guy in leather pants.

"You need a light?" he asked.

"Uh, sure," I said.

I held out the cigarette. Agnes chortled.

"You put it in your *mouth* first," she said. "Are you *sure* you're a smoker?"

I nodded, and looked across the lawn at Kristen. She waved at me. I waved back.

"Yup," I said. "We just, uh, do it a little differently in California."

"Like, *how* differently?"

I pretended not to hear. I put the white part of the cigarette in my mouth.

"WRONG END!" shrieked Agnes, and then she fell back

onto the grass, laughing hysterically. I prayed that Kristen couldn't hear.

I put the brown end in my mouth. The guy in leather pants held out his silver lighter. A blue flame leapt up. I put the cigarette in my mouth, leaned over, and dipped it into the flame. What next? I glanced up at the guy. It looked like he was wearing mascara.

"Inhale," he whispered.

I inhaled.

What felt like a brush fire went through the cigarette, into my mouth, and down my throat. I started choking. Some kind of phlegm rose up in my throat. Before I even knew what was happening, I'd spat out the cigarette onto the grass and was crouched over on the ground, hacking. Agnes wailed with laughter. The guy in leather pants was shaking his head.

"Thanks, anyway," I whispered, my eyes burning with tears, and jogged back across the lawn toward Kristen.

It felt like small demon was running around inside my throat, setting fire to my tonsils.

"What happened?" Kristen asked.

I was planning on just giving up and telling her the truth. I really was.

But then That Thing happened again.

"Those *cigarettes*," I said. "That guy had the worst cigarettes."

"Oh, really?"

"Yeah. I'm, like, extremely picky about the cigarettes I smoke. And those were really gross. Blech."

"What kind of cigarettes do you normally smoke?"

"Um. This really expensive French kind."

I wanted to punch myself in the face.

"I guess we'll go buy some later," Kristen decided, and patted a spot on the ground next to her. "Now tell me more about LA."

I sighed with relief.

I had a friend.

Now I just had to make sure not to compulsively lie to her.

"LIGHTS OUT!" Agnes bellowed, running up and down the hallway. "LIGHTS OUT, YOU LITTLE SUCKERS!"

Another big surprise about Putnam Mount McKinsey: It felt a little, just a little, like a prison.

All freshman and sophomores, Agnes informed us during our orientation meeting, had dinner at 7:00 PM, study period from 8:00 to 10:00 PM, and then lights out at 10:30.

I couldn't believe it.

In LA, I went bed at midnight. At the earliest.

Alice Bingley-Beckerman and I sat on the edge of our parallel twin beds, waiting for Agnes to knock on our door. Alice was wearing a beautiful black satin nightgown, and her blond hair rippled down her back.

I was wearing a pair of Pradeep's old boxer shorts and a tank top.

We were ignoring each other.

I felt ugly.

Even worse, I was starting to get this weird stomachache. I tried to remember another time I'd felt this way, and the only thing I could think of was this summer vacation Pradeep and I took when I was ten. We'd never met our mother's parents before and so they sent the two of us to Bangalore, India, to meet them. After a sixteen-hour plane trip, we spent two weeks in a tiny, hot house outside of the city, listening to a grandmother we'd never met before lecture us on how we were leading pointless, immoral lives in America. Between lectures, she'd chew dates and spit the pits into the palm of her hand.

There were also servants we weren't allowed to touch.

And one night I was forced to eat goat.

Anyway, the whole time we were in Bangalore, I had a stomachache. Maybe it goat-induced indigestion, but mostly I think it was homesickness. I missed my mom. I missed my dad. I missed my friends. I missed my dolls. I missed running in and out of the sprinkler in our backyard.

And the second I got back to LA and was folded into my mother's warm, rose-scented bosom, the stomachache went away.

Now I was sitting in a strange little room at this strange little boarding school in Massachusetts, next to a snotty blond girl who was ignoring me, waiting to be checked on by a scary older girl who seemed to be the only parental figure around, and it was that same feeling again. That same stomachache. That same feeling of homesickness.

And then I realized something even scarier: I wasn't even sure what I was homesick *for*.

I didn't want to go live with my mother and Pria.

I definitely didn't want to go live with my father and Shanti Shruti.

I was missing something that didn't exist.

I was missing the past.

I was pastsick.

There was a loud knock on our door.

"Yes?" Alice murmured.

Agnes threw open the door. "Yo," she said. "Just making sure you're both here."

"Yo," I said sadly.

She peered at me. "You know you can't smoke in the dorm rooms, right?"

Alice whipped her head around and stared at me. "You *smoke*?" she asked.

It was the first sentence she'd spoken to me all evening.

"Er," I said, "Yeah. I guess."

Agnes laughed in her horrible condescending way, and shut the door.

There was a long pause. I glanced in Alice's direction. She was bent over, her chin cupped in her hand, and her hair fell across her face.

"I guess I'll turn the lights out," I said.

She nodded.

I stood up, flicked off the light switch, and the room was plunged into total darkness.

"Good night," I said.

"Good night," Alice whispered, and I groped my way toward my bed, holding my hands out in front of me and trying to see its outline in the darkness. I felt the edge of my mattress with my knee, and touched my pillow with my finger. Then I let my body collapse onto my new, hard, cold, and unfamiliar bed.

I listened to the sound of my breath. I listened to the sound of Alice's breath. Someone had left a single glow-in-the-dark star sticker on the ceiling. I stared at it for a long time.

Then my cell phone rang.

Alice bolted upright.

"Sorry, sorry!" I yelped, and reached down to the floor to fish it out of my purse. Pradeep's name appeared on the screen. I took the phone and burrowed under my covers.

"Hello?" I whispered.

I heard Alice exhale in disgust.

"REEN!" Pradeep yelled into my ear. I could hear music playing and people talking in the background.

"Quieter, please," I murmured.

"REEN!"

"What?"

"IT'S AWESOME HERE!"

I didn't know what to say. Was he kidding?

"Aren't you in bed?" I asked.

"Aw, no way! Our RA is awesome! He's letting us stay up and party!"

"Oh."

"Are you okay?" Pradeep asked.

I sighed. "Um. I guess."

"Do you like your roommate? Mine is awesome. He's from *Nova Scotia*. Isn't that crazy? He, like, goes moose hunting for fun!"

In the background I could hear hooting and laughter.

"I don't know," I whispered.

"Wait. What? You don't know what?"

I sighed, exasperated.

"What are you talking about?" he asked again.

"Pradeep."

"What?"

"I have to go."

"Oh. Okay. Cool, cool."

"I'll see you tomorrow."

We hung up. I stared at the ceiling. I had never felt more alone in my life.

And it was all Shanti Shruti's fault.

SIX

Molly

Radicchio.

I couldn't believe it. My first day at boarding school and there was already a *word* I didn't *know*.

An unprecedented event.

Right after dinner I ran upstairs to my dorm room and looked up *radicchio* in the OED.

"A variety of chicory," I whispered out loud.

The door opened and then slammed shut. I looked up from my bed. My new roommate was standing in front of me, hands on her hips. Her violet eyes blazed with anger.

"Is this what it's going to be like?" she demanded.

"Hi, Kristen," I said.

She pursed her lips and stared at me for a long time.

"Is this what *what's* going to be like?" I finally asked.

"Living together. Are you always going to be in here, like, reading?"

"Um, no. But I do like to read."

She sighed and flounced down onto her bed. My heart did a terrified little leap. My roommate—Miss Kristen Diamond of Westport, Connecticut—uncannily reminded me of the popular girls at North Forest High. Except with more money. And more rage.

I had sort of thought everyone at Putnam Mount McKinsey was going to be thoughtful and nerdy and quiet and friendly. Like me.

Kristen kicked off her flip-flops and lay on her back. I tried to focus on the OED and listen to the whirring of the window fan.

"Do you have a boyfriend?" she finally asked.

I chortled, not taking my eyes off the dictionary.

"What's so funny?"

"I've never had a boyfriend."

"Never?"

"Nope."

"Have you ever been on a date?"

"No."

"God. That is tragic."

I stared at the OED entry. *Radicchio. From the Italian.*

"I've had, like, ten different boyfriends," Kristen announced.

"Good for you."

"Are you being sarcastic or something?"

"Nope. Not at all."

Normally having reddish purple, white-veined leaves. Not used in the English language until 1978. So I'd never had a boyfriend. Big deal. Not that I didn't want one. It was just that . . . no guy had ever really expressed an interest in me. And I'd never met a guy I thought was that great.

Except for that one guy in the pink shirt, the one I'd seen

years before in my father's diner. The Putnam Mount McKinsey student with the book of Emily Dickinson poems sticking out of his pocket. He was perfect.

That guy had probably already graduated.

Kristen snapped me out of my reverie. "...sex," she was saying. "I've only had sex four times. But I plan to get a lot more practice here."

I nodded numbly.

"I've already seen a bunch of really cute guys."

There was no way I was going to be able to focus on my reading. I put down the OED and lay on my back while Kristen chattered away about her ex-boyfriends. My heart thumping quietly, I stared at the ceiling and thought about my new life. Everything had changed so quickly. Putnam Mount McKinsey was nothing like what I thought it would be, and my memories from that very morning—Spencer standing in the driveway in those terrible high heels—seemed incredibly far away. I didn't miss North Forest yet, not at all, and yet I couldn't really comprehend the fact that I didn't live there anymore. It was kind of hard to believe that I could climb in a car and just *drive away* from the place I'd hated my whole life.

But could I?

Because I was still thinking about it. I was thinking about my mom at Silverwood, sitting by the window in her rocking chair, staring out at the sinking sun. I was thinking about Candy kissing my father good night and making another snide comment about my skirt. I was thinking about Sandie and Randie squatting together under a tree and digging for earthworms.

I was just . . . living somewhere else now.

Kristen kept chattering away, and I kept nodding and saying, "Mmhm," even though I'd stopped listening.

Where were the people who were going to become part of My New and Better Life?

I wanted to meet them. As soon as possible.

Early the next morning, I stood outside the student union with my fellow transfer classmates and listened to a psychotically cheerful junior scream into a megaphone.

"STUDENT LIFE AT PUTNAM MOUNT MCKINSEY IS ALL ABOUT TRUST!" she yelled.

A couple of people snickered. Kristen, who had made a point of standing as far away from me as possible, nudged a beautiful Indian girl who was standing next to her and winked at her.

Even though Kristen was my new Least Favorite Person Ever, I felt a twinge of jealousy. I wanted someone to wink at me.

"YOU HAVE TO TRULY TRUST YOUR FELLOW CLASS-MATES TO CREATE A PRODUCTIVE AND HARMONIOUS EN-VIRONMENT," the girl bellowed. "SO WE'RE GOING TO DO A FEW EXERCISES TO GET EVERYONE FEELING COMFORTABLE AND OPEN!"

At least fifteen kids groaned.

"COUNT OFF IN TENS!"

A halfhearted muttering passed through the crowd. I barely heard the girl next to me whisper, "Five."

"Six!" I said loudly.

Someone nearby burst out laughing.

"OKAY," the junior announced. "ONES, OVER THERE. TWOS, OVER THERE. THREES, OVER THERE . . ."

When she got to the sixes, she pointed vaguely at a patch of shady grass off in the distance, and I trudged toward it. Kristen was already standing there, tapping her foot impatiently. She looked at me in horror.

"Oh, God," she said. "You're kidding me."

"Nope," I said.

"Is it just the two of us?" she asked. "Because if it is—"

I never found out what she was going to say. A smiling boy had suddenly stepped into our little patch of shade. Kristen and I fell silent.

"Hey," he said, his hand outstretched, "I'm Pradeep."

Kristen and I both stared at him, speechless. Then, for some miraculous reason, I recovered my composure.

"I'm Molly," I said, and shook his hand. He grinned at me.

"What up, Molly?" he said.

He had thick black hair and skin the color of maple syrup. He had a gap between his two front teeth. He had hazel eyes. He had a crooked grin. He had ears that were just a little too big for his head. He had a gorgeous lips. He had the tiniest bit of chest hair poking out from underneath the neck of his V-neck T-shirt. He had bony wrists. He had a pronounced Adam's Apple that throbbed slightly when he smiled. He had—

"I'm Kristen," said Kristen. She stepped forward, her red hair falling across half of her face, and delicately offered him her hand.

The boy blinked. I watched his hazel eyes take in Kristen's perfect skin, her perfect hair, her perfect dress, her perfect body. *No!* I tried to telepathically communicate to him, *don't!*

"It's weird that you shake people's hands," Kristen said to him, raising one eyebrow.

He tilted his head to one side and stared at her, mock serious. "You got a problem with that?" he asked.

"Yeah," she said, her lips thrumming with a half-concealed smile. "I do."

They grinned at each other.

Great. Just great.

"OKAY, EVERYONE!" screamed the megaphone girl. "I WANT TWO PEOPLE IN EVERY GROUP TO PAIR OFF!"

"Well, I'm definitely not pairing off with you," Pradeep said to Kristen.

"You neither," she giggled, and they moved toward each other as if by magnetic force.

"Oookay," I said. "I guess you guys are the pair."

They ignored me.

"NOW!" the girl said. "THIRD PERSON, FACE AWAY FROM THE PAIR!"

I sighed and faced away from Kristen and Pradeep. I could see a Japanese-style pond in the distance, with tall reeds and stone benches. I pictured sitting on one of the benches with Pradeep and whispering word origins in his ear. *You're so smart,* he'd murmur, and then our fingers would touch.

"FALL BACK!" the girl yelled into the megaphone, interrupting my fantasy.

My heart froze. I turned around to face Kristen and Pradeep.

"What'd she say?" I asked.

Kristen stared at me, already annoyed. "She said fall back. Fall back and we'll catch you."

"Um," I said. "I don't want to."

"It's okay," said Pradeep. "You can trust us."

I looked at him for a long time. He smiled reassuringly at me, and I watched his amazing Adam's apple bob up and down. What would it be like to touch his neck?

"For God's sakes, Molly," Kristen said. "Fall."

"Okay, okay," I said, and turned back to face the Japanese garden. I paused. I didn't want to fall. Why was this a necessary part of boarding school orientation? What did this have to do with math and English class?

"FALL!" I heard through the megaphone. "FALL!"

I closed my eyes. The sun shone through my closed lids and made everything a pulsing orange color. I smelled the new-cut grass and the sunscreen on people's skin. Okay. I had to do it. I had to take risks. This was my new life. Everything was different now.

I took a deep breath. I rocked back on my ankles. Once. Twice. A third time. And then, my body rigid, my hands pressed against my side, I fell.

For a while everything went black.

I woke to find a bright buzzing light shining into my eyes. I squinted. My head hurt.

"She's awake!" someone whispered, and then a head floated into my line of vision.

It was Pradeep. I smiled groggily at him and assumed I was dreaming.

"Uh, hey," he said. "Molly? That's your name, right?"

"Mmhm," I murmured, and his beautiful eyes swam in and out of focus.

"I'm really sorry, dude," he whispered.

Unable to help myself, I kept grinning at him.

"Can you understand me?" he asked.

I bobbled my head around, trying to nod.

"It was really lame, what happened," he said. "We just . . . we were talking, and we forgot, and it was a total accident, but it was . . ."

I wasn't sure what he was talking about, but I didn't like the words he was using. Lame. Accident. *We.*

"Where am I?" I whispered.

"Oh, dude," he said. "You must be really out of it. You're at the nurse's office."

A stern-looking woman's face appeared above me. "You have to leave now," the face told Pradeep.

He nodded, and his head floated away.

My forehead suddenly throbbed with pain. I winced. I heard the door click as Pradeep left the room. The woman stared down at me.

"You, my dear," she said, "have a concussion."

"Nope," I said. "That's impossible."

"It is the very opposite of impossible," she said. "It's fact. Your friends forgot to catch you and your head hit the concrete."

I felt a stinging sensation in the back of my eyes.

Of course.

This was the kind of thing that could only, only happen to me. This particular brand of pathetic humiliation was Classic Molly Miller.

"They're not my friends," I whispered.

"What did you say, sweetheart?" she asked.

"They're not my friends!" I said, and then burst into hot, burning tears.

I drifted in and out of sleep. A day passed. Maybe two. I awoke to a ray of midafternoon sun streaming in through the window and falling across my legs. I could see thousands of dust particles in the air, fluttering in the beam of light like little insects.

"Molly," someone said.

The voice sent a chill down my spine. I recognized it but couldn't place it.

A hand reached out and shook my wrist.

"*Molly*," the voice said again.

I raised my head up, painfully. Candy was sitting in a chair across from my bed, her hands folded across her lap.

It took all of my strength to stop myself from groaning out loud.

"How are you feeling," Candy said. She said it like a statement, not a question.

"I'm okay," I murmured. "Where's Dad?"

"At home with Sandie and Randie."

"Why aren't *you* at home with Sandie and Randie?"

"Do not mouth off to me, missy."

"Okay, okay."

There was a long pause.

"I want you to come back to North Forest," Candy said.

I shot up in bed. Pain seared through my skull. "*What?*" I yelped.

"You should come home."

"Why?"

"We need your help."

I stared at her. Her face was expressionless. Her mouth formed a tight little line. Her blue eyes looked dull and blank.

"You need my help doing what?"

"Your father and I are both working full-time. Spencer is practicing for the statewide twirling competition. Sandie and Randie need someone to—"

"No." My head throbbed. My whole body was trembling. My fingers clutched at the edges of the sheet. I made direct eye contact with Candy. "I will not come home."

"You don't belong here, Molly."

"Yes I do."

"Look at you. You get a, a *concussion* within twenty-four hours of—"

"Shut up!" I yelled.

Candy shook her head. "You're being irresponsible," she said after a while. "Your father and I need someone else to help out. The fact that you think you can just abandon your family and—"

"You're not my family," I told her.

"Excuse me?"

"You're not my family."

"Oh, yeah? Then who's your family?"

My stomach sank.

Candy gave me a rueful smile. "The rest of your family is checked into the loony bin."

"It's a residential treatment facility."

She laughed. "Right. Whatever."

"I'm never going back to North Forest," I said, trying to sound full of conviction.

87

"You're abandoning your sisters."

Spencer's face flashed through my mind. I shook my head and tried to push it away. "I'm not leaving."

"We'll see how you feel after first semester."

"No. No. No."

She stood up and folded her purse into her chest. "Well," she said, gazing down at me, "you might not have a choice."

And then, her high heels clicking neatly across the linoleum floor, she was gone.

SEVEN

Alice

It was a pleasant, breezy morning. The sun was peeking through streaks of gauzy white clouds. The bells of Putnam chapel were ringing.

I was miserable.

It was the first official day of classes. I had managed to get through three days of orientation without making a single friend, and now I was walking up a grassy hill toward the humanities building, toward my first class, all by myself. Surrounding me were clumps and pairs of my fellow students, giggling and talking and swinging their book bags by their side.

I walked through a set of big double doors and stopped in the lobby. It was a beautiful old building, with wooden floors and beams of light shining through stained-glass windows. I squinted at a sign with little arrows indicating classroom numbers and locations and then walked down a narrow hallway. My mouth was dry. I was worried nothing would come out if I tried to talk.

"Hi, Alice," a high, nasal voice piped up next to me.

I turned and looked. It was the same shrimpy girl with glasses from the first night of school. Except this time she had a white band of gauze wrapped around her head.

"Hi," I croaked, and kept walking down the hall.

She trotted alongside me. "You like artichokes, right?"

"What?"

She giggled. "Remember? From the name game? You couldn't think of a word that started with *A*?"

Great. Even the nerdy girl thought I was a loser.

"I'm Molly Miller, by the way," she added.

"Oh. Right." I glanced up and down the hall, trying to find an escape route.

"I like the all-black thing," she said. "It's very Hamlet. Have you read *Hamlet*?"

I shook my head.

"You have to. By Shakespeare? It's my favorite play. Hopefully we'll get to read it sometime this year. Are you in Humanities 101?" she continued brightly.

"Um, yeah."

"Me, too!"

"Oh. Cool."

"Hey!" she exclaimed, and stopped in her tracks. "This is our classroom!"

She flung open a door on our right and held it out for me like a bellhop.

I sighed. Maybe this made me a Bad Person, but I really didn't want to walk into class at the same time as Molly Miller. She was kind of a . . . dork. And I wanted to make friends.

People who looked like Molly Miller didn't usually have friends.

I entered the classroom with my head ducked down and slid into a seat. I could see my classmates talking and laughing out of the corner of my eye. I was too freaked out to look at any of them directly. Molly immediately plunked herself down in the desk next to me and leaned over, propping her chin in her hands.

"English is my favorite subject," she said in a loud whisper. "By *far*."

I nodded.

"I wonder what's gonna be on the reading list."

I nodded again. The last thing on my mind was the reading list.

Someone cleared his throat, and the classroom fell silent. I looked up. A young man—he was probably in his late twenties—was leaning against the desk at the front of the classroom, his arms folded. He was small and compact, with sparkling eyes, and his black hair was streaked with gray.

"Hi, everyone," he said.

There was a general murmuring in response.

"My name is David Newman," he said. "Welcome to Humanities 101. I'll be your teacher for the entire school year. So here's hoping we don't all hate each other."

There were a couple of chuckles. Molly let out a burst of high-pitched laughter. I winced.

"In this class," David Newman began, moving behind his desk and sitting down, "we're going to spend most our time studying the Greats. *Gilgamesh. The Odyssey. Henry the Fifth.* Wharton's *House of Mirth*."

I could see Molly Miller nodding vigorously to the right of me. I had no idea what he was talking about.

"But," he continued, "I'm going to start us off with a

piece of twentieth-century literature. This is a fantastic work by a contemporary novelist, and it synthesizes many of the disparate themes and works we'll be discussing this fall."

My brain was somehow unable to absorb anything this guy said. I looked around the classroom desperately. Could anyone else understand him?

He reached into his desk, pulled out a book, and held it up in the air. I couldn't see the title, but it somehow looked familiar. Something about its color and the blurry illustration on the cover . . .

"This is *Zen Ventura*," he announced. "Has anyone heard of it?"

My heart stopped.

Molly Miller's hand shot up into the air. Slowly I raised mine, too. David Newman glanced in our direction.

"Okay. Two of you. Well, this was a seminal book in 1978. Just about everyone read it and was influenced by it. Nelson Bingley is one of the great writers in the post-1950 generation of—"

His words starting blending into each other. *Zen Ventura*. My father's first and most famous novel. The one I never bothered to read because it looked too thick and boring.

Now we were talking about it on the first day of school.

It had never occurred to me that this could happen.

I glanced over at Molly Miller. She was in the middle of talking.

"—one of my most favorite authors," she finished, her cheeks flushed with excitement.

"I'm so glad," David said. He nodded in my direction. "And what about you? When did you read it?"

I tried to swallow. My tongue was glued to the roof of my mouth.

"Um," I said. There was a long pause. Everyone in the class turned to look at me. I stared into the sea of their blank, disinterested faces. "Uh . . . I actually haven't read it. I've just . . . ah . . ." I trailed off.

"Heard of it?" asked David.

Another attempt at swallowing. "Yeah."

"Okay. Well. That's fine." He turned to the rest of the class. I breathed a sigh of relief. "There should be twenty-five copies waiting for you guys at the school store. By this time next week everyone should have read the first three chapters. Okay?"

General shuffling and nodding and whispering.

"Okay." He smiled at all of us. "So I guess that's it. I see no point in keeping you guys. I'm here to talk to you about literature, and since you haven't done the reading yet . . . we have nothing to say to each other."

Molly Miller let out another high-decibel squeal of laughter. Everyone rose to their feet and started trudging out of the classroom. I saw my roommate, Reena, and her new redhaired best friend whispering to each other and glancing over their shoulders as they walked out the door.

I sighed. They were probably talking about what a big loser I was. Reena had managed to ignore me for the past three days, except in the middle of our second night when she'd reached across the gap between our beds, poked my shoulder, and yelled: "YOU'RE SNORING!"

"Sorry," I'd muttered, my cheeks hot with embarrassment, and then I'd spent the rest of that night and the one after lying awake, paralyzed with fear.

So I was also pretty tired.

"Alice!" someone yelled.

I looked up. Molly Miller was standing in front of me, clasping her book bag to her chest. Except for us, the classroom was empty.

"I can't believe you like Nelson Bingley, too!" she said, and shook her head in happy bewilderment.

I buried my head in my hands.

"Alice?"

I didn't respond.

"Alice. Are you okay?"

I lifted up my face and gazed out the window. Green leaves shimmered in the sunlight. It was amazing how you could be in such a beautiful place and still feel miserable. I looked back at Molly Miller. She was staring at me. The gauze bandage around her forehead was starting to come undone. God, was she dorky.

"Why are you wearing a bandage on your head?" I asked. My voice sounded so cold and distant. Hearing it made me wince.

Her cheeks flushed. "Um . . . I fell."

"You fell? How?"

She looked down at the ground. "I actually don't want to talk about it."

There was a long pause. I stood up, slung my bag over my shoulder, and started walking out of the classroom.

"Hey, Alice?"

She was relentless. I turned around. "What?"

"You're really not at all interested in talking about Nelson Bingley? He's, like, one of the greatest writers in the—"

I couldn't stand it anymore. I threw my bag down on the ground.

"No. I don't want to talk about Nelson Bingley. You know why? Because he's my dad. And he's a huge traitor. You think I want to be here at this school? Well, I don't. But my mom died and he married a crazy person, so here I am."

Molly stared at me, her mouth open.

"Happy?" I asked. "That's what I have to say about Nelson Bingley."

I picked up my bag and walked out of the classroom, my heart pounding in my ears. I strode through the long hallway, burst out through the double doors into the sunlight, and stopped on the pavement. I squinted up at the treetops and bit my lip to stop myself from crying.

A small shadow approached me from behind.

"Please go away," I said.

There was a long silence.

"Mine is named Candy Lamb," Molly whispered.

"I have no idea what you're talking about."

"Her name is Candy Lamb."

"Who—whose name is Candy Lamb?"

"My evil stepmother."

I turned and looked at her.

"I have one, too," she said quietly.

And then dorky little Molly Miller did the strangest thing. She held out her arms.

So I fell into them. And cried harder than I'd cried in a long time.

"There are like a million stars!" I exclaimed. The wet grass prickled the back of my neck.

"This is nothing," Molly said.

"You can see, like, *three* in New York City. On a good night."

"Oh, you should see them from the top of Mount Austin in North Forest. It'll blow your mind."

I breathed in the crisp night air. The two of us were lying on our backs on the lawn in front of our dorm. For the first time in four days I didn't feel terrible.

"Show me Orion again," I said.

Her pale hand rose above our heads into the black air. "See those three little stars? In the diagonal line?"

"Uh-huh."

"That's his belt."

"And see that big one?"

"Mm-hm."

"That's his knee."

"Cool!"

The chapel bells rang out from the top of the hill. Molly sat up. "Oh, my God. I totally forgot. It's the fall commencement ceremony. We have to go."

I yawned. "Let's skip it."

"Are you kidding me?"

"Nah. That kind of thing is stupid."

Molly's little face hovered indignantly over mine. "You are such a cynical brat."

I laughed.

"Come on. Seriously. All the seniors come in wearing robes and candles. I think it sounds magical."

"It sounds dumb."

"*Alice . . .*"

"Okay, okay."

She held out her hand and I grabbed it. She hauled me up,

giggling, and the two of us ran up the hill toward the chapel, holding hands.

So . . . okay. Maybe Molly Miller was a huge dork. Actually I knew Molly Miller was a huge dork. Not only did she have all the outward signs of dorkiness—huge glasses, a squeaky voice, pimples, frizzy hair—but over the course of the evening, she'd informed me that her favorite book—besides *Zen Ventura*—was the dictionary. ("And not just the dictionary," she'd said pointedly. "The *Oxford English* Dictionary.")

But I was kind of starting to like her anyway.

And it wasn't just because she had a cold, distant father and a crazy, daughter-hating stepmother and a mother in an insane asylum.

I mean, that helped. We'd spent the entire afternoon talking about our horrible family situations.

But I was starting to realize that Molly Miller was also—in her own, bizarre way—kind of fun.

We ran up to the chapel, and it did look pretty beautiful. Its stained-glass windows glowed in the night sky, and crowds of students were pouring inside, their voices echoing as they made their way up the stone steps.

Molly clutched my hand tighter. I looked at her. Her eyes were shining. It was weird. She was totally into the, like, romance of boarding school.

It was kind of infectious.

The two of us filed into the chapel, and squeezed into a pew near the back. The place was packed. An old woman with a shock of white hair was softly playing the organ, and a middle-aged man with glasses and a big red beard was standing at the podium, shuffling through a pile of papers.

"That's Headmaster Oates," Molly whispered.

"*Him?*"

The guy definitely didn't look like a headmaster. He looked more like . . . an organic vegetable farmer.

"He's a former PMM student himself," Molly said reverently.

She'd clearly read the entire school brochure and transfer welcome packet from front to back.

The old lady started playing a slower, grander melody on the organ. The chapel was filled with the sounds of shuffling and breathing while everyone turned around in their seats and looked toward the front entrance.

The first senior walked through the door in a white robe, cupping a small votive candle in her palm. She was followed by another robed student, and then another . . . I pleasantly zoned out and watched the lights from the candles bob and blur while the organ played and the senior class filed in one by one and made their way toward the podium.

Until I saw him.

And then I'm not exactly sure what happened.

My heart stopped for a second and then started again. A little voice inside my head said: *Uh-oh.* Then I felt like a bucket of cold water had been dumped over my head. Followed by a bucket of hot water. Followed by another bucket of cold water.

He was walking near me, just next to me (his candle's flame seemed to burn more brightly and sorrowfully than any flame I'd ever seen before), and then he moved past me. He was gone.

I blinked. I swallowed. My brain started and stopped, like a car engine trying to rev to life.

"*Who,*" I whispered to Molly, "*was that?*"

She looked at me, puzzled. "Who was who?"

I couldn't believe it. She hadn't noticed him?

"That," I said hoarsely. "That *person*. That *guy*."

"Which guy?"

"The, uh . . ." I lifted my hand up and pointed, trying not to be too obvious. "He just walked by."

"A hundred guys just walked by. Are you talking about the one with the earring?"

I shook my head numbly.

"Alice. Are you okay?"

I shook my head again.

"Oh, my God. Are you breathing?"

I shrugged. The organ song came to a dramatic end.

"What's going on? You look like you saw a ghost or something!"

A girl sitting in our row leaned over. "*Shhh!*" she hissed.

Molly rolled her eyes. I turned toward the front of the chapel, trying to will my vision into focus. The hundred or so entering seniors were all standing in front of the podium, shifting their weight from foot to foot and cupping their little candles. Headmaster Oates looked up at all of us and smiled nervously.

"Hello?" he said into his microphone, and it shrieked and hissed in response. Everyone in the audience moaned and put their hands to their ears. Except me. I was still looking for . . . him.

"Oops," said Headmaster Oates, chuckling. "Sorry about that, guys."

And then there he was. His face was half-obscured by a tall girl with a blond ponytail, but I could see his gorgeous left eye . . . and his gorgeous left shoulder . . . the gorgeous left corner of his mouth . . .

I'd never reacted like this before. To anyone.

"Welcome," Headmaster Oates said. He beamed out at all of us. "Welcome, new students. Welcome back, old students. This fall is going to be an exciting one. We've hired some incredible teachers, built a new science building, and we're introducing an intramural Frisbee league that I'm sure will—"

His voice faded away. I stared at what I could see of the Guy, and my imagination was starting to run away with me. I pictured the two of us walking over the Brooklyn Bridge at sunset, the silvery East River gleaming below us. I pictured the two of us sitting across from each other at a romantic Italian restaurant. I pictured what it would be like to be the votive candle cupped inside his palm. What did his palms smell like? What did his sweat smell like? What words did he whisper in his sleep? What was his preferred brand of toothpaste? What was his favorite movie? What did he look like in a tuxedo? What was the name of his third grade teacher?

"Oh, no," Molly murmured.

I turned to her. "What?"

"No, no, *no*."

"What's wrong?"

She nodded toward Headmaster Oates.

"—a chance for parents and teachers to interact," he was saying. "And a chance for parents to be incorporated into extracurricular and dorm life. We're a family here at Putnam Mount McKinsey, but we also care about the families you came from."

"Parents Weekend," whispered Molly. "Apparently it's the week after next."

My brain snapped back into focus.

If my dad came by himself, it might be okay. Or . . . not.

Because then everyone in my English class would know my father was Nelson Bingley. Which would be weird and . . . humiliating. But if my dad came with R., it would be even worse. She'd find a way to ruin whatever life I'd already established here. She would traipse around campus in her purple pashmina shawl, charming the pants off of everyone or freaking them out, depending on what mood she happened to be in. ("I thought you said your stepmother was evil," Molly would say, hypnotized, her pupils forming tiny concentric spinning circles. "But R. Klausenhook is *lovely*!")

And what would Miss Perfect Paruchuri think about my totally weird and dysfunctional family? It would only give her new reasons to make fun of me and talk about me behind my back.

I had to find a way to make sure my Dad and R. weren't coming.

I also had to find out the name of the Guy.

EIGHT

Reena

These were the cool kids.

Jamie Vanderheep, crouched in the corner of his dorm room, riffling through his pile of old records, a cigarette dangling out of his mouth.

Rebecca Saperstein, sprawled across Jamie's couch, idly drawing on her big toenail with a purple Magic Marker.

Jules Squarebrigs-Farroway, sitting at my feet, playing a video game and hooting whenever his character blew somebody up onscreen.

And Kristen Diamond. My new best friend. Laughing, lying next to me on the bed, her head in my lap while I ran my fingers through her long red hair.

I was In.

I'd always been pretty good at finding my way In. When we moved to Beverly Hills in the middle of my seventh-grade year, it took me exactly two weeks to befriend

Samantha Foote, the most popular girl in my grade, and then only two more weeks to make out with Frankie Olevsky, the most popular guy in my grade. I didn't even like Frankie Olevsky; I just knew that he and Samantha were my ticket In.

It always happened the same way, whether it was at a new school or summer camp—there was that first paralyzing moment of fear: the what-if-I-don't-make-it moment. But that was always quickly followed by the triumphant I-made-it-after-all moment; the moment right after I'd cracked everyone up, or caught the cutest boy in the room glancing at me as I walked by.

So I guess it went the same way at Putnam Mount McKinsey: one brief bout of fear, one brief bout of embarrassment (I blushed whenever I thought about the cigarette incident—and I was still constructing elaborate lies to convince Kristen I was a smoker), but finally, three days after I arrived, I received an invitation to a post-fall-ceremony-hanging-out session in Jamie Vanderheep's dorm room. And the deal was sealed.

"*You . . . are . . . hilarious*," choked out Rebecca Saperstein. She lay curled up on the couch, shaking with laughter. I'd just done a spot-on imitation of Headmaster Oates, and now I was basking in the warmth of everyone's response. Kristen, her head still in my lap, grinned up at me. The two of us were the only sophomores in the room. Jamie and Rebecca were both seniors, and Jules Squarebrigs-Farroway was a junior. (You know you're really, truly In when you're not only hanging with the cool kids in your grade, you're also hanging out with the cool kids who are two grades above you.)

So I should have been happy.

I wasn't.

For one thing, I kept obsessing about my roommate, Alice. There was something about her that drove me crazy. For one thing, why did she hate me? And why did it seem like she was one of those people whose life was just... perfect? like nothing had ever gone wrong for her?

And then I kept wondering what I was going to do about Jamie Vanderheep. He kept crawling over to me on the floor and showing me these old jazz records he'd bought over Christmas break in Pittsburgh. "Oh, man!" he kept saying, shaking his head and snapping his fingers. "You gotta hear this! The trombone, like, *sings*!"

Obviously he wanted to make out with me.

And he was cute—he really was. He had big blue eyes and sandy brown hair that curled around his ears and he was wearing a really awesome threadbare Jane's Addiction T-shirt from, he claimed, "like 1992." He was popular. He was a senior. He was co-captain of the Ultimate Frisbee team. He was known to walk around campus followed by a wide-eyed group of drooling junior girls.

But I couldn't stop thinking about David Newman.

I was completely, horribly, utterly, devastatingly, crushed out.

"How old do you think David is?" I asked Kristen, absentmindedly weaving a little braid into her hair.

"David who?"

"David Newman, dummy."

"Oh. God. *Old*."

"Like over thirty?"

"Maybe."

Jamie Vanderheep spasmed on the floor, listening to a record he'd just put on. "The bass!" he cried out in ecstasy.

Kristen squinted up at me. "Wait, why do you care?" she asked.

"Oh. I was just wondering."

"Do you have a—"

My phone rang. I snatched it out of my bag, relieved, and looked at it.

"Who is it?" Kristen said.

"Ah, nobody. Just my brother, Pradeep."

Kristen sat straight up and looked at me. "Wait. Pradeep?"

"Yeah."

"Does he go here?"

"Yeah. He just transferred with me. He's a junior. He—"

She clapped a hand over her mouth. "Oh, my God. I *met* him the other day."

"Really?"

"He's adorable."

I winced.

"I mean, I don't mean that in a weird way . . ."

"Uh-huh . . ." Girls always went nuts over Pradeep. It really grossed me out, especially when they were my friends. One thing I loved about my friend Katie in LA was that she always thought Pradeep was—as she put it—"a total doofus."

"Are you gonna answer your phone?"

I sighed and looked at it.

"You should totally invite him over!"

"Okay, okay." I pressed Talk and put the phone to my ear. "Hey, Deep."

"*Deep,*" Kristen whispered. "That's so cute."

Ew.

"Hey," said Pradeep. His voice sounded drained of all emotion.

"What's wrong?" I asked.

"I need to talk to you. In person."

"Do you want to come over? I'm in East Dorm."

There was a pause. Then: "That's a boys' dorm, Reen."

"Yeah. I know. I snuck in."

Another pause.

"There are lots of people here," I added. "Not just boys. You should come over."

Kristen nodded eagerly, listening.

"I want to see you alone," he said. "Can you meet in front of the horse?"

There was an enormous bronze statue of a rearing horse in the center of campus, right near a grove of pine trees. According to Jules Squarebrigs-Farroway, it was *the* clandestine meeting spot for fights, make-out sessions, and drug deals.

And, apparently, brother-sister crisis counseling.

"Fine," I sighed. Then I hung up the phone. "Sorry," I told Kristen. "Apparently this is family only."

She smiled at me, her eyes glazed over. "God. Do you, like, love him?"

"Uh. Well. He's my brother."

"He must be, like, the best brother ever."

"I don't know about that."

"He's, like, really really funny."

I nodded and got to my feet, slinging my purse over my shoulder. "Thanks for having me over," I told Jamie, who was curled up in a fetal position on the floor, playing air trombone. "It was fun."

He blinked up at me. "You're leaving?"

"Family emergency."

"Well, you should come back sometime." He propped himself up on his elbow and gazed at me with his big blue eyes. "We can hang out, just the two of us."

I smiled feebly. "Yeah. Sure. Of course."

I reached out to put my hand on the doorknob.

"Wait!" Jamie screeched. "Stop!"

I turned around. "What?"

"You can't leave now. My RA is doing the rounds. You'll get caught."

"You're gonna have to climb out the window," commented Jules Squarebrigs-Farroway, not taking his eyes off the TV screen.

I stared at them. "Are you kidding me?"

"There's a maple tree right outside. You just climb out and slide down the big branch, and then you—"

"No. No way. I am not climbing down a tree in *this*." I grabbed hold of my pink angora miniskirt and raised my eyebrows threateningly. Everyone looked unimpressed.

"Don't be a baby, Reena," said Kristen from the bed. Suddenly there was a weird, urgent look in her eyes—a you-better-not-screw-this-up-for-us look.

"*Fine*," I said, exasperated, and marched over to the window. I wrenched it open. A late summer breeze came wafting into the room. I stared out into the night. The biggest branch of the maple tree was a long, long leap away.

"It's easier than it looks," Jamie said, standing behind me.

"Yeah, right," I said. A flurry of tiny butterflies released it-self inside my gut.

He shrugged. "Just, like, sling your legs over, and then if you reach out, like, really far, you can actually grab hold of it."

"Just do it," piped up Kristen from the bed.

Painfully, awkwardly, I slung one leg out the window.

"Ack," I said. "I'm stuck."

Jamie grabbed hold of my other (bare, I might add) leg and lifted it up and out. One of his hands briefly grazed my thigh.

"Get your hands off me," I hissed.

"Chill out," he whispered, and then, suddenly, I was sitting on the windowsill, my legs hanging out above the twenty-foot drop.

"I can't do this," I announced.

"Just reach forward and grab hold of the branch."

"Impossible."

And then Jamie Vanderheep did something unforgivable.

He shoved me.

For a second I was nowhere. The night air rushed around my ears. Time slowed down. I pictured myself falling for hours, days, months. Then I realized I'd stopped falling. My hands were grasping—precariously—the tree branch.

"See?" called out Jamie from the window. "It's easy! Now just put your feet on the branch underneath!"

I breathed in and out, shakily, but I still had the feeling of falling in my body. The sensation was terrifying. It chilled me to the bone.

"HEY!" Jamie yelled again. "ARE YOU OKAY?"

I took another breath, placed my feet on the branch below, and then dropped neatly onto the ground.

"Hey! Reena! Are you all right?"

I looked up at his little lit-up window,.

"GO SCREW YOURSELF, VANDERHEEP!" I yelled.

Then I ran away into the night, my heart pounding.

Maybe, just maybe, I was done being In.

At first I couldn't find him. Then I saw a pair of New Balance sneakers poking out from underneath a fir tree. A few seconds later, I heard the faint sound of rustling plastic.

Pradeep was always—without fail—eating some horrible form of junk food.

"Yo," I whispered. "Butthead."

The sound of rustling plastic got louder. Then a hand extended itself out from underneath the branches. I grabbed it, and it pulled me into a little dark cave hollowed out in the center of the tree.

Pradeep's round face faced mine, illuminated only by a slice of moon peeping through the branches.

"Wanna honey-roasted cashew?" he asked.

"Ew. Gross."

"Actually, buttface, they're delicious."

"You're disgusting. What is this place?"

"It's cool, right? Jamal showed it to me."

"Who's Jamal?"

"My friend. Don't you have any friends yet, buttface?"

"Shut up, butthead. I have plenty of friends. Care to tell me why I'm here?"

Pradeep stared at me ominously, chewing away on his cashews.

"Pradeep."

He swallowed and cleared his throat. "Okay. It's about Shanti."

"What about Shanti?"

"She's, um, nuts."

There was a long pause while I waited for him continue. He giggled, somewhat hysterically.

"Okay, I don't understand. Why is this funny?"

Pradeep bent over and pressed his face into his knees. His shoulders trembled with laughter.

"What the hell is going on?"

He could barely get the words out. "I'm . . . sorry . . . it's . . . it's just . . . that—"

"It's just what?"

He lifted his face up, wiped the tears from his eyes, and then let out a high-pitched chuckle. "It's just . . . everything is just, like, *so* screwed."

"Oh, come on, Deep. It could totally be worse."

He nodded. "Yeah, yeah, I know . . . it's just . . . uh . . . well, I talked to Mom tonight, and, um . . . she's, like, freaking out."

"Why?"

"Ah . . . she's living with Pria, you know, but she's running out of cash, and she's saying she's gonna have to sell her clothes and stop going to that really fancy hairdresser on Wilshire and—"

"Is that such a big deal?" I interrupted.

"Well, to Mom it is. You know her. She's used to a certain lifestyle." His eyes narrowed. "And you should talk, Miss Marc Jacobs Shoes."

I glanced self-consciously down at my pink high heels (now covered in dirt and pine needles).

"Why isn't Dad just giving her a little money to tide her over?" I asked.

Pradeep started giggling again.

"Deep. This is really annoying."

"I'm sorry. I'm sorry. It's just, uh, it's like I'm so upset I'm not even upset anymore, you know?"

I actually did know. So I nodded.

"The reason," Pradeep finally said, "that Dad is not giving Mom a little money to tide her over ... at least, according to Dad, whom I also talked with tonight ... is that he doesn't have any extra money to give. I mean, aside from the money he's putting toward his crazy divorce lawyers."

"That makes no sense," I said. "Dad is rich."

"Yeah. Well. He was. Until ..." Another insane-sounding giggle. "Until Shanti decided ... that she ... that she, um, wanted a penguin."

I stared at him.

He continued: "You know that documentary that came out last year? About all the penguins and, like, how they have babies and—"

"Yeah ..."

"Well, Shanti saw it, and she decided that she wanted, ah, a baby penguin. So apparently Dad made a bunch of calls—"

"You're kidding me. You have to be kidding me."

He shook his head no, his eyes gleaming white in the moonlight. "Apparently Dad called a bunch of places, like zoos and stuff, and this one zoo in Colorado had an extra penguin. It's not a baby, but—"

"Pradeep. Please tell me this is a joke."

"No. So Shanti is adopting this penguin, but it needs, like, a really cold, like *arctic* environment . . . so they're building an addition on the house, this, like, special terrarium or something with ice and water . . . and it's costing Dad like a million dollars . . . so," he finished, almost out of breath, "Dad doesn't want to cut Mom a break and just hand her some cash because he, um, needs all the cash he can get for Shanti's penguin's . . . home."

We looked at each other for a long time. I felt the edges of my mouth start to tremble.

"See?" Pradeep whispered. "It's so bad it's *funny*."

And then we both started laughing. Hysterically. I actually fell over and hit my head on a root. Pradeep spilled his cashews everywhere.

"Oh," he choked out, while I was convulsing with laughter on the ground, "and one more horrible thing—they're coming."

"Who? Where?"

"Dad and Shanti. They're coming for Parents Weekend."

I sat up with a bolt. "No."

"Yes."

"They can't be."

"Wait a second. This is upsetting you more than Mom having a nervous breakdown? That's really weird, man."

"It's just . . . they can't come. They can't. It'll ruin my life."

"Um, Reen? It sucks that they're coming, but it will definitely not ruin your life."

But I was thinking about Alice Bingley-Beckerman. I was thinking about her smug little face, and her perfectly combed hair, and her perfect New York City parents with their perfect little faces and blond hair, and I was picturing all three of them standing in the middle of our dorm room and laughing at me. Me and my crazy family.

And suddenly the situation wasn't very funny at all.

NINE

Molly

The thing that really broke my heart was the stuffed animal sitting on her pillow. It was this white bear with beady eyes, and it was holding a plush red heart that said, GET WELL SOON.

It made me feel like she was a little kid or something.

Spencer and I sat with her next to the window and watched the cars drive in and out of the parking lot. The leaves were starting to change their color, and this one tiny maple tree had already turned already bright orange. I held Mom's hand and pointed in its direction.

"Isn't that pretty?" I asked.

It was kind of a dumb question.

But I was having a hard time thinking of smart questions.

She smiled at me with what seemed like great effort. I smiled back and stroked her soft, knobbly hands. My mom has the softest hands in the world. It's weird how soft they are.

"The food is terrible here," she announced after a long pause. I nodded eagerly.

Spencer, who'd barely said anything since we arrived, began humming under her breath and tapping her fingers against her chair.

It was the Saturday after the first few days of classes. I'd been friends with Alice Bingley-Beckerman for less than a week, but it had made me realize how important it was, having someone to talk to. It had made me think about my mom sitting all by herself in a white room for months on end. So I'd telephoned Spencer and demanded that she meet me outside Silverwood on Saturday morning. I'd called a cab and Spencer had taken the free bus that lumbered between the small Chesterton County towns at about five miles an hour.

It was the first time either of us had seen Mom since the spring.

All summer, Dad had discouraged us from going—apparently Mom wasn't been "ready" for visitors. But when I asked him to phone the hospital during the past week, they'd said that she was "slowly on her way to recovery" and willing to see guests.

I looked out the window again. A young couple was leaning against their station wagon in the parking lot and kissing. Suddenly I was filled with anger. Why were these people being gushy in the parking lot of a mental institution? Why were they being gushy, period? Life was way too screwed-up to allow for gushiness. I stared at the couple. They looked so small from Mom's third-story window. It made me feel like I could reach out and just . . . crush them between my thumb and forefinger.

"How are you, Mol?" Mom asked.

I snapped out of my reverie. "Oh. Um . . ."

"How's school?"

"It's okay. I mean, I'm having a little trouble adjusting, but . . . it's good. I mean, it'll get better. And the classes are really good."

Her eyes wrinkled happily. "I'm so glad. And what about you, Spencer?"

Spencer kept staring at the window.

"Spencer," I said.

She tore her eyes away from the couple in the parking lot. "What?"

"Mom just asked you a question."

"Oh." Spencer's eyes flickered guiltily in Mom's direction.

"How are you, darling?" Mom repeated.

Spencer shrugged. "I'm okay. School is dumb. But cheerleading is awesome. And jazz dance. Oh, and baton. Candy is teaching me all these cool new moves."

I winced. Did she have to mention Candy?

"Did you know," Spencer continued, growing more cheerful, "that Candy was actually a twirling champion herself in—"

"Okay, enough," I said loudly.

There was an awful silence. Spencer went back to looking out the window. Mom stared down at her hands.

"Mom?" I finally asked.

"Yes, honey?" she whispered.

"When do you think . . . when do you think you're gonna get out of here?"

We looked at each other. Her eyes seemed to dull and fade.

Almost like my question had made a little part of her go to sleep. I tried to backtrack.

"I mean . . . not that you know yet . . . I just thought *if* you knew . . ."

"I'm not sure, Molly," she said.

"That's fine. Of course. That's fine." I stared down at my lap. "It's just . . . next weekend is Parents Weekend. I was thinking that if you did happen to be—"

Mom stood up abruptly. Her white hospital gown was all wrinkly. She started smoothing it down nervously with her hands.

"Definitely not by next weekend, okay?" She walked over to her nightstand and started fiddling with the dials on the radio.

I swallowed. "Okay. Yeah. Sorry. Sorry for asking."

She stopped playing with the radio dials and started fingering the leaves of this little green plant next to her bed. Then she started pacing all over the room and touching everything—the knobs on the closet door; the TV antennae; our jackets hanging on the wall.

"Mom?"

"I'm fine." Now she was rubbing the wallpaper with her forefinger, her brow furrowed, like she wanted to see if it would rub off.

"Are you sure?"

She whirled around to face us. "Yes," she snapped. "But can you stop breathing down my neck for *one* minute?"

I stared at her. I stared at this new, unfamiliar person, standing in front of me in a white gown, hair disheveled, face red with anger.

There was a loud knock on the door.

"Lunch!" called someone gaily from the hallway.

Mom looked at us.

"I think," she said after a long pause, "that I probably should eat alone."

Spencer bolted up out of her chair and ran out of the room. Mom sighed. Then she moved toward me and embraced my neck with her soft, bony arms. Her cheek pressed against mine.

"Come back next Saturday, okay?" she said.

I extricated myself from her arms and turned away.

"Good-bye, Mom," I whispered, and hurried out the door, brushing past a smiling woman in a white uniform carrying a steaming tray of food.

Spencer and I stood at the bottom of the long driveway that led to Silverwood and waited for the Chesterton County bus in silence. When it finally came, Spencer immediately dropped down into a seat, took out her new nano iPod (a birthday present from Candy, she'd informed me), and stared out the window. I couldn't see the nano itself, just its little white wires extending out from under her head of blond hair and into the pocket of her jeans.

I took out my worn copy of *Zen Ventura* and tried to start reading it for the fourth time.

But I couldn't really focus.

I looked over at Spencer. The trees we passed along the side of the highway made an orange-and-red stream behind her head.

"Spence," I said. I wasn't sure she could hear me.

"Leave me alone," she muttered.

"Why are you ignoring me?" I asked

"You think you're so much better than us," she murmured, still not looking at me.

"What?" I exclaimed. "I do not! Better than who?"

The bus pulled into the parking lot of the North Forest post office. Spencer tore off her nano and started putting on her jacket.

"There's Candy," she said, and pointed through the bus's dirty window at a little figure in a huge pink ski jacket waiting next to our Dad's old Chevy.

Just the sight of her made me shiver involuntarily.

The bus cranked to a stop and Spencer ran down the aisle (cutting in front of several old ladies) and down the steps. I peered through the window and watched her bound over to Candy and embrace her. The two of them started gabbing immediately. Spencer said something into Candy's ear and then pointed in the direction of the bus. Candy started laughing.

Great. My little sister, who'd always seemed somewhat foreign to me, even when she was baby, had now officially gone over to the Dark Side.

Sighing, I gathered up my things and disembarked. It was Saturday. I'd agreed to spend the night in North Forest before returning to Putnam Mount McKinsey. But suddenly twenty-four hours seemed like an unbelievably long amount of time.

"Hi, Molly," said Candy as I trudged over to the car, slouching under the weight of my backpack.

"Hi," I said.

We gave each other long, stony stares while Spencer did a little dance, shifting her weight back and forth between her right and left feet.

119

"I'm cold!" she yelped. "Let's go home!"

I spent the car ride sitting silently in the backseat while Spencer and Candy discussed the junior high's new cheerleading uniforms.

Candy didn't ask either of us how the trip to visit Mom had gone.

What actually bugged me more was that Spencer didn't seem to mind.

We pulled into the driveway. Spencer immediately leapt out of the car and disappeared into the house. Sandie and Randie were running through the front yard, waving strange yellow foam swords around in the early evening light. The second I stepped out of the car they descended upon me and started stabbing random parts of my body.

"Agh," I said, and tried to push them away as gently as possible.

"Your stepsisters are happy to see you, Molly," said Candy pointedly.

"Mmhm," I muttered, and tried to wrench Randie free from my knee, which she had managed to wrap herself around.

"Stupid sister!" yelled Sandie, and shook a marker-stained forefinger in my direction.

Candy laughed. "They just missed you a lot."

"I'm not stupid," I informed Sandie.

She seemed to consider this possibility, then shouted: "You're made of poop!"

This made Randie laugh so hard that she loosened her grip on my knee, and I managed to wiggle free of both of them and run toward the back door.

Dad was standing in the kitchen, stirring a boiling pot of

pasta. When the door banged behind me, he lifted his eyes up and gazed at me, a vague, pleasant smile on his face.

"Hi, Dad," I said.

"Hi, sweetheart," he said, and then went back to stirring the pot.

I moved toward him, stood on my tiptoes, and awkwardly kissed his grizzled check.

"That's nice," he murmured.

"How are you?" I asked.

"Fine. Just fine."

I leaned against the refrigerator and waited for him to ask me how I was. He didn't. There was just the sound of his spoon scraping against the bottom of the aluminum pot.

"I really, really like Putnam Mount McKinsey," I announced.

"Aw, that's great."

"It's like: I never want to leave!"

I watched him carefully to see his response. I don't even know what kind of response I wanted, to be honest. I think maybe I wanted him to wish I would come home—but because he missed me, not because Candy needed a caretaker for Sandie and Randie. And even though I wanted him to wish that I would come home, I didn't want him to make me come home.

My feelings were kind of complicated.

But I got no response from him at all. He just stared down at the stove, moving the spoon around in concentric circles.

Candy and Sandie and Randie all came crowding in through the back door, and Randie scored one final sword jab in the small of my back.

"WASH UP FOR DINNER!" yelled Candy, and after they skittered out of the room she moved behind my father and put her arms around his waist.

"Mmm," she murmured. "Cuddle-duds."

Involuntarily I snickered.

Her arms still around Dad, Candy whipped her face in my direction.

"What's funny?" she asked.

"Nothing," I said.

"I'm glad you think you're so much better than your family already, Molly. That's nice. That's really nice."

"I don't think I'm better than anyone. I just thought I heard you say, 'Cuddle-duds.' But apparently I was mistaken." I smiled triumphantly at her. Saying "but apparently I was mistaken" made me feel smart. Like I had the upper hand.

"Cuddle-duds is my nickname for your father."

"Uh-huh . . ."

"What's so funny about that?"

"Okay, okay," my father finally said, and turned around to frown at us. His glasses were all steamed up from the pasta. "Quit it, you two."

"You two?" asked Candy incredulously. Her eyes suddenly filled up with tears, and covering her face with her hands, she ran out of the room.

My father sighed and looked at me.

"What?" I asked. "I didn't do anything."

"Be nice to Candy, Molly. Please. Okay? She's having a hard time."

"I'm having a hard time, too, you know!"

He sighed. "You get to live at your fancy boarding school and do whatever you want, and Candy has to—"

"You think that's what it's like? I get to do whatever I want? You don't think I work hard or—"

"That's not what I'm saying. Just . . . please. Be sensitive, okay?"

I couldn't believe it. He was even crazier than Mom. At least she knew she was crazy.

"Mol?"

I rolled my eyes. "Sure. Okay. I'll be sensitive. Whatever that means."

He turned back to the stove. "Will you set the table? We don't need knives. Just forks and spoons tonight."

I gazed at his stooped shoulders and the fuzzy gray nape of his neck. It was strange. I missed him terribly, even though he was standing right in front of me.

"Yeah, fine," I said. "Whatever."

I grabbed a handful of forks and spoons from the silverware drawer and headed out into the little dining room, where Sandie and Randie were already sitting at the table, drinking juice from plastic glasses decorated with pictures of Scooby-Doo.

"Hey, dudes," I said, trying to sound cheerful, and plunked down the silverware in front of them.

"Mom is crying," announced Sandie.

"Yeah, yeah," I said. "I know, I know."

"She's sick," said Randie.

I looked at her. "Sick?" I asked. "What kind of sick?"

"No," said Sandie, shaking her head emphatically. "Not sick. Prenant."

A spoon fell from my hands and clattered down on the table. "What?"

"Prenant."

123

"Pregnant?" I desperately tried to think of another word that sounded like "prenant," but couldn't. Where was the OED when I needed it?

Sandie nodded. "Yup."

"Yup in a cup," added Randie, and they both giggled.

I pulled out a chair and sat down in it with a thud.

"Great," I told my stepsisters. "Now *I* feel sick."

Spencer walked into the room, her nano firmly lodged in her ears, and slunk into a chair at the table, her eyes lowered.

A minute later Dad came into the room carrying a big bowl of pasta, and Candy came in from the other room, wiping her eyes and sniffling. They both sat down at the table and looked at me.

"Um," I said, "I'm sorry I laughed at you, Candy."

Somehow Sandie and Randie found this hilarious and started laughing themselves.

"Shh!" hissed Candy. They fell silent.

We all started to spoon out the pasta and pour drinks. I was barely able to form a coherent thought in my mind.

Pregnant?

Impossible.

"So does this food seem pretty boring to you, Molly?" asked Candy after a long silence. "Since you get to eat fancy gourmet food at boarding school?"

"Um," I said, "I actually don't to get to eat fancy gourmet food at boarding school. I get to eat really disgusting Sloppy Joes and this totally gross vegetable mush they recycle every night. This is much better," I added, and tried to smile.

Candy smirked. "So now she's complaining about boarding school," she commented to my father across the table.

"I'm not complaining!" I said.

"Do you want them to serve you champagne in teacups or something?" asked Candy. "Filet mignon?"

Spencer giggled.

"That's not what I meant," I said. I glowered down at my plate and thought about what it would be like to punch my fist through the bay window in the hallway.

Pregnant?

"Have you thought any more about what we discussed at the nurse's office, Molly?" Candy asked.

"I don't know what you mean."

"Oh, come on. Yes, you do."

"I don't." Without being too obvious, I tried to glance under the table to see if her stomach was bulging beneath her stirrup pants. It was kind of hard to tell.

"We discussed the fact that your father and I would like you to come back home and start helping out a little."

I looked at my father. He looked out the window.

"Oh," I said finally. "Yeah. I have thought about it. Not a chance."

Candy stood up. My father reached out and grabbed her arm.

"Candy . . . ," he said.

"Ungrateful," she said to me. "You're ungrateful."

"And you're crazy."

Randie started crying, softly.

"Tell her," Candy said to my father. "Tell her now."

My father sighed and rubbed his temples with his fingers.

"What?" I said. "Tell me what? That you're pregnant?"

They both stared at me, shocked.

"How did you know?" Candy asked. "Did Spencer tell you?"

"I didn't say a word!" shouted Spencer, and she pushed back her chair and ran upstairs.

Candy's eyes slid accusatorily in Sandie and Randie's direction. They both became very interested in eating their vegetables. Randie sniffed back her tears.

"I could just tell," I said.

Candy sat back down in her chair, patted her hair nervously, and gazed at me. "Are you happy about it?" she asked.

I sighed. "Sure," I said. The truth was, I was absolutely terrified.

"Doesn't that make you want to move back in?" Candy asked.

"No," I said. "It doesn't."

"Herb," said Candy, the color rising in her cheeks, "tell her she *has* to. We need the extra set of hands."

My father opened his mouth to speak, but before he could, I rose from my seat and ran out of the dining room and into the kitchen. The door swung behind me. I stopped at the sink and stood there, breathing heavily, trying to figure out what to do next.

"MOLLY!" bellowed my father from the dining room. "GET BACK IN HERE! WE NEED TO FINISH THIS CONVERSATION!"

Quickly I considered every possible outcome to the conversation in my mind. And then I realized there was just one thing I had to do.

Never come home again.

"MOLLY!" my father yelled again.

I snatched my jacket off the coat hook, flung the back door open, and started running. I figured that if I ran until I reached the highway, and then hitched a ride, I could be back in time for Agnes and lights out.

126

As I sprinted past the dimly lit-up houses of North Forest, the chilly autumn wind blowing my hair back and the dried leaves skittering around my feet, I felt a smile spread across my face for the first time all day.

TEN

Alice

We were both standing by the WELCOME, PARENTS sign, waiting. He looked as anxious as I felt.

Did he even realize I was there?

At first there had been about a hundred of us waiting around near the entrance to campus, chatting among ourselves, peering over one another's heads to see if the station wagon approaching was the station wagon that contained our parents.

Except Dad and R. didn't drive a station wagon. They drove a 1956 gold Cadillac, a gift from Andre Blackmun, the famous theater director who had taken R. under his wing when she was just seventeen.

Anyway. Station wagon after station wagon drove onto campus, and normal-looking, ruddy-cheeked parents leapt out and embraced their normal-looking, ruddy-cheeked children, and then everyone piled back into their cars to go get ice cream before the afternoon's activities began. The crowd of students began to dwindle. After a while, there were about thirty of us.

Then a dozen. Then five. Then Judah Lipston the Third, my silent friend from the Boston van ride, fell sobbing into the arms of a plump middle-aged woman and a tall emaciated man (I could only assume he was Judah Lipston the Second), who had just emerged from a parked car, and suddenly it was just me.

Me and the Guy.

I hadn't seen him since the night of the fall commencement ceremony.

I was pretending to find the grass at my feet extremely fascinating.

It was strange. I'd been thinking about him for almost a month. His face—or what I could recall of his face—had been my constant companion. It floated above me when I lay in bed at night. It stared back at me when I looked at my reflection in the mirror. It hovered between the peaks of distant hills when I sat with Molly Miller outside Middleton and watched the sun set every evening.

Now he was standing right in front of me, in the flesh, and I couldn't even bear to look at him.

In fact, his presence was so overwhelming that I forgot—briefly—how much I was dreading seeing R. again. Although, all things considered, I was pretty lucky; that morning Reena had brusquely informed me that she was meeting her parents in the town of Putnam itself for lunch. That meant that she wouldn't be waiting at the station wagon parade with me. And that meant maybe, just maybe, I could successfully avoid having her see or meet my father and R., period. The goal was to show them my dorm room when I was sure she wouldn't be there, quickly usher them out, and then avoid her and her functional family for the rest of the weekend.

"She's late," the Guy said.

I nearly jumped a foot in the air. Then I turned and looked at him. His hands were stuffed into his pockets, and he was staring off into the distance.

"Yeah," I said.

I prayed that I would think of something else to say. But nothing came to me. So I closed my eyes against the mid-afternoon sunshine and just . . . waited.

"She's always late," he said. "My mother, I mean."

"What about your father?" I asked, and then instantly regretted it. I sounded too curious.

I felt him turn and look at me. After a second, I turned and looked at him. I wanted to faint. It felt like his brown eyes were boring a hole into my forehead. But I forced myself to keep making eye contact. And there was something about him that made me want to tell him . . . everything.

"My dad is gone," he said.

"My mom is dead," I blurted out.

He looked shocked. I clapped a hand to my mouth.

"Aw, man," he said. "I'm sorry."

"Jamal?" someone asked.

I whirled around. A petite woman in sweatpants and a Yankees baseball cap was standing in front of us.

"Mom!" said the Guy, and then he and the little woman embraced each other. I tried not to stare.

"I got lost," she said, "and then I parked in the wrong lot, and then—"

"Don't worry about it," he said. "Let's go get lunch."

They slung their arms around each other and started to walk away. He glanced over his shoulder at me, smiled, mouthed, "Good luck," and then turned back to his mother and began talking to her. Something he said made her giggle, and then they rounded a bend and were gone.

I took a deep breath.

His name was Jamal.

Jamaljamaljamaljamal.

We had actually spoken to each other.

He knew my mother was dead.

He was a Yankees fan.

I was a die-hard Mets fan.

It was like Romeo and Juliet.

Suddenly I heard the whirring and clanking of an ancient engine. I squinted into the sunshine, and saw R.'s gold Cadillac come rushing in my direction. It was unclear whether or not she could see me. In fact, as the car approached, it kind of looked like she was going to run me over. I waved my hands in the air and yelled. When it was about two feet away from me, the Cadillac screeched to a dramatic stop.

My family had arrived.

"It's so *windy*," R. moaned.

The three of us were sitting on a picnic bench in front of the ice cream stand in Putnam's town center. There was a pleasant breeze wafting through the branches of the trees and rustling the red and yellow leaves.

R. was clutching the edges of her silk shawl and shivering dramatically. She was also wearing a tiny hat with a peacock feather sticking out of its center. "It's so interesting," she informed me. "You're only three hours north of New York City, but there really is a huge difference in temperature."

As if I'd chosen to leave New York and move up to a tiny cold town in the mountains.

Dad and R. had only been in town for fifteen minutes, and I was already feeling lonelier than I had since arriving at Putnam Mount McKinsey. Sitting in your room doing homework alone is one thing; feeling alone in the presence of your only living parent and his wife is another. The first thing R. had told me—before we even said hello—was that she was making "a huge sacrifice" by coming to Parents Weekend (as if I wanted her there at all). Rehearsals had just started for her new play, a Broadway revival of *The Cherry Orchard*, and she was missing two of them by coming to Putnam.

Now the sixty-degree weather was making her miserable.

I clearly was The World's Most Evil and Unreasonable Stepdaughter.

Dad was sitting off to the side, wearing a wrinkled pin-striped suit and scratching absentmindedly at the surface of the bench with his thumbnail. Both Dad and R. looked—to put it mildly—out of place in rural Massachusetts.

"So, how are you?" Dad asked. "How's your roommate?"

"Oh. Yeah. Reena. She's okay."

"I'm looking forward to meeting her."

"Well. Yeah. Actually, I think she's pretty busy for most of the weekend."

R. let out a high-pitched shriek as another cool breeze wafted over us. "Are we *really* staying here until Sunday?" she asked Dad. "Because I'm going to get frostbite if we do."

There was a long pause.

"Hey, Dad," I said finally. "Guess what? We're reading *Zen Ventura* in English class this semester."

Dad looked up and blinked. "You're kidding me."

"Nope."

He shook his head. "That's absurd."

"Why is it absurd?"

He sighed. "Because, Alice. It's not *Johnny Tremain*. It's not an easy book."

"It's a very complicated text," R. added eagerly.

"Well," I said, "Mr. Newman is actually a really good teacher."

Dad guffawed. "I'm sure." Then he turned and gazed at R., pushing back a tendril of her hair. "Those kids are going to bludgeon my book to death, darling," he said.

I was horrified. He was actually starting to talk like her.

I stood up, abruptly. "Can we go now?"

"What's the hurry?" R. asked.

"I want to show you guys my dorm room before...," I trailed off.

"Before what?"

"Before the Welcome Dinner." What I really meant was *before Reena Paruchuri and her parents come back to campus and witness how totally bizarre you are.*

We climbed back in R.'s Cadillac and drove to campus. On the road next to the student union, I thought I spotted Reena's black hair and light blue headband. I ducked my head below my window before I could see who was walking with her.

"What are you doing?" asked Dad.

I held my breath until we were a safe distance away, and then I sat up again. "Oh. Nothing. I thought I saw some gum on the floor."

We parked next to Middleton and got out of the car. R. stared up at my dorm, shielding her eyes from the sun with her ring-bedecked fingers.

133

"Oh," she said. I could sense the disapproval in her voice.

"Yeah, yeah," I said. "I know. I got the ugly dorm."

"Uck," she said. "It's just that late sixties architecture . . . I hate it." She shuddered and flailed her arms, as if the cootie-infested goo of late sixties architecture had actually rubbed off on her body.

"Let's go inside," I said. I wanted to get this over with as quickly as possible.

They followed me into the dark, carpeted dorm lounge ("Eeek!" shrieked R. when a poster from the bulletin brushed against her shoulder), and up the flight of stairs to the second floor. I opened the door from the stairwell to the hallway, and almost knocked over . . .

"Alice!" said Molly. "Hey! What a surprise!"

"Hey, Mol," I said. "What are you doing on my floor?"

Molly and Kristen Diamond (who, Molly and I had decided together, after an evening of carefully tallying up their offenses, was an even worse roommate than Reena Paruchuri) lived on the fourth floor.

"Um . . . I was just dropping something off." She pushed up her glasses, and her eyes flitted to the right and behind me, where Dad and R. were standing.

"Oh," I said, and stepped aside. "Dad and R., meet my friend Molly. Molly, meet my father and, um, stepmother."

Molly smiled so widely that I thought her face was going to fall off. I also noticed that she had a tiny piece of spinach between her two front teeth. She thrust out her hand and forced my surprised-looking father to shake it.

"Mr. Bingley," she said. "A pleasure. An total and absolute pleasure."

I stared at her.

And then it hit me. I had completely forgotten.

Molly Miller was obsessed with my father.

"Yes," my father responded, looking a little uncomfortable. "Uh, likewise."

R., never one to be left out, offered up her hand. "I'm R. Klausenhook," she said. "You must be one of Alice's little friends."

Molly shook R.'s hand limply, not taking her eyes off my father's face.

"Yes," Molly said with great reverence. "We just love Alice here at Putnam Mount McKinsey."

We? Who was she talking about?

"Mmhm," said my father, and shot me a get-me-out-of-here look.

"What are your plans for the weekend, Mr. Bingley?" Molly asked brightly. "Hiking? Swimming? Skiing?"

"Skiing?" I echoed. She was really starting to freak me out. "It hasn't even snowed yet."

Molly blushed. "Well. Um. Of course. I mean . . ."

"Mol," I said, "you'll have to excuse us, but I wanted to show Dad and R. my dorm room before the Welcome Dinner starts, and—"

"Of course, of course!" Molly cried, and moved aside.

"I'll see you later tonight," I told her. "Maybe—"

"I'm sorry, Alice," Molly said loudly, interrupting me. "But could I maybe just ask you and your wonderful family for one favor?"

Dad and R. stopped in their tracks, chagrined. I stared at Molly.

"Um, what?" I said.

Molly looked at my father. Her eyes shone with pathos.

"Unfortunately," she said, "no one in my family was able to make it to Parents Weekend. My mother is in a mental institute, and my father and I have had a kind of . . . well, falling out."

My jaw dropped. Why was she telling my father this? Did she think he was some kind of god or something?

"I'm so sorry," my father murmured, although he didn't look sorry at all. He looked bored.

"So I was wondering," Molly continued, "if maybe I could accompany your family on some of this weekend's activities?"

I briefly closed my eyes.

"If," she added, turning to face me for the first time, "it's all right with Alice, of course."

"It's all right with me if it's all right with Alice," my father said tiredly.

Molly stared at me with gigantic, pleading eyes.

I groaned. "Fine, Molly. Whatever."

Molly clapped her hands with joy, and then darted down the second-floor hallway, beckoning my father and R. to follow her.

"Just you wait until you see the inside of Putnam Chapel," she told them, already taking on the role of official tour guide. "The stained-glass panels go all the way back to the nineteenth century, and they're going to change your life. . . ."

I followed, lagging a few feet behind.

It was just my luck.

My only friend at boarding school was already more interested in my father than she was in me.

"HA HA HA," Molly bellowed, and heartily slapped her own knee.

I couldn't believe it. I had no idea that people actually slapped their own knees in real life—it always just seemed like a cliché in books. But here was my new best friend, sitting to the left of me in the dorm cafeteria, and she was actually doing it.

"You have *got* to be kidding me!" she said to my father.

He smiled modestly and toyed with his silverware.

The four of us were having dinner in the dorm, surrounding by other kids and their parents. Although my dad had initially seemed somewhat horrified by Molly Miller, it had taken him less than ten minutes to realize that she was, in fact, his favorite thing in the whole world: a fan. A fan who thought everything he said was fascinating, and every story he told hilarious. Now he was eating up the attention, and R. and I first were staring off in to the distance, bored out of our skulls.

"That just seems so unlike Sam Shepard," Molly said, shaking her head.

"We writers are rarely who you readers think us to be," answered my father, raising his eyebrows.

"When you were writing your first novel," said Molly, putting her elbows on the table and propping her chin up with her hands, "how did you have the strength to keep going? How were you not totally consumed by self-doubt and anxiety?"

My father nodded. "I *was* totally consumed by self-doubt and anxiety. But I kept telling myself to just finish it, and then I could start tearing it apart. Writing is a delicate process."

"Mm*hm*," said Molly adamantly, as if she, too, had bravely plowed her way through a first novel.

"Also," my father said, after a hesitating for a second, "my wife—my wife at the time, Susan—Alice's mother . . ."

I froze. I hadn't heard Dad mention Mom . . . since I could remember. At least since before he met R. I also felt R. freeze, across the table from me, and I watched her eyes slide slowly in Dad's direction.

Dad cleared his throat. "Susan was a novelist, too, and although she was already an established writer at the time, she was incredibly encouraging. She really believed in me, and I trusted her opinion. So that . . . that helped." He nervously glanced over in R.'s direction. She shot him a tight-lipped smile.

Molly, in the meanwhile, had turned white. "Hold on," she said, and turned to me for the first time since dinner started. "Your mom's name is Susan . . . and you're Alice Bingley-Beckerman. . . ."

I frowned at her. What was she getting at? "Uh-huh . . . ," I said.

"So your mom is—was—Susan Beckerman?"

I sighed. "Yes, Molly."

"*The* Susan Beckerman?"

"Um, Susan Beckerman the writer, yes."

Molly put a hand to her heart. "Oh my God. I cannot believe you didn't tell me that."

"I told you that I had a mom, and that she—"

"But you didn't tell me who she was!"

I looked at Molly. "I'm sorry," I said, aware of the iciness in my voice, "I thought I had."

And then, refusing to look at her again, I went back to eating my horrible cafeteria meat loaf. Dad and R., in the meantime, had fallen into a traumatized silence. I could only imagine the fight that would erupt between them later that night in their hotel room.

Molly continued talking, not noticing the pall she had cast across the entire table. "That's just so weird. Because you'd think with your parents—I mean, your parents are like two of the greatest writers in the latter half of the twentieth century—you'd think that you, Alice, would be some kind of like crazy genius or something."

I kept staring at my meat loaf, my cheeks hot with anger.

My father chuckled. "How do you know Alice isn't a genius, Molly?"

"Well—"

I stood up. "Excuse me," I said. "I'm going to go get some dessert."

I marched away from the table, gripping my tray so hard that my knuckles turned white.

Clearly Molly Miller wasn't my friend at all.

She was just a brown-nosing fan.

Now I had zero friends. Zero friends and no real family to speak of.

"Hey, Alice," someone said.

I looked up. Of course. It was Reena, standing at the salad bar, looking stunning in a yellow off-the-shoulder top.

"Hi," I said sullenly.

"Are those your parents?" she asked, pointing in the direction of my table. I looked. Molly was still chatting away, R. looked like she was going to kill somebody, and Dad was staring uncomfortably into his lap.

"Oh," I said. "Um, no. Those are, um, Molly Miller's parents."

She squinted. "Really? That isn't how I imagined them."

I laughed uncomfortably. "Yeah. I know. It's strange. They're, like, really weird people. Kind of crazy."

She looked at me, and for a second it looked like a wave of insecurity passed over her face, although I had no idea why.

"Yeah," she said finally. "Crazy. Sure."

"Where are your parents?" I asked. This was maybe the longest conversation we'd ever had with each other. Somehow we'd manage to communicate entirely through disdainful grunts whenever we were alone in our room together.

She flushed. "Um. Oh. I . . ."

Suddenly, for no particular reason, her cafeteria tray slipped out of her grasp, and her plastic cup went clattering to the ground. Apple juice started spreading in a puddle across the linoleum floor. I bent down and began mopping it up with my napkin. Reena squatted down, too, and distractedly dabbed at the spill with a tissue.

"They're not here," she said.

"Who?"

"My parents. They . . . went out to dinner."

We both stood up.

"Why didn't you go with them?" I asked.

Her face dropped. "Oh. I . . . I wanted to eat with Kristen."

Without even thinking, I looked around the cafeteria, trying to spot Kristen's distinctive red hair.

"She's outside!" blurted Reena. "She's outside! I actually have to meet her there right now!"

And, putting her tray down on the salad bar and just leaving it there, she scurried out of the cafeteria.

I stared after her, and for a minute I was distracted enough to forget about my horrible family and the traitorous Molly Miller.

There was definitely something weird going on with Reena Paruchuri.

And I wanted to find out what it was.

ELEVEN

Reena

She was wearing a sari.

Even worse, it wasn't a real sari. It was the kind of sari middle-age white ladies buy at their local "exotic goods" shop. You know—those shops that sell incense and mood rings and wind chimes and books telling you about whether your astrological sign is compatible with someone else's astrological sign. And random "foreign" objects, like vests covered in mirrors and tablecloths with little African elephants all over them.

Saris, in case you didn't know, are the traditional garment worn by Indian women. They're basically like this long rectangle of fabric that goes down to your feet, and you wrap it around your waist and sling it over your shoulder. I've only worn a sari a few times in my life, like whenever there's a wedding thrown by any of my more traditional cousins or family friends. But my mother wears one almost every day. And, you know—I hate to admit it—because they're like the opposite of what you're supposed to wear if you're a cool

Los Angeles high school student—saris can actually look kind of sexy.

Obviously Shanti Shruti had figured this out.

Her sari was hot pink, and made out of this cheesy shiny synthetic fabric (my mother wore saris made only from cotton or silk). It had little sparkly beads sewn around the hem, and it made this horrible swishy, chime-y sound when she walked.

So when she and my father entered the pizza parlor on the edge of town (a meeting spot that Pradeep and I had come up with together, hoping to avoid as many of our peers as possible), my jaw dropped. Then I turned and looked at Pradeep, who was sitting next to me, and saw that he was shaking his head back and forth in disbelief.

"Hello, my dears," said my father.

He looked exactly the same. Big white hair, big white beard, gray suit jacket, pot belly, khaki pants.

"Hi, Dad," I said, and I awkwardly stood up and kissed him on the cheek.

Pradeep didn't stand up. After a silent standoff—he and my father stared at each other for what seemed like a full minute, unblinking, each Paruchuri man refusing to back down—my father grabbed Pradeep's shoulder and shook it. Then he tousled Pradeep's hair.

"Hello, son," my father said.

"Mmrf," said Pradeep. He bent over and shoveled half of his pizza slice into his mouth.

Shanti stepped forward and tucked a long strand of blond hair behind her ear, smiling nervously. Then she threw her arms around me. We were exactly the same height.

"You look *so* beautiful," Shanti whispered.

I broke out of the hug, and she held me out at arm's length.

"Wow," she said, "I am totally intimidated by how beautiful you look."

Ew. Gross. First of all, I didn't believe her. Shanti looked like an almost impossible mix of a Barbie doll, Gywneth Paltrow, and a swan. Second of all, I didn't look any different than I had during the summer. Third, she was my stepmother. She was supposed to be old and wise and kind, not intimidated by how beautiful I was.

But maybe that was unavoidable. After all, she was barely out of college.

Shanti turned away from me and looked at Pradeep.

"Hi, Pradeep," she said sweetly.

Pradeep picked up a jar of oregano and began sprinkling it over his pizza slice. He didn't look up.

"Pradeep," my father said.

Pradeep put down the jar of oregano. "Nice sari," he said, still avoiding eye contact.

I watched Shanti's face flush red. "Um, thanks," she said. She leaned against my father and rested her head on his shoulder. He stroked her hair.

We all paused there for a minute, silent: Pradeep sitting at the table, me and Dad and Shanti standing up, no one sure what to do next.

I actually heard the guy behind the counter flip a piece of dough up into the air and catch it.

"It is nice to see both of you," my father said stiffly.

Pradeep coughed into his hand. It seemed like a fake cough, but I wasn't sure.

"You, too, Dad," I said.

Pradeep peered up at me resentfully.

"I would like to see where you two live," my father said to us.

I winced. There was a good chance Alice Bingley-Beckerman's parents wanted to do the same thing. And I really, really, *really* didn't want them—or Alice—to see or meet or even come within a hundred of miles of my father and Shanti Shruti.

I tried to sound casual. "Oh, the dorm isn't that interesting. Just little rooms, you know, and bunk beds ... Wouldn't you rather just go out to dinner or something?"

Shanti shook her head. "No, no," she said. "I'm dying to see the inside of Middleton Dorm again."

I blinked. "Again?" I asked.

"I lived in Middleton *my* first year," she told me excitedly. "Remember? I'm a PMM alum."

Oh, yeah. That was how I'd ended up in freezing-cold Massachusetts in the first place. I nodded. Then she leaned forward and grabbed my arm. "I'll show you how to sneak boys into your room," she whispered, "if you haven't figured it out yet."

"Shanti!" exclaimed my father.

"*What?*" she asked, and giggled again in her horrible way. Then she and my father gazed at each other, their eyes dancing. Shanti reached out and toyed flirtatiously with my father's hairy earlobe.

Barf.

An idea dawned on me. I looked at my watch. It was 4:30 PM. The Welcoming Ceremony was at 7:00 PM. Most of the kids and their parents would probably be there, including Alice and her parents. If we could all go see Pradeep's room now, and then eat an early dinner, and then skip the ceremony, and go up to my room when no one was going to be there . . .

I proposed my ingenious plan.

"That way," I finished, "you guys don't have to sit through Headmaster Oates's really boring welcome speech. It'll put you to sleep."

My father looked dubious.

"Dad. Seriously. Trust me."

He shrugged. "Fine. I don't care."

"I don't care either," said Shanti, "as long as I get to see Middleton at some point before I go."

Pradeep looked at me like I was crazy.

"Trust me," I mouthed to him.

Pradeep sighed. "Whatever Reena wants," he said grouchily.

My plan was working.

Maybe I was going to get through Parents Weekend after all.

Two hours later, I stood out on the green lawn in front of the cafeteria, panting.

I had just narrowly avoided another Alice Bingley-Beckerman-meeting-my-parents disaster.

I stared up at the darkening sky and tried to calm down.

First of all, why did Alice Bingley-Beckerman also have to be in the cafeteria eating an early dinner?

But more important, why was she eating an early dinner with Molly Miller's family? Where were her parents?

I had just told Alice that I was meeting Kristen outside and had basically just made a run for it.

But Kristen was in Connecticut for the weekend. What if Alice knew that?

Once again, I was starting to drown in an ocean of my own lies.

My family was still inside the cafeteria, waiting for me to come back from the salad bar. But I couldn't come back. Not until I was sure that Alice Bingley-Beckerman had left the building.

Shivering—I'd left my jacket inside—I leaned against the trunk of a big maple tree and waited. And waited. After a few minutes, my cell phone rang. I took it out of my pocket and answered without looking at it.

"Hello?" I asked.

There was a long pause. Then, in a barely audible whisper: "Is she there?"

"Mom?"

An exasperated sigh. "Yes, it's me. I'm asking you a question. *Is. She. There?*"

"Shanti?"

"REENA!" she shrieked in horror.

I laughed. "She's not here, Mom. She's inside the dorm with Dad and Pradeep."

There was a sigh of relief. Then, suspiciously: "Where are you?"

"I'm waiting outside. For someone. I'm . . . it's a long story."

"A boy?"

"No, no."

"Do you have a crush on a boy, Reenie?"

I paused for a second too long.

"You do!" she crowed.

"Oh, God, Mom. Leave me alone."

"What's his name?"

"Some other time, okay?"

"Fine." She returned to her original topic. "So, tell me what she's wearing."

I giggled. "You're not going to believe this."

"What?"

"A pink sari."

"You're kidding."

"I'm not."

For some reason I'd thought that my mother would think this was funny. Instead there was an ominous silence.

"Mom?"

"Does she look pretty?" she asked quietly.

"Oh, Mom."

"She does, doesn't she?" I heard a muffled sob.

"Oh, God. No. She doesn't. She looks really really dumb. Trust me."

"Has your father mentioned anything about money?"

"Uh, no."

"I had to sell the Blahniks, Reenie."

"The what?"

"The Manolo Blahniks! My favorite high heels!" She erupted into a fresh round of tears.

"Mom. I have to call you back later."

There was a short, high-pitched moan, and then the phone clicked off.

Great.

I'd just made my mother cry.

I was almost as bad as Shanti herself.

Suddenly I spotted a blond head of hair moving down the steps of the dorm and onto the grass. I darted behind the tree and peeked out. It was Alice. Walking with . . . Molly Miller's parents. With Molly Miller nowhere in sight. Weird.

Something fishy was going on.

I waited until Molly Miller's parents and Alice were a safe distance away, and then I darted up the stairs, into the dorm, into the cafeteria, and back to my family's table. Pradeep was staring at his plate. My dad and Shanti had their arms draped around each other's shoulders. Was it possible for them to stop touching for more than a second?

They all looked up at me.

"Where were you?" asked Pradeep.

"I, uh, ran into a teacher."

Pradeep burst into a wicked grin. "That David guy?"

I shot him a death glare. "No."

Shanti clapped her hands. "David? David who?"

"No one," I said. I sat back down at the table and stepped on Pradeep's sneaker with the heel of my stiletto boot. He yelped. Dad and Shanti looked at us, confused. Pradeep and I both gave them big, fake smiles.

"It is *so* weird to be back here," Shanti said, and stared dreamily around the cafeteria. "Everything looks the same."

"How's your penguin?" Pradeep suddenly asked.

I blushed, but Shanti didn't seem bothered by the question at all.

"His name is Ganesh," she said "And he's the sweetest thing in the world."

Pradeep nodded vigorously in a way that I recognized to be a complete mockery of everything Shanti was saying. But she didn't seem to catch on.

"He is just *so* cute, Reena," she told me. "You would die."

"Isn't he lonely without any other penguins around?" I asked.

She blinked. "Um. No. I don't think so. He has me, after all."

"How much does it cost to maintain his, uh, environment?" Pradeep asked.

Shanti suddenly looked uncomfortable. "Um . . . I'm not sure. . . ." Her eyes darted over to my father.

"That's an inappropriate question, Pradeep," my father said.

"Why?" asked Pradeep.

"Because—"

"Because it's money Mom should be getting but instead it's going toward an enslaved penguin?" Pradeep said, his voice icy cold.

Shanti's eyes widened and filled with tears. "Ganesh is *not* enslaved."

Pradeep burst out laughing.

"Pradeep," my father hissed, "if you don't stop right now, I promise you you will be sorry."

Pradeep stood up and pushed his tray forward. "I'm actually done," he announced, "with this delicious cafeteria dinner. I propose we go upstairs and see Reena's room. All in favor say aye."

Shanti sniffed. My father put a protective arm around her waist. I shrugged. Alice was safely out of the building. Now was as good a time as any.

"Aye," I said.

We trudged down the long, dimly lit second-floor hallway, Pradeep and I taking the lead, Dad and Shanti trailing behind us, holding hands.

"Wow!" exclaimed Shanti. "This dorm hasn't changed at all!"

"Yeah," I said. "Exactly. It could really use a renovation."

150

I peeled a piece of plaster off the wall and showed it to her while we walked.

We reached my door.

"Welcome," I said grandly, "to the Paruchuri abode."

Pradeep snickered. I threw the door open.

And then I heard someone scream. From inside the room.

I shrieked in response and fell back against the door.

"What in God's name is going on?" my father asked.

I took a deep breath and peeked inside.

Alice Bingley-Beckerman was standing in the middle of our room. With . . . Molly Miller's parents. She looked as pale as a ghost.

"Reena," she said. "Um . . . I didn't think you'd . . ."

"Hi," I said. "Yeah . . . I thought . . ."

We were unable to finish our sentences.

"I left my purse behind!" said Molly Miller's mother cheerfully. She was a tiny, beautiful woman, but her eyes seemed to gleam with a kind of psychotic rage. She was also wearing way too much makeup.

"Um . . . ," said Alice. Her mouth was moving, but no words were coming out. She seemed to be in some kind of physical pain. "Um," she said again. "Reena, I'd like you to meet my father and my stepmother." Her cheeks flushed, and she refused to look me.

I frowned. "Wait. I thought you said—"

She suddenly looked up, her blue eyes connecting with mine, and I suddenly saw that she was pleading, *begging* with me not to finish my sentence.

And for some reason—even though Alice Bingley-Beckerman had officially been my nemesis for the past three weeks—I didn't.

151

And then I thought: *Stepmother?*

"Hello," the woman said, and she glided forward and offered me her miniscule, jewel-encrusted hand. "My name is R. Klausenhook."

"Nice to meet you," I said. I had no idea what was happening. Why had Alice told me that this was Molly Miller's mother?

"I'm Nelson, Alice's father," said the tall, stern-looking man at her side, and instead of shaking hands he gave me a little nod.

"Reena?" asked a sugary sweet voice from behind me. "Aren't you going to introduce us?"

My heart fell. In the shocking moment of discovery that Alice Bingley-Beckerman, Miss Perfect, was the possessor of a stepmother, and weird-seeming one at that, I'd forgotten that I had one, too.

"Oh, yes," I said, and stepped aside. "Alice, this is my father and, um, stepmother." Now I was the one who couldn't look anyone in the eye.

"I'm Shanti Shruti," said Shanti Shruti loudly. I winced. Did she have to say her last name, too? The fake Indian-ness was too absurd for words. I glanced at Alice, who now looked as surprised as I'd felt a minute before.

"Hello," Alice said, and I saw her eyes move up and down Shanti Shruti's body, taking in her blond hair, her tanned skin, her lithe, young body, and her . . . sari.

"I'm Rashul," boomed my father, and for the next minute everyone shook hands with everyone else. Even Pradeep, who was sulking near the doorway, eventually introduced himself and offered out a limp hand to Alice and her father and stepmother.

"Well," said Shanti, beaming at Alice. "I'm so glad we got to meet you. It actually seemed like Reena was trying to hide you from us."

I closed my eyes, chagrined. But when I opened them I saw that Alice was looking at me and . . . smiling.

"No, no," she told Shanti. "Not at all. If anyone's been hiding, it's me."

And to my surprise, I found myself smiling back.

TWELVE

Molly

All around me were teenagers trying, valiantly, not to cry.

It was Sunday afternoon, and Parents Weekend was finally over. And it was funniest thing: My fellow students had looked so miserable and self-conscious for all of Friday and Saturday, like they were just dying for their families to leave. Even the most popular and frightening kids on campus—the gorgeous Jamie Vanderheep, the icy Rebecca Saperstein—were rendered sulky and uncomfortable in the company of their plump, cheerful, fanny-pack-toting parents. The look on everyone's face, for all of Parents Weekend, was *Get these people away from me.*

But now the parents were taking off, piling into their cars and driving away, everyone was feeling the inevitable pang you feel when your parents finally do go, no matter how annoyed you've felt with them: suddenly you experience a strange, sinking, *oh my God don't leave me* sensation. Even the most bulky and imposing football player on campus was sitting alone and cross-legged near me on the student union green, toying with a dandelion and gulping back what looked like sobs of genuine loneliness and woe.

I just felt relieved.

I'd been one of the only kids on campus who didn't have a single family member visiting all weekend, and it had made me feel more like a freak than ever. I hadn't been in touch with my father and Candy since the night I ran away from their house—my father had phoned my dorm room repeatedly, I'd refused to return his calls, and then they'd finally just petered out—and there was no way my mom was going to be able to come. I'd called Silverwood a few days before and the staff had informed me that she wasn't even taking visitors for the next few weeks. Clearly things had gone downhill. I was trying not to think about it.

But it was hard. For forty-eight hours I'd been surrounded by hundreds of smiling, well-meaning families, and hundreds of kids not appreciating how lucky they were just to have one.

Alice Bingley-Beckerman, for example.

She'd spent the past month complaining to me about how evil her stepmother was (and, after meeting R. Klausenhook, I kind of had to agree—she was pretty awful), but her father was *Nelson Bingley*. One of the twentieth century's great geniuses. I couldn't even imagine what it would have been like to grow up with an intellectual, educated, perceptive father. Let alone the fact that her mother had been Susan Beckerman, another great novelist. Alice's childhood in Brooklyn Heights sounded idyllic. And hanging out with her father was like an honor in itself.

So I couldn't understand why shortly after dinner on Friday night, Alice had abruptly informed me that she needed some "alone time" with her father and R.

And then that "alone time" had extended itself to . . . the rest of the weekend.

Didn't she understand that I had no one to visit with, and nowhere to go?

Alice was supposed to be my new best friend. But during the past two days she had already hurt my feelings beyond belief. I'd spent the entire weekend alone in my room, lying under my covers and reading the Oxford English Dictionary. And even the fascinating discovery that the word *stepmother* has existed in some form in the English language since the year AD 725 didn't really make me feel any better.

Now I was lying on my stomach on the student union green, rereading *Zen Ventura* for Newman's humanities class, and hoping that Alice—now that her father and R. had most likely taken off—would come and find me.

I was mad and hurt, but I still wanted to see her.

A mosquito started flying around my head. I batted it away, annoyed. Every year in Massachusetts it seemed like the mosquitoes were around just a little longer than they should be. After all, it was already October. The mosquito buzzed closer to my ear. I could hear its wheedling, whingeing little voice get louder and louder. Suddenly I felt like it was actually flying around inside my brain.

"*Aaa!*" I yelped. I sat up and slapped the side of my head.

Then I heard giggles coming from a short distance away.

Assuming that the laughter was coming from the smirking mouths of kids like Vanderheep and Saperstein, I tried not to look in their direction. But then my eyes slid to the side in embarrassment, and I suddenly recognized the bright yellow head of hair.

It was Alice.

She was sitting with—could it be?—Reena Paruchuri.

The two of them were talking. And laughing. In fact, given all the solitary, red-eyed teenagers sitting by themselves on the green, Alice and Reena seemed almost inappropriately happy.

Without even thinking about it, I stood up. "Alice!" I called out.

Her bright blue eyes flashed in my direction, and then dulled at the sight of me. "Oh, hi, Molly," she said. Her voice sounded flat.

Reena, who had been in the middle of saying something, glanced up at me distractedly and then looked away.

I walked over toward them. My legs felt numb.

"Hey," I said, smiling at Alice.

She didn't say anything in response. I shielded my eyes from the sun with my hand and tried to keep smiling.

"How was the rest of your weekend?" I asked.

"Fine."

A long silence.

"What about you, Reena?" I queried hopefully.

Reena Paruchuri and I had never even really spoken to each other before. She and Kristen would sometimes hang out in our dorm room, but Kristen made a point—and it seemed like she told all her friends to make a point—of pretending I didn't exist.

"Terrible," Reena said, and sighed. "I hate my stepmother."

My mouth dropped open. "*You* have a stepmother?"

"Yeah. An evil one. Alice and I have totally bonded over our mutual bad luck."

"I have one, too!" I exclaimed.

Reena suddenly looked at me with interest. "Really?"

Alice cleared her throat and stood up. "Reen, let's get back to our room. I want to show you something."

"But Molly was saying—"

"But I really, *really* want to show you something."

"What?"

"Just . . ." Alice shot Reena an imploring look that I probably wasn't supposed to notice. "Please."

"Okay, okay." Reena hauled herself to her feet. "See ya later, Molly."

Alice grabbed Reena's arm and yanked her away. Stunned, I watched the two of them walk together across the green and back across the road toward Middleton.

I couldn't believe it.

What had gone wrong?

I suddenly felt myself turn into Molly Miller at Age Eight again, standing on the playground at North Forest Elementary and watching my (I thought at the time) best friend Suzanne get beckoned over to the crowd of "popular kids" standing next to the jungle gym. *"I'll just be gone a minute,"* she'd whispered to me.

But Suzanne had never come back. Not that day, or the next one, or the one after that. Years later, I would still see her huddled in some impenetrable corner of the North Forest Junior High School parking lot, smoking cigarettes, laughing, and pretending not to recognize me while I trudged by with my oversized backpack.

Now it was happening all over again.

But somehow it made even less sense this time.

Alice was smart. Alice and I had genuinely liked each other.

Was the attraction of someone like Reena Paruchuri—beautiful, fashionable, witty, friends with Jamie Vanderheep—really that strong?

I shook my head and tried to fight back tears. I'd thought better of Alice. I really had. But, I reminded myself, the world was a cruel, stupid place. My short-lived friendship with Alice Bingley-Beckerman had just made me momentarily forget that. Now I was in touch with reality again.

Suddenly I felt something thwack against my right shoulder. A shooting pain made its way down through my entire arm. A Frisbee thudded off my body and crashed onto the ground.

"Sorry!" I heard a guy call out.

That did it. Hot tears started dripping down my cheeks. Dizzy with anger, I picked up the Frisbee and hurled it off into the distance, far away from the green and toward the road.

"*Hey!*" I heard the same person say.

I turned around and realized, to my utter dismay, that it was Pradeep Paruchuri, looking confused and standing with another boy in a golden patch of sunlight.

A sob rose out of my stomach. Bending my head down in shame, praying he wouldn't recognize me, I ran away as fast as I could, back toward the familiar loneliness—and relative safety—of my little overheated dorm room.

But I had forgotten that Kristen was coming back.

Her absence had been the one nice thing about Parents Weekend. It was unclear why she'd gone back to Connecticut, instead of having her parents come to Putnam Mount McKinsey, but I, for one, certainly wasn't going to ask. I'd just felt relieved to have forty-eight hours away from her. Now it was Sunday evening and the time of her inevitable return.

I smelled Kristen even before I saw her. Her signature scent washed over me the second I opened the door to our room: a combination of artificial berry lip gloss, artificial berry shampoo, and artificial berry perfume.

Then I heard the muffled thumping of dance music coming out of the tiny speakers on her desktop computer.

Luckily, all these signs of Kristen gave me time to wipe the tears from my eyes and clear my throat before she actually saw me.

Then I stepped inside the room and took a deep breath. Kristen was unpacking her little leather suitcase and hanging her clothes back up in the closet. Her red ponytail swung back and forth as she bopped her head to her music.

"Hey," I said.

"Hey," she said, barely glancing in my direction.

I held my breath. No snide comment? No underhanded insult?

Kristen hummed cheerfully under her breath as she unfolded a pink silk skirt and smoothed it out with her hand.

Apparently not.

I was almost disappointed.

I plopped down on my bed, stared at the ceiling for a little while, and then reached into my bag and took out *Zen Ventura*. I stared at the cover. It had been my favorite novel since I was in sixth grade. So rereading should have made me feel better.

But now I kept flipping it over and looking at the author's photo on the back cover. There he was. Nelson Bingley. Alice had his clear, blue eyes, and long, straight nose. Her lips were different, though, and her cheekbones—

I shook my head. I didn't want to be thinking about Alice. Or her family. After all, she'd totally just rejected me. Maybe Nelson and R. thought I was stupid and uneducated. Maybe they could tell I wasn't from New York or some other snooty city. I began to stew in my own anger. I was just as smart as anyone! Smarter, in fact! I was *years* ahead of everyone else in Newman's humanities class, even though all the other students had attended snooty private schools their entire lives. Newman himself had said in our one-on-one conference that I was reading and writing at a college level. So who did the Bingleys think they were? Just because I wasn't a Beverly Hills fashionista like Reena or a New York intellectual like—

There was a knock on the door.

"I'll get it," said Kristen.

She delicately tiptoed her way toward the door through the mass of clothing strewn across our floor. I opened *Zen Ventura* and pretended to be deeply involved in it.

"Hey!" I heard Kristen exclaim.

My heart sank. A part of me had been hoping it was Alice, coming over to make peace. *Don't be so naïve*, I chided myself, and I went back to pretend-reading.

"What?" I heard Kristen ask. "You do?"

I peeked around the pages of my book. Reena Paruchuri was standing in the doorway, talking softly to Kristen. Just the sight of her made me angry, so I quickly turned on my side and faced the wall. A few seconds later, I heard the door shut, and Kristen stepped back inside the room.

"Molly," Kristen said.

"What?" I replied, not moving.

"Um . . . I have no idea why, but Reena wants you to come talk to her."

I sat up, shocked. "What? Where?"

"She said to tell you that she'll be waiting for you in the third-floor lounge." Kristen looked annoyed. She folded her arms, pursed her perfect pink lips, and stared out of our window.

"What I don't understand," she said finally, "is why she wants to hang out with you before she even asked me about..." her voice trailed off, and she seemed to space out for a few seconds before whirling around and staring at me accusatorily. "Well, aren't you going to go talk to her?"

"Uh... yeah. I guess so." I stood up, pushed my glasses up with one finger, and started walking toward the door.

"I mean, did you guys, like, become best friends over the weekend or something?" Kristen suddenly asked, just as I was about to step into the hallway.

I turned around and looked at her.

"No," I said slowly, "not at all."

Kristen's violet eyes widened in relief, and then, within seconds—it was almost miraculous—shifted back to their normal condescending glare. "I didn't think so," she said, and then turned around and started folding her clothes again.

When I got to the third-floor lounge, I found Reena, sitting cross-legged on an old beat-up beige couch and eating a bag of microwave popcorn.

I stood on the stained gray carpet and eyed her warily.

"Want some?" she asked, and held out the still-steaming, grease-stained bag.

I shook my head.

"It's so weird," she said, "I eat more microwave popcorn in a week here than I did during, like, five years in LA."

I didn't respond. I actually felt the same way—in fact, I

felt like our entire dorm had permanently absorbed the smell of Orville Redenbacher and emitted its fumes even when no one was actually making popcorn—*but now,* I thought to myself, *is not the time to be agreeing with Reena Paruchuri.*

After all, she'd just stolen my best friend.

"Sit down," Reena said, and patted the saggy couch cushion next to her.

I sat.

We looked at each other.

"You and I are very different, Molly," Reena said.

I nodded. What was she getting at?

"But," she said, pressing a well-manicured fingertip thoughtfully against her chin, "I think we also have a lot in common."

I stared at her.

"Don't you think so?" asked Reena.

"Um," I said, "I don't think I understand what you're talking about."

She smiled. "You will." Then she reached into her pocket, pulled out a small white envelope, and gave it to me. Written across it in calligraphy was

Molly

I stared at it. "What is this?"

"It's an invitation. Don't open it yet. Just promise me one thing."

"What?"

"You won't tell Alice about it."

I stared at her. "Reena. For reasons that are beyond me,

Alice is not, like, even speaking to me anymore. So I don't think you have to worry."

She nodded. "Okay. Yeah. Good. Just . . . don't tell her."

I hesitated, then swallowed. "Do you happen to know why she's not talking to me?"

Reena suddenly stood up. "I gotta go, Molly."

"Wait. I . . ."

"Seriously. I, uh, I have a lot of homework." She tossed the popcorn bag in a trash can and made a beeline for the door. Then she stopped and turned around. "Just remember: Don't tell Alice. Or anybody, for that matter."

"I don't even . . . tell anybody what?"

She grinned. "You'll see."

And then she was gone.

I sighed and sank back on the dingy couch. Alone again. I could hear sounds of kids talking and laughing from down the hall. I looked down at the little white envelope in my hands. I wondered if it was some kind of practical joke. Then I ripped it open. Inside was a small blue card, and written across it in the same calligraphic script was the following:

> *You are invited to the first meeting of*
> *The Poison Apples*
> *To Be Held on the Roof of*
> *Middleton Dorm,*
> *October 17th, Midnight*
> *Invitation Only*
> *RSVP Unnecessary*

I read the card about five times, trying to decipher its meaning. But I couldn't. Reena Paruchuri was definitely a lot weirder than I'd given her credit for.

Who were the Poison Apples?

And why couldn't I tell Alice?

I stood up and stuffed the card in my pocket. Maybe it was some kind of practical joke, concocted by Reena and her horrible popular friends. Maybe Kristen was involved. *I should probably forget about it and not show up at all*, I told myself.

But somewhere inside of me I knew that I was going to find a way to sneak out of my room, climb out onto the roof, and see what Reena Paruchuri was all about. After all, today was October 17th, and midnight was only five hours away. Despite the risk of humiliating myself at the hands of the evil and more popular, I had to admit it: I was intrigued.

THIRTEEN

Alice

"I don't get it," I said. "Who else is gonna be there?"

"No asking questions," Reena said. She stepped onto her bed, her high heels sinking into the mattress. One of the many pictures of steroidal male models on her wall was starting to sag, and—with her tongue sticking out between her teeth in concentration—she was reaffixing it with a roll of Scotch Tape.

"What does 'Poison Apple' even mean?" I asked.

She turned around and mock frowned at me. "Just shut up," she said affectionately. "Okay?"

I couldn't help but smile back. My life had completely turned around in the past twenty-four hours.

Reena Paruchuri and I were friends.

Our friendship had started as quickly as our enmity had. Two nights before, after we'd bumped into each other in our room with our respective parents and stepparents, everything had changed. After Dad and R. left for their bed-and-breakfast,

I walked back to the room and found Reena standing in the middle of room, her arms folded, grinning.

"Hi," I said.

"You didn't tell me," she said, her grin getting even bigger.

"Tell you what?"

"About your stepmother."

Then it was my turn to grin. "Well, you didn't tell me about yours."

And we'd both burst out laughing.

Because it was like the big balloon of tension that had filled up the room since the first day we moved had suddenly . . . popped.

Now it was Sunday evening, and Reena (my roommate! my friend!) was handing me some kind of strange invitation with the words *Poison Apples* on it and insisting that I show up on the roof of Middleton at midnight.

She refused to go into any more specifics, and I eventually gave up asking.

I set the alarm for 11:50, went to bed at 10:30, and tried to sleep as much as I could in the time between. But Reena was snoring in the bed next to me, and some kind of weird owl was hooting in the elm tree outside our window. I also couldn't stop mulling the weekend over—how Dad had changed even more in the month I'd been gone than in the whole two years that passed after Mom's death. And how R. acted as if there was nothing weird about me being three hundred miles away at boarding school. As if it was perfectly natural. As if she'd had nothing to do with it.

Reena said Shanti Shruti had done the same thing: just acted as if nothing was wrong. That way if she, Reena, had thrown some sort of temper tantrum or been anything less than 100 percent friendly, she would have seemed crazy.

The thing was, acting friendly and normal sometimes seemed like the craziest thing of all.

A loud beeping sound interrupted my thoughts. It was the alarm. Reena rolled over in bed and groaned.

"Go ahead without me," she said.

"But you're the one who invited me."

"I'll be there in a few minutes."

I had a feeling she was just going to go back to sleep.

I hauled myself out of bed, slipped on my winter coat over my pajamas, and tiptoed out into the hallway. I had to be careful. Agnes the RA seemed to have the uncanny ability to smell freshman and sophomores who were sneaking out of their rooms at night.

I found my way to the stairwell in the semidarkness and walked up the winding staircase to the roof, wincing whenever I made the old wooden steps creak. I reached the top and stared up at the tiny metal ladder above my head. I'd never been up on the Middleton roof before. Agnes had informed us, time and time again, that it was strictly off-limits.

I stepped onto the ladder, the metal cold against my bare feet, and attempted to wrench open the door. I was sure that some kind of alarm was going to go off. But the door opened, and I didn't hear anything except the wind whistling up above me. I climbed up and hauled myself clumsily over the ledge and onto the slanted, shingled roof. The cold air blew against my face. A million stars shone above my head.

"Hi, Alice," someone said.

I turned around. Molly Miller was sitting right next to the chimney, wrapped in a blanket and shivering.

"What are you doing here?" I blurted out.

She shot me a resentful glare. "I could ask you the same question."

"Reena invited me."

"Good for you, big shot. She invited me, too."

I felt a gust of wind lift my hair up above my head. "I don't believe you."

Molly stood up, wobbled a little, and grabbed onto the chimney for balance. "What is that supposed to . . . ," she spluttered. "What is wrong with you?"

"What is wrong with *you*?" I retorted. "I thought you were my friend!"

"What are you talking about? You were the one who—"

"SILENCE," a voice boomed out.

Molly and I both froze, then slowly turned around.

Someone was standing behind us.

And it took me a few seconds to realize that someone was Reena Paruchuri.

First of all, she was carrying a huge flashlight (she must have stolen it from the janitor's closet) that she was holding below her chin and shining up into her face. The bluish light made her look absolutely terrifying. Secondly, she was draped in some kind of enormous cloth that made her look floating and shapeless, like a ghost. Thirdly, she seemed to be wearing some sort of . . . crown.

"Reena?" I whispered.

"SILENCE, MORTAL," the draped figure shouted. Then she burst into giggles, and her crown fell off. "Sorry, sorry," she said. She picked it up and put it back on again.

"Is that a Burger King crown?" asked Molly from her perch next to the chimney.

169

"NO QUESTIONS," Reena bellowed.

Molly sighed.

"What are we doing here, Reen?" I said.

Reena cleared her throat. "We are attending the first meeting of the Poison Apples."

"And what's that?"

"Please, please," Reena said, and held out her hand, palm forward. "Patience. As founder and president of the Poison Apples, I insist that before initiation we—"

"Initiation?" asked Molly, laughing.

The whites of Reena's eyes gleamed indignantly in the moonlight. "Yes, Molly Miller. Initiation. But I insist that before initiation begins we resolve any existing disputes between members."

Molly and I stared at her.

Reena sighed. "I believe there is a dispute between the two of you."

"Me and Alice?" Molly said.

"No," Reena said, "You and the other blond girl standing on this roof." There was a long pause, after which she tittered quietly at her own joke.

"Well," Molly said, "I'll be honest. I'm confused. I wasn't aware that there was a dispute between me and Ms. Bingley-Beckerman until this afternoon when she started totally ignoring me and acting like a jerk."

"And I wasn't aware until Friday evening," I added, "that Ms. Miller is only interested in being friends with me because my father is her favorite writer."

"Excuse me?" shrieked Molly.

Reena clapped her shawl-covered hands. "Good, good. Get it all out in the open."

Molly stood up and walked over to me, stepping carefully around the shingles. She faced me and put her hands on her hips. The moon reflected in big white circles off her glasses.

"I was never interested in being friends with you because of your father," she said, her voice trembling. "What made you think that?"

"Because," I said, trying hard to make sure that my own voice didn't tremble, "you basically ignored me and only talked to him. And then you made a big deal about my mom being famous, like that even matters..." (Oh, no. It was happening. My voice was shaking and tears were starting to well up in my throat. I continued anyway.) "...like that even matters...when she's dead."

There was a long silence. The wind blew a high-pitched song above our heads.

"Oh, Alice," Molly said.

"That's good," whispered Reena from behind us. "'Oh, Alice' is good. That's what I imagined you'd say."

"Shut up, Reen," I said, turning around.

Reena nodded obediently.

Molly and I looked at each other.

"I'm sorry," Molly said. "You have to believe me...that's not why I became friends with you. I became friends with you because you're smart and funny and weird."

"I'm not weird," I said, slightly offended.

"Yes, you are," Molly said. "In the best way. You're extremely weird. And I acted dumb around your dad because he *is* my favorite writer. But that has nothing to do with me liking you for the wrong reasons. And..." Molly hesitated.

"Don't hold back!" piped up Reena.

171

"I was hurt that you didn't let me spend more time with you guys. Because even though you have a crazy family, at least they *came*. I didn't have anyone to complain about, because no one was even *around*."

She took off her tear-streaked glasses and wiped them with the edge of her shirt.

"I'm sorry, Mol," I said. "I was really hurt."

There was a long silence.

"This," announced Reena, "is exactly what I was talking about. Resolving existing disputes. Not as hard as it sounds."

Molly and I looked over at Reena. Her paper crown was sitting crookedly on top of her head, and the flashlight, now tucked under her arm, was illuminating her left earlobe. She looked thrilled.

"Reena," I asked, "why are we here?"

"Okay," she said. "Good question. Now that the existing dispute has been resolved . . ." She paused for a second. "Wait. It's been resolved, right? Do you guys agree that it's been resolved?"

Molly and I looked at each other.

"Yeah," I said finally.

"Yeah," said Molly.

My stomach flooded with unexpected relief.

"Okay. Good. Now we can begin. Please be seated."

Molly and I sat down on the cold shingles. We crossed our legs and looked up at Reena. She cleared her throat ceremoniously.

"Welcome," she said.

We nodded impatiently.

Reena reached underneath her enormous shawl and removed something. "Please step back," she said.

Since we were already sitting, we scooted back on our butts.

"Behold," she said, and held out her hand. "The Poison Apple."

It was pretty dark, but it looked like Reena was just holding a regular red apple.

"Is that a Red Delicious from the cafeteria?" asked Molly.

"No," Reena snapped. "It's a Honey Crisp. I bought it at the fruit stand next to the highway. It's much . . . crisper. And more expensive."

Molly and I giggled until Reena gave us both the evil eye.

"So why is it a *poison* apple?" I asked.

"This apple," said Reena, "is symbolic. Don't you guys remember Snow White?"

Molly gasped. "Oh, my God. *The Poison Apple*. I'd forgotten."

"What about it?" I asked. "I don't remember a poison apple."

Molly turned to me, excited puffs of fog coming out of her mouth. "Yes, you do. You have to. Snow White is hiding out with the Seven Dwarfs and then her, um, her evil stepmother . . ."

Reena nodded encouragingly.

". . . Her evil stepmother dresses up as an old woman and comes to the house and, like, offers Snow White an apple. But it's poisoned, and Snow White falls asleep, or, like, dies or something, until the Prince comes along and kisses her and she wakes up."

Just the mention of kissing made Jamal flash through my mind. I blushed. Luckily, neither of them could tell in the dark.

"So . . ." Molly stopped and frowned. "Wait, I'm confused."

"We're the Poison Apples!" Reena declared. "We're a society of mistreated stepdaughters! And we're coming together to take revenge!"

Revenge.

The word sent shivers down my spine.

But I didn't know if they were bad shivers or good shivers.

"But it's the evil queen who gives the apple to Snow White," Molly pointed out. "Not the other way around."

"Okay, Miss English Lit," Reena said. "But think about symbolism. Hasn't Newman taught you anything? The apple represents our unlucky fates. It represents our stepmothers' plots to ruin our lives. So we're reclaiming the apple. It's *ours* now. Two can play that game."

"What game?" I asked.

"The game of . . ." she trailed off for a second.

"The game of power," Molly finished for her.

Reena nodded. "Exactly. If they can be our evil stepmothers, we can be their evil stepdaughters. Right?"

"Right!" shouted Molly.

"Do we really want to be *evil* . . . ?" I started to ask, but Reena had already taken a chomp out of the apple and was handing it to Molly.

"We'll each take a bite," Reena said, "as a gesture of our loyalty and camaraderie. We are a group of unlucky heroines. And we are going to take action. We are going to take our lives back."

Molly sunk her teeth into the apple and then chewed on her piece. "Mm," she said. "You're right. This *is* better than the cafeteria apples."

"Your turn, Alice," Reena said. Molly held out the apple.

I stared at it. It gleamed red and yellow in the moonlight.

Okay. Reena had just said that the apple symbolized our fates. But, if I understood the fairy tale correctly, it also symbolized evil. And deceit. And trickery.

On the other hand, a society of mistreated stepdaughters sounded pretty great. It sounded kind of like a . . . family.

"Take a bite!" barked Reena. "We don't have all night!"

"That rhymed," said Molly, and giggled.

"Fine," I said. I took the apple out of her hands and bit into it. I let the sweet, slightly sour juice sit in my mouth for a minute, and then I swallowed and handed the apple back to Reena. She held it aloft.

"They cannot poison us!" Reena yelled. "We will fight back!"

She drew her arm back and pitched the apple out into the night sky. I watched it sail past the stars for a few glorious seconds, and then it fell, invisibly, down to the dark earth below.

PART
TWO

ONE

Reena

David Newman was looking at me.

I mean, he was looking at everyone. But he was looking at me just a little *more*. His eyes would move around the classroom, come to rest on my face, flicker a little, and then move on again.

He is so cute, I scrawled on a piece of scrap paper. I passed it to Molly, who was sitting at the desk to my right. She read it and rolled her eyes.

I guess she wasn't mature enough to recognize real love when she saw it.

It was the middle of November. Everyone at Putnam Mount McKinsey was waiting for the first big snowfall. A few days before, a few lonely flakes had drifted down out of the white sky while Pradeep and I were taking a walk, and the two of us had whooped and leapt around and shouted at the clouds to give us MORE, MORE, but nothing happened.

Now it was the Wednesday before Mount McKinsey Weekend, and the bored-sounding man on the radio that morning had predicted that we'd be in the middle of a full-fledged snowstorm by nighttime. David Newman's entire Humanities class was fidgeting excitedly in their seats and turning around every five seconds to look out the window. I was pretty much the only person in the room who wasn't interested in looking at anything but the seemingly endless depths of Newman's eyes.

Halfway through his lecture about the "culture of rebellion" surrounding the characters in *Zen Ventura* (which, by the way, although I wasn't going to admit it to Alice, I thought was totally boring), Newman pushed back his chair, stepped out from behind his desk, and howled in frustration.

Everyone snapped to attention.

"What is this about?" he demanded. "Why is everyone except Reena Paruchuri staring out the window?"

I blushed.

"There's going to be a snowstorm," Judah Lipston the Third announced sulkily from his desk.

"Ah," said Newman. "I should have realized." He stepped forward and stood in front of my desk. "And Ms. Paruchuri—why are you superhumanly able to focus on your class work when your fellow students are thinking about sledding?"

"Snowboarding, actually," Judah Lipston the Third said.

I shrugged. Molly snorted into her hand.

"Please," Newman said to the class, "it's Wednesday. You've got a three-day weekend coming up and a big trip to Mount McKinsey. Try to focus a little before Friday, when you'll cease to remember that Humanities class even exists."

I would never forget, I tried to telepathically communicate to him.

The bell rang. Everyone leapt out of their seats.

"Finish the book by tomorrow!" Newman hollered.

"I finished it a week ago," Molly whispered triumphantly, "for the fourth time."

"Oh, shut up, Mol," said Alice, who was sitting to my left. She stood up and started gathering up her things. "You're such a Goody Two-Shoes."

"Reena's the one who's 'superhuman,' remember?" Molly said, and poked me in the ribs.

Alice shook her head and stuffed her copy of *Zen Ventura* into her backpack. "I just don't think Newman gives us enough time to do all the reading. I mean, doesn't he know we have homework for our other classes?"

I studied Alice as she bent over her bag, her blond hair falling in strands across her pink cheeks. "Are you okay, Alice?"

"I'm fine," she snapped, and disappeared into the crowd of students filing out of the classroom.

"Whoa," I said.

Molly shook her head. "Don't take it personally. She's just upset that she can't get through the novel."

"What do you mean?"

Molly pushed her glasses up her nose and leaned in confidentially. "We were studying together in the library yesterday and she had *Zen Ventura* sitting in front of her for like two hours. You know how many times she turned the pages? Three."

"Well, maybe she was distracted."

"Maybe. But it looked like she was trying pretty hard." Molly held up her own well-worn copy of *Zen Ventura* and pointed to the author's photo on the back. "It must be tough to have a hard time getting through your own father's book."

I shrugged. The book wasn't hard for me to understand, but I did think it was pretty dull. The plot consisted of a bunch of New York intellectuals sitting around in living rooms, drinking wine, discussing politics, and occasionally deciding to get divorced.

By this time the classroom had pretty much emptied out. Newman approached me and Molly. My heart began to palpitate wildly.

"How do the two of you like the book?" he asked. Molly opened her mouth to speak, but then he shook his head. "Scratch that, Miller. I know you love it. How many times have you read it? Three?"

"Four," she said happily.

"What do you think, Paruchuri?" Newman asked, his head cocked to one side.

I found myself unable to look him in the face, so I gazed down at my hands and picked furiously at one of my cuticles. "It's okay."

"Okay?" he asked, and laughed. "Okay means you hate it."

I looked up. Our eyes connected. "Well," I began reluctantly, "I guess I just think everyone in it is kind of a . . . jerk."

Molly gasped in indignation. Grinning, Newman put up a hand to shush her. "Interesting. Why is everyone a jerk?"

"Well, they just talk about their problems all the time. They're so self-involved. They never get up and actually do anything."

Newman smiled. "Well, exactly. You've just articulated my favorite thing about the book."

I frowned. "*What's* your favorite thing?"

"That sense of stasis. These sad people sitting around

wanting to do things differently, but they're never actually able to get off the couch and change their lives."

I tried to nod, but the real world was fading around me. I was drowning in the shiny black pools of David Newman's pupils.

"And it's so realistic," Molly added, waking me from my dream state by shaking my elbow. "I mean, *Zen Ventura* is showing us what real people are actually like."

"Yes," Newman nodded. "It's all so painfully real and human."

I shook my head. "I don't think it's realistic," I said, "I'm not like that. I don't sit around and complain like those people. I get things done."

Newman smiled, beautiful crinkles springing up around the corners of his eyes. "Oh, really?" He turned to Molly. "Is that true, Miller? Does Paruchuri get off the couch and get things done?"

She considered this, chewing on her chapped bottom lip. "Yeah," she said after a pause, "I guess she does."

I could have kissed her.

Newman rocked back on his heels and observed me, his head still cocked to the side in that mischievous way. "I'm impressed, Paruchuri. And jealous. I'm definitely just a good-for-nothing *Zen Ventura* kind of guy." He picked up his big leather bag, which was stuffed full of our term papers, and nodded to us. Then he walked out of the room.

I sighed, closed my eyes, and pressed a palm to my burning forehead. Molly scrutinized me.

"Ew, gross," she said.

"What?"

"He's way too old for you."

"Love knows no bounds, Mol."

"Oh, my God. Don't make me retch all over myself."

We walked out of the building together and stood outside on the pavement, shivering and staring up at the sky. Gray clouds were floating ominously overhead.

"Okay, hold on," I said. "Newman just said that he was a *Zen Ventura* kind of guy. Do you think he was trying to, like, communicate something to me?"

Molly scrunched up her red nose. "What are you talking about?"

"Well, he's shy. He can't 'get off the couch.'"

Molly's mouth hung open as she stared at me, uncomprehending.

I sighed in exasperation. "He was telling me to make the first move!"

Molly shook her head. "No. No."

"Don't be so quick to—"

"I'm sorry, Reena, but you have completely lost your mind." She pulled on her wool cap and mittens and started walking back toward the dorm. "Come on. Let's go find Alice and eat lunch."

I refused to move from my spot on the pavement. "I don't think you understand."

"I do understand. You've gone berserk. Newman is not trying to subtly communicate to you that you should make a move. He's like forty."

"Thirty-two," I corrected her.

"Whatever." Her frizzy hair stuck out goofily from beneath her cap and her glasses were half-steamed up from her breath. "Let's go."

I wasn't done yet. I had to make her understand. I'd grown to love Molly in the past few weeks, but sometimes she acted so . . . immature.

"I know that the idea of dating an older man is difficult for you to comprehend, Mol," I said. "But you and I are very different."

"Oh, yeah? How?"

"Well, I don't think you understand romance in quite the same . . ." I trailed off. It was hard to explain. "I mean, it just seems like you don't think about boys that much. You don't even have a crush on anyone, and you—"

"How do you know?" Molly snapped.

I raised my eyebrows. "You have a crush on someone?"

Her face turned bright red. "No, I just . . . I just . . ."

"Who?"

She folded her arms against her bulky jacket and stared at the ground. "No one. Never mind."

"See?" I said. "I just don't think you know what it's like to have really, really strong feelings for someone."

Molly pulled her cap farther down over her ears and refused to look at me. "You know what? Do whatever you want. I don't care."

"Thank you."

I walked over, linked arms with her, and the two of us started heading back toward the dorm. Molly kept staring at the ground. She was clearly brooding about something.

"Don't worry, Mol," I said. "You'll find someone eventually."

She didn't respond.

"I mean, who knows—maybe you'll even meet a guy during Mount McKinsey weekend!" I added hopefully.

Molly nodded. Suddenly I noticed a few specks of white falling on the collar of her jacket.

"Oh, my God," I gasped. "I think it's . . ."

We stopped in our tracks and looked up. Cascading out of the sky toward our upturned faces were thousands of snowflakes. One landed in my eye and dripped down my face. I yelped happily and did a little dance, sticking my tongue out into the cold air.

"My first snowfall!" I yelled.

Molly nodded and held out her mittened hand, watching clusters of snowflakes form in her palm. "Funny," she said. "I think I've seen about a thousand of these."

It was Friday, and Mount McKinsey weekend had finally arrived. The storm had—to the delight of the entire school— lasted for all of Wednesday night and most of Thursday. We'd gotten almost a foot and half of snow. I'd basically spent the last two days staring out of our dorm window and whispering: *"Amazing."*

Now every Middleton resident was standing on the snowy walkway outside the dorm, waiting for the bus that was going to take us thirty miles north to the top of Mount McKinsey. Everyone was talking and laughing so loud that I could barely hear myself think. So I just looked down at the snow and admired my hot pink galoshes.

I looked pretty good in them.

A yellow bus came rumbling up the road and screeched to a halt in front of us.

"No more than two in a seat!" shrieked Agnes the RA, but

she was drowned out by the sound of fifty girls all jostling one another to get on the bus first.

I pushed my way into line behind Alice and Molly, but then suddenly felt a hand on my arm. I turned around. It was Kristen.

"Hey," she said. "Long time no see."

I nodded, feeling guilty. I'd been kind of avoiding Kristen for the past few weeks. Well, not kind of avoiding. Definitely avoiding.

The thing was, I really, really liked Alice and Molly. I liked them because they were smart and interesting and, most important, they made me feel comfortable. Like I could be myself. And ever since that night in Jamie Vanderheep's dorm room, I'd been wondering why hanging out with the cool kids had always mattered so much to me in the past. My friend Katie in LA was one thing; she was popular and well-dressed, but she was also really nice to everyone. But making my way into the cool crowd so effortlessly at Putnam Mount McKinsey made me reevaluate why being part of the cool crowd was, in itself, so important. Kristen, in particular, had started to drive me crazy, even before I became friends with Alice during Parents Weekend. For one thing, Kristen was never into talking about our families. It seemed like she had a perfect life, and judged anyone who didn't. Her favorite activity was sitting around, painting her toenails, and talking about who needed to get a decent haircut and start dressing better (Molly's name would come up frequently).

So, slowly, I'd started to pull away from her. And after Parents Weekend and the first official meeting of the Poison Apples (which made me happier than I'd been in a long, long time), I'd pretty much decided that I didn't really want to be friends with Kristen anymore. At all.

But she was having a hard time picking up on my cues. In her defense, I think it was the first time anyone had ever stopped wanting to be friends with her. She was clearly one of those people who had, since her first day at preschool, radiated power and popularity.

"Where have you been?" she demanded, a weird, aggressive smile plastered across her face. "You didn't come to Rebecca's party the other night!"

"Yeah," I said, digging a little hole in the snow with the tip of my pink boot. "I know. I had a lot of homework. Sorry." The truth was, I'd stayed up late with Alice that night drawing goofy self-portraits of ourselves and laughing.

"We had an amazing time," Kristen said. The line to get on the bus moved forward, and I saw, to my chagrin, Alice and Molly get lost in the swarm of students.

I nodded. "Yeah. It sounded really cool."

There was a pause, and I saw a wave of insecurity wash over Kristen's face. She looked amazing—her long red hair was streaming out beneath a green cashmere cap that perfectly matched her green woolen peacoat and her short green-and-blue skirt and leggings—so seeing her turn pale with self-doubt was sort of incredible. It was like she'd never experienced rejection before, on any level, and so the feeling of rejection didn't come naturally to her. It clashed with her outfit. It clashed with her perfectly made-up face.

"Well . . ." Kristen hesitated. "Are you, like . . . okay?"

I was kind of touched. Kristen had never ever asked me if I was okay before. Her normal way of greeting me was grabbing my elbow and whispering something mean about the girl across the table in my ear.

"Yeah," I said. "I'm actually doing great."

She looked completely baffled.

"How are you?" I added.

"Um," she said. "Oh. Yeah. I'm fine. I'm fine. Yup. Fine."

"Good."

The line moved forward, and I climbed up the steps to the bus, Kristen right behind me. Sitting in the third row of seats were Alice and Molly. Together. Of course. I mean, why wouldn't they sit together? I'd lagged behind.

"Hey guys," I said, relieved to just see them again, and started to squeeze into the seat with them.

"Um, Reen," Molly whispered, "it's just two to a seat."

I blanched. "Oh."

"Sorry," she said, and looked at Alice for help. Alice shrugged and made a what-are-we-supposed-to-about-it? face.

I felt a hand grabbing my arm again.

"Reena," Kristen said from behind me. "We're sitting together, right?"

"Oh," I said. "Um . . . yeah. Sure."

"Vanderheep and Saperstein are going on the second bus. Which sucks. Because," and she leaned forward to whisper this last part loudly in my ear, "that means we're stuck with all the dorks."

I glanced at Molly, who had clearly heard everything Kristen said.

"Well," I began, trying to think of a way to defend my friends without getting into some kind of weird argument, but Kristen had already yanked me down into the seat right behind Molly and Alice and was pulling celebrity magazines out of her purse.

"You *have* to see this picture," she said, and started flipping through the latest issue of *People*.

I nodded weakly.

Hopefully the bus ride—which, I saw now, was going to be excruciating—wouldn't be representative of the entire weekend on Mount McKinsey.

After all, I had three extremely important goals for the trip:

1. Relax and have fun.
2. Conduct the second official meeting of the Poison Apples.
3. Kiss David Newman for the first time.

And, I told myself as the bus pulled out of the Putnam Mount McKinsey campus and onto the snowy highway, using the very words my father had said to me before taking his medical boards fifteen years before: *A Paruchuri Always, Always Achieves His (or Her, in this case) Goals.*

TWO

Molly

The sun was setting when we arrived at Mount McKinsey Lodge, and the silhouette of its roof made a sharp black triangle against the burning orange sky. As the bus came to a halt, we all fell silent, amazed.

It was a gigantic, sprawling old building, with three chimneys and two verandahs and a huge stained-glass window above the front entrance that—with the glow of the setting sun shining through it—cast strange, otherworldly shapes onto the floor of the lobby, where the entire school stood, agog, with our suitcases.

"MIDDLETON GIRLS!" Agnes yelled, and we all clustered around her.

She began handing out room assignments. I unfolded mine, ran over to Alice and Reena, and asked: "Room 405? Room 405?" They looked at their assignments, squealed with delight, and the three of us slapped five.

"Did I hear someone say Room 405?" a familiar voice inquired from behind us.

I turned around, horrified. It was Kristen.

"Yes," I said slowly. "Is that—"

Kristen pushed me aside and hugged Reena. "We're roomies!"

Reena bugged her eyes at me over Kristen's shoulder in a help-me expression. I ignored her. I wasn't going to feel bad for someone whom Kristen actually *liked*. And I was the one who had to deal with being her roommate all the time.

The four of us hauled our suitcases up four flights of creaky, windy stairs and were panting by the time we reached Room 405.

Reena turned the key in the latch and flung open the door. We all gasped.

"It's like we're in the nineteenth century," Alice said dreamily.

"More like the thirteenth century," said Kristen. She bent down, touched the floor with her forefinger, and then showed it to us. "Gross. Everything is covered in dust. Doesn't anyone ever clean this place?"

"Who cares?" I said. "It's beautiful."

The ceiling was slanted and crisscrossed with wooden beams. There were four single beds, each one with its own individual red velvet canopy and a tiny, tasseled, red lamp beside it. There were even four tiny desks and four wooden rocking chairs. I walked over to the one of the dusty oval windows and stared out at the winter landscape. There were the snowy bluffs of Mount McKinsey, then miles of evergreen forest, then the thin gray line of the highway, and then a little cluster of buildings that was probably the town of Putnam. I squinted even farther out into the distance, and thought I saw, nestled between snow-covered hills in the distance, a dark spot that might have been North Forest. Or maybe I was just imagining it.

North Forest. The thought of my hometown sent shivers down my spine.

I hadn't spoken to either of my parents in almost a month.

"Molly!" said Alice. "Can you hear me?"

I spun around. "Yeah. Sorry. I spaced out. What?"

"Are you coming down to dinner?"

"She's always like this," Kristen commented from the door, where she was waiting with Reena. "She's always staring into space, thinking about something nerdy."

I stared at Kristen. Nerdy. Right. The disintegration of my family was nerdy. "You're right," I said to her, my voice icy with rage, "I should be spending my time the way you do, coming up with ways to get Jamie Vanderheep to pay attention to me."

Kristen blushed a little, but then put her hands on her hips and tried to look nonchalant. "And what's wrong with that?"

"It's just a little pathetic when he so obviously has a crush on Reena."

Reena gasped. "Molly!"

"What? It's true."

Kristen's face had crumpled involuntarily, but now she was twirling a piece of red hair around her forefinger and clearly trying to come up with a comeback. Still—for once—it looked like I rendered her speechless. After a few awful seconds, she turned and left the room. We all stood there for a minute and listened to her high-heeled boots clatter down the hallway.

"Molly," Alice whispered, "that was really mean."

"Mean?" I asked. "You're calling me mean? That girl is the Queen Bee of Mean."

"Yeah, but two wrongs don't make a—"

"Alice," I said, "do not finish that sentence."

Reena, still standing in the doorway, giggled softly, covering her mouth with her hand.

"You think this is funny?" Alice asked. "Kristen looked like she was gonna start crying."

"I'm just impressed, that's all," Reena said. "Miller has guts."

"That's a strange thing to say," Alice informed her, "for someone who's totally unable to say no to Kristen, like, ever."

"I can say no!" Reena retorted. "And maybe you're just jealous because she doesn't even notice—"

"Okay, okay," I said, walking forward and linking arms with both of them. "Let's not fight. Who cares about Kristen? This trip is about the Poison Apples."

"You're right," Reena said as the three of us walked down the hallway and started descending the spiral staircase toward the sounds of our classmates chattering in the dining room. "We need to have our second meeting sometime this weekend."

Just as we were about to enter the lobby, Alice froze in her tracks, her foot hovering in the air between the last step and the floor. "Act normal," she whispered. "Just . . . act normal."

"Are we not acting normal?" Reena asked, confused.

"*Shhh,*" Alice hissed.

A cluster of PMM seniors passed by us, talking and laughing. A vaguely familiar-looking African American boy lagged behind for a second and smiled at us. "Hey, Alice," he said.

Because her arm was still linked in mine, I actually felt the goose bumps spring up on Alice's skin. Her temperature also seemed to drop about thirty degrees. Her eyes widened and she looked like she was about to faint.

"Um, what?" she asked the boy.

He frowned. "Wait, what?"

"I ..." Alice hesitated for a second. "What?"

I could see Reena out of the corner of my eye, biting her lip to keep from laughing.

"I, uh ... I just said hello," the boy said, looking uncomfortable. "But I should probably go, uh, catch up with my friends."

Alice nodded vigorously. "Yeah. Yeah. Of course."

He raised his hand, gave an embarrassed half-wave to me and Reena, and then dashed away.

For the next few seconds, Alice remained absolutely still. I watched her delicate nostrils flare as she attempted to inhale and exhale. Reena and I sent each other what-do-we-do-now? looks. Finally Alice whispered something inaudible.

"What did you say?" Reena asked.

"Kill me now," Alice muttered. "Just ... kill me."

"It wasn't that bad," I told her, trying to sound positive. "You were both just a little ... awkward. What's the big deal?"

"He's pretty cute," Reena said.

Alice turned to her, her face drained of all color. "Jamal Chapman is more than cute. He's the most beautiful boy in the world."

Nope, I corrected her in my mind, *Pradeep Paruchuri is the most beautiful boy in the world.* But I had to be careful to never, ever say that out loud. Reena would never let me live it down. And she'd probably run and tell Pradeep within five minutes.

"Oh my God," gasped Reena. "You totally have a crush on

him! I can't believe you didn't tell your own roommate about this!"

Alice shook her head back and forth. "I refuse to talk about it. Later. Right now I just feel like I'm going to die."

With Alice trembling between us, Reena and I proceeded to the dining room, where the sounds of silverware clinking against plates echoed like music off the tall cathedral ceilings. The windows were almost twenty feet tall, and they opened onto long, snow-covered verandahs. The sun had just set, and the sky outside was light violet. Ornate, sparkling chandeliers hung from the ceiling. There were dozens of round tables, each one covered in red cloth. Our PMM classmates, usually so raucous and obnoxious, seemed to have absorbed the dignity of the room they were sitting in, and were conversing softly—even laughing—in an uncharacteristically grown-up manner.

"I want to live in Mount McKinsey Lodge," I whispered, as we surveyed the room for a place to sit.

"They say it's haunted," Reena whispered back.

That was the first thing that distracted Alice from her stupor of humiliation. Her eyes widened. "Haunted?" she said. "Don't say that. Come on. You're kidding."

"I'm just repeating what I heard."

I groaned. "You guys are acting like little kids."

We found an empty table and sat down.

"I'll save our seats while you guys go to the buffet table," I told Alice and Reena. "Then I'll go by myself." I just wanted to sit and absorb the atmosphere for a while. I'd never been anywhere this elegant in my life.

They nodded and left, and I leaned back in my chair and

gazed up at the ceiling contentedly. There was something about Mount McKinsey Lodge that fit perfectly into fantasies I'd had when I was little girl. Everything about it was so old-fashioned and refined. There were even pictures in the lobby of all the famous writers who had stayed there when it was a working hotel. Being at the lodge made me feel like a totally different person. Instead of Molly Miller from North Forest, Massachusetts, I was Molly Miller from Paris, France. Molly Miller from Zurich, Switzerland. Molly Miller from Venice, Italy. Actually—even better—I was a world-traveling high-society woman from Monaco. I wore long white gloves and a single gleaming magnolia behind my ear. I went to masked balls and sat at the roulette table in Monte Cristo casinos, laughing and smiling and whispering sweet nothings into the ears of handsome men. At night I slept between silk sheets. I lived in a thousand different hotels, always arriving by steamer and carrying a golden birdcage that contained a single green parakeet named—

"Pradeep."

I gasped and jolted forward in the chair that I'd been ab-sentmindedly tipping backward.

Pradeep Paruchuri had just sat down across from me at the table.

"Pradeep," he repeated. "That's my name. Do you remem-ber me from Orientation Week?"

Did I remember him from Orientation Week? Was he try-ing to be funny?

I nodded. "I remember."

"Molly, right?"

"Uh-huh."

"My sister keeps telling me all these great things about you."

Something in my chest burst into flame, traveled up my throat, and burned my cheeks. I lowered my head and stared at the tablecloth.

"Well, Reena is great, too," I whispered.

"I just wanted to say again that I'm sorry about what happened during that—"

"It's okay," I interrupted him.

"During that orientation activity? Dropping you and all? I felt horrible about that."

"Pradeep," I heard myself saying, with uncharacteristic firmness, "please stop apologizing. The whole thing becomes exponentially more humiliating every time you say you're sorry."

His smile turned into a huge grin. "Ha. Reena was right. You are funny."

This left me completely speechless, and luckily Alice and Reena showed up at that moment and plunked their trays of food down on the table.

"You've got to get some of this," Reena informed me. "It's like real food. So much better than at school." Then she turned to her brother. "What are you doing here?"

"Talking to your friend. Is that such a big deal? Or am I not allowed to sit with you guys?"

Reena rolled her eyes. "Do whatever you want to do, butthead. Actually you and Molly should talk to each other. You're both big nerds."

"What is that supposed to mean?" Pradeep asked.

"You both spend all your time with your faces buried in books."

"Oh, yeah?" Pradeep gazed at me curiously. "Who are your favorite authors?"

I took a deep breath. *You are a nineteenth-century lady from Monaco,* I told myself. *You wear white gloves. You are charming. You think nothing of talking about books with a handsome young man.*

I propped my chin in my hand, trying to look casual and thoughtful at the same time. The author that always came to mind was Nelson Bingley, but I had to be careful these days not to freak Alice out.

"Emily Dickinson," I said. "Um...also Walt Whitman. I guess those are both poets. In terms of novelists, I really love Dickens. Especially *David Copperfield*. Um. I also really like—"

"*DAVID COPPERFIELD* IS MY ALL-TIME FAVORITE BOOK!" Pradeep shouted.

Reena buried her face in her hands. "Geez, Pradeep. Make sure the whole cafeteria hears how nerdy you are."

"It's really your favorite book?" I asked. My nervousness was ebbing away and actual curiosity was taking over.

"Yeah. I've read it like seven times. And I *love* Walt Whitman."

I looked straight into his eyes and smiled. "Weird."

Suddenly he leapt up out of his seat. "Shoot. I forgot to give Jamal back his iPod. I gotta go." He kissed Reena on top of her head, eliciting an indignant "ew!" and then he darted away.

Even though I felt as if I'd just been inside a dream, I attempted to act normal. "I didn't know your brother was a big reader," I told Reena.

"Yeah, yeah. He's always—"

"Did he say *Jamal*?" Alice interrupted.

"Oh. Yeah."

"Pradeep is friends with Jamal Chapman?"

"I guess."

Alice stared at Reena, her mouth open. "You didn't tell me."

Reena's fork clattered down to the table. "You are such a psychopath! I didn't know until *five minutes ago* that you had a crush on Jamal Chapman!"

"Shh!" Alice shrieked.

I stood up. We were all starting to go a little crazy. Maybe the high altitude was affecting our brain chemistry. I headed over to the buffet table and started spooning steaming lumps of roast beef and potatoes onto my plate. I looked to my right. There was Pradeep again. Helping himself to a generous portion of butterscotch pudding.

"Dessert for dinner," he commented.

"Mm-hm." I nodded and, wielding a pair of silver tongs, attempted to pick up some Brussels sprouts and deposit them on my plate. They fell onto the white tablecloth, making a horrible little thump.

"You gonna be at the dance tonight, Miller?" Pradeep asked. He pointed to a banner hanging above the entrance to the dining hall. WINTER WONDERLAND BALL, it read, FRIDAY NIGHT, 9:00 PM.

I nodded. "Um. Right. The dance. Uh ... well ... I'm not like a really big dancer or anything."

He shrugged. "Well, me neither. But it'd be nice to see you there." He awkwardly patted me on the shoulder and then walked away, joining a table of laughing juniors and seniors.

It'd be nice to see you there. I kept repeating that to myself while I stood, frozen in place, over the steaming tray of Brussels sprouts.

Was it the high altitude?

Or was Pradeep Paruchuri interested in me?

The three of us lay on our three red beds, swinging our socked feet off the edges of our beds and staring at the ceiling.

"Dances are stupid," Reena said finally. "They're so ... adolescent."

There was a long pause.

"But we *are* adolescents," Alice said.

"I just wish they could have come up with a more grown-up activity."

"Like what?" I asked.

Reena crossed her foot over her knee, tucked her hands behind her head, and thought for a while. "Fine," she said after a while. "I don't know. We'll go to the stupid dance."

Alice sat up and clapped her hands. "Yay! It'll be so much fun! We'll all dress up!"

My stomach sank. I didn't have anything to wear. Well, that wasn't true. I'd brought the awful orange maid-of-honor dress Candy had made me wear to the wedding.

And Volume XI of the Oxford English Dictionary.

But you can't wear the OED to a dance.

Alice peered over at me from her bed. "What are you gonna wear, Mol?"

"Uh ... just this, like, hideous orange puffy thing."

"You don't like it?

I shook my head. "Whatever. I'm fine." A complete and total lie.

Alice gave me a long look. "Hmm. Hold on a sec..." She

leapt off the bed and ran over to her suitcase. "Just try some-thing on for me, okay?"

An hour later, the three of us were standing in front of the mirror, our arms around one another's shoulders.

Reena was wearing a crimson red strapless minidress with matching high heels and lipstick. Her hair was swept up in a messy bun, and she'd sprinkled—to my shock and awe—tiny bits of red glitter over her entire head, so in certain lights her black hair literally sparkled.

In keeping with her all-black-clothing-all-the-time theme, Alice was wearing a black peasant dress with embroidered flowers around the collar and little embroidered vines around the cap sleeves. She wore pale pink lip gloss and a shimmering of gray powder over her eyes.

And then there was me.

Alice had lent me one of her mother's old dresses. It was maybe the nicest thing anyone had ever done for me. Alice had saved it from her mother's closet just before her dad and R. cleaned out the brownstone in Brooklyn Heights and threw everything away. "This was her favorite dress," Alice told me. "She always wore it when I was a kid. It reminds me of her."

The dress did fit me perfectly. It reached my calves, so I didn't look dowdy or like I was trying too hard. It was made out of a soft, simple cotton, but leading up to the high collar was a line of tiny brass buttons—"Very neo-Victorian," Reena had informed me. The sleeves were ever-so-slightly puffed, and they tapered out just before my elbows, making my arms look unusually slender.

I made eye contact with my reflection and then, not able to help myself, I smiled. Reena had insisted on applying "just a touch" of mauve shadow to my eyelids, and wielding a beige stick of foundation, Alice had pinned me to the bed and covered up a few of my worst pimples.

I looked good.

"We look good," Reena announced.

Alice blushed and grinned, then looked around the room. "Wait a second. Where's Kristen? I haven't seen her in like three hours."

Reena shrugged. "Who cares? The dance already started. Let's go now."

We descended the stairs. The dining room had been completely transformed in the two hours that had passed since dinner. Tinsel and glass icicles hung from the chandeliers, and mountains of cotton were piled up in the corners, simulating snowdrifts. The lights were dimmed to a low, pinkish hue that reminded me of the times when I'd wake up in the middle of the night in North Forest and know, just from looking at the color of the sky out of my bedroom window, that there'd been a snowstorm. A dozen or so people had started slow dancing, but most of the students were lined up against the walls, murmuring nervously to one another.

"Ew," Reena commented as we paused in the doorway. "*So* cheesy."

Clearly this was nothing compared with the dances at Beverly Hills High. On the other hand, it was the most beautiful dance I'd ever been to. The North Forest High dances were always held in the gymnasium under a broken disco ball and usually involved shaving cream attacks on underclassman.

Alice and Reena and I made our way over to an empty section of wall and tried to look like we weren't obsessively scoping everyone else out. Or at least Alice and I did. Reena, confident as always, let her eyes pass critically over the room, and then narrated her impressions to us while we leaned against the wall and stared at our hands.

"Oh my God. Look at Millie Fitch. *Look* at her."

Alice and I refused to look at her.

"Her dress is so short you can see her butt, I swear to God. Oh, no. Judah Lipston is wearing a purple tie. And I think it's a clip-on . . . wow. Rebecca Saperstein must have spent like three thousand dollars on her dress and she still looks incredibly strange. Sad. But . . . but . . . you guys . . . Jules Squarebrigs-Farroway is walking over to her. I think he's gonna ask her to dance. Yup. It's happening. Man. She's had a crush on that guy since their sophomore year, apparently. Well, good for her. Wow. They're actually dancing. *So* awkward. Anyway."

Abruptly Reena stopped her monologue.

"Keep going," Alice whispered.

Reena shook her head. "I can't."

We both looked at her. Tears were brimming around the edges of her perfectly made-up eyes.

"Reen?" I asked. "Are you . . . ?" I couldn't even say the word. I'd never seen Reena cry before. Or even come close to crying.

Reena wiped the tears from her eyes with her red fingernails. "I'm fine. I'm fine. I just realized . . . um . . ."

Alice rested her palm on Reena's shoulder. We waited for her to continue.

"I just realized," she said, gulping a little, "that I'm always, like, standing on the sidelines and criticizing everybody."

"That's okay," I said, "that's what great artists do."

"But I'm not an artist."

She had a point.

"It's just..." She tucked a tendril of hair behind her ear and sighed shakily. "I just... I've never had a boyfriend. Like, I've kissed people, but I've never had a boyfriend."

"Well, neither have we," Alice said. "We're all in the same boat here."

"I've never even kissed anyone," I said cheerfully.

Reena gawked at me. "Oh, my God. That's terrible."

"Reen," Alice chided her.

"Sorry," Reena said. "I just wonder if... like, if I'm really honest with myself... if sometimes I make fun of people who make me jealous. It's just... look." She gestured toward the dance floor. "My instinct is to make fun of all those people, but the truth is, they really look like they're having a good time."

We all looked. She was right. Couples were swaying together, smiling together, whispering to each other, putting their heads on each other's shoulders. Rebecca Saperstein looked like she was in seventh heaven. And it all just seemed so foreign and unattainable. Like all those people knew something I didn't—like they'd learned some secret language or code used to communicate desire, mutual attraction, and romance. I didn't understand how you could like someone, how they could like you back, and then how one of you could work up the guts to tell the other one. It just seemed like a confluence of statistical impossibilities.

Alice slung her arms around our shoulders and sighed. "Romance," she said, "is just something that happens to Other People. Never me."

Reena and I nodded.

"Totally," I said. "That's just what I was thinking. And another weird thing is that—"

"Alice?" someone inquired.

Alice's arms slowly slipped from our shoulders to her sides, and I felt her temperature fall again.

Jamal Chapman was standing in front of us, wearing a gray pin-striped suit. He wore a white flower in his lapel and he looked ... spectacular. He also seemed (and I couldn't understand this, since he was a senior and incredibly popular) nervous.

"Hi, Jamal," Alice said. At least she was able to form a sentence this time.

"Would you like to dance?" he inquired.

I couldn't believe it. It was like I was inside some kind of dream. Or like I was inside one of Alice's dreams.

"Um, sure," Alice said, blushing.

Jamal held his hand out and she took it. Then the two of them walked slowly out into the center of the dance floor. Alice put her hand on his shoulder, Jamal put his hand on her waist, and then it was just ... *happening*. Like that. They were dancing. Alice had left my reality and entered the reality of Other People. All within ten seconds. I shook my head, stunned.

"Did that just happen?" I asked Reena, not taking my eyes off Jamal and Alice.

There was no response.

"Reen?"

I turned to my right. She was gone.

Confused, I spun around in a circle, looking for her. But she was nowhere to be found.

I was completely alone.

My heart thumping in my chest, I started walking around the dance floor, trying to find Reena. I pushed past crowds of my classmates, dancing, talking, drinking punch. I asked people if they'd seen her and was rewarded with apathetic shrugs. I kept going. I waded through piles of cotton balls. I grazed my head on a low-hanging fake icicle. I was starting to feel insane. Both of my friends had just disappeared. One for a boy, and one for . . . no reason at all. My face felt hot, and I cast my eyes around the room desperately.

"Miller? Are you okay?" Pradeep Paruchuri was standing in front of me in a blue shirt and a silky black tie.

"Pradeep." I stopped, put my hands on my hips, and tried to catch my breath. "Um. Yeah. I'm okay. I'm just looking for Reena."

"My sister?" He squinted out onto the dance floor. "I haven't seen her anywhere. Are you sure she's even here? She hates dances."

"Yes, I'm sure." I was trying to sound calm, but my voice cracked a little. "We came here together."

"Weird. Yeah, sorry. I have no idea." He smiled at me. "But I'm glad we ran into each other again. I wanted to talk to you."

I stared into his big hazel eyes. "Um, yeah. Definitely."

"It's just really nice to find someone else here at this school who actually reads for fun. It's, like, most people I know read because they have to for, like, school, not because they actually enjoy it."

I couldn't believe it. Was Mount McKinsey Lodge a magical place? Were we all living in some kind of surreal dream? Was Pradeep Paruchuri really cornering me at the Winter Wonderland Ball and telling me he wanted to talk about books? I crossed my hands behind my back and pinched the soft part of my palm.

It hurt.

Was he going to ask me to dance?

"Anyway," Pradeep continued, "another thing I wanted to say about *David Copperfield* was—"

He stopped short.

"What?" I said, trying to smile encouragingly.

"Um . . . ," his voice was fading out, and his eyes were fixed on something above and behind my right shoulder. "I . . . um . . ."

I turned around.

Kristen Diamond was walking toward us. As mysteriously as Reena had left, Kristen had appeared, and she was wearing a short dress made entirely out of tiny white feathers. Her red hair was in sausage curls that fell down her impressive chest and stopped just above her miniscule waist. Her skin glowed, her lips were parted, and her violet eyes were fixed, determinedly, on some point in the distance.

It only took me a few seconds to realize that that point was Pradeep.

And then she was upon us.

"Hi, Molly," she said sweetly. "Hi, Pradeep."

Pradeep and I stared at her, mutually agog.

"Pradeep?" she asked. "Would you like to dance?"

I felt as if someone very far away, very tiny and sitting inside a cave inside a mountain inside an uninhabited country in a remote part of the world, was screaming, *Nooooooooooo!* But because the voice came from such a great distance, it registered as a tiny, terrible tremor, and then faded away.

I blinked.

"Sure," Pradeep said, grinning nervously. "I would love to."

It was like I had completely ceased to exist for Pradeep the minute Kristen entered the room. On the other hand, the acknowledgment he was about to give me felt so humiliating that I found myself wishing I *had* ceased to exist.

"Stay cool, Miller," Pradeep called over his shoulder as Kristen led him away.

And then she turned around herself and shot me a blinding and triumphant smile.

"Yeah," she echoed, her white teeth gleaming, "stay cool."

THREE

Alice

You spend a good part of your childhood lying in bed at night and thinking about the future. You're picturing what kind of job you'll have; what kind of person you'll be; what you'll look like. When you're in third grade you try to picture what sixth grade will be like. When you're in sixth grade you try to picture what ninth grade will be like. And one of the great, eternal questions you ask yourself during those long years of anticipation is:

When will I meet my first boyfriend?

What will he look like, how will he sound, what will he wear, and, most important, *what will it feel like to kiss him?*

I'd been asking myself those questions for as long as I could remember. And as I got older and older, and all the girls I knew met their first boyfriend, kissed him, broke up with him, met their second boyfriend, kissed him, broke up with him, and had already moved onto their third boyfriend before I'd even had a boyfriend at all, I started to worry that I would still be asking myself those questions when I was a fifty-five-year-old woman with chin hairs and pink curlers.

"You're crazy, Alice," my friends at the Brooklyn Montessori School would tell me. "It'll happen eventually, and then you'll stop worrying."

But it didn't happen ... and it didn't happen ... and it didn't happen ...

And then, on a Friday night in November, at the Winter Wonderland Ball on top of Mount McKinsey, it did.

Everything happened so fast. Jamal Chapman asked me to dance, and then we were dancing, and smiling at each other, and his hand was resting on the small of my back, and then he rested his head on my shoulder, and then I rested my head on his shoulder, and then after a few songs he pulled away from me—my heart froze in fear—Was this the end? Would I ever see him again?—and asked if I wanted to take a walk.

Holding hands, we walked off the dance floor (I caught a glimpse of half the girls in the room staring at me with utter hatred) and out into the cavernous lobby.

Jamal took a deep breath. "It's nice to get some air."

I nodded. My heart was beating so hard that I was sure he could hear it.

Our hands still clasped, we walked up the length of the lobby and right up to the big bay windows facing the snowy bank that lay right behind the lodge.

Then we stood there for a while in silence, staring out at the night.

"It's weird," Jamal said, "I really don't know you at all, Alice."

I nodded again, gulping.

"But I kind of feel like I do. I have no idea why. It's creepy."

"I feel the same way," I admitted. "What's weird is that it's, like, mutual."

There was another silence.

"I want to know everything about your life," he said finally. "But I don't know where to begin, I guess."

Everything? No one had ever said anything like that to me before. What sprang into my mind were visions of my childhood. Sitting with my mother in Prospect Park in the springtime, drinking soup from a thermos. My mother and father setting a birthday cake in front me, candles ablaze. Walking by myself to school for the first time, my feet crunching over piles of autumn leaves, my backpack thumping on my shoulders. My mother kneeling in the doorway, opening her arms as I clambered up the steps of our front stoop in the sunshine . . .

Jamal was looking at me quizzically.

"Sorry," I said. "I kind of spaced out. Um . . . I had a pretty good childhood, I guess. Until my mom died. Then my dad married a psychopath and she sent me off to Putnam Mount McKinsey and so . . . here I am."

It was unbelievable. Something about this guy just made the truth fly out of my mouth. I had no control over it.

Luckily he started laughing. "Wow," he said, leaning forward and pressing his forehead against the windowpane. "That was an incredible summary."

I blushed. "I mean, it's more complicated than that."

He laughed even harder. "I would assume so. But I love the way you just *say* everything."

"Usually I don't. Usually I don't say anything."

We looked at each other. Whenever our eyes met, I felt like I was being sucked through a black hole into some kind of alternate universe. It was definitely a scary sensation. But I liked the way that alternate universe of me-and-Jamal felt. Things made more sense in it. Suddenly all the bad things that had happened to me in the past three years didn't seem as bad. And I did feel a weird freedom around him—like I could say whatever I wanted. Like all the fear and anxiety I normally walked around with had the potential to just . . . ebb away.

"What about you?" I asked.

"What about me?"

"Tell me everything." I giggled.

"Oh, man. I don't know if I can sum it up as well as you did."

Feeling suddenly bold, I reached out and touched his arm. "Try."

He gazed out the window. "Well . . . I grew up with my mom."

"Yeah. I saw her. That first day of Parents Weekend."

He nodded. "I remember. Let's see. The two of us are really close. Um . . . she raised me all by herself. I'm an only child. I grew up in Washington Heights, which is in the northern part of Manhattan."

"I know that," I said. "I'm from Brooklyn."

His face lit up. "You're kidding!"

I shook my head.

"I assumed you were this really rich girl from the suburbs of Connecticut or, like, southern California. That's so cool!"

My stomach fell a little. I was kind of a rich girl. After all, I'd gone to private school my whole life.

"Where in Brooklyn?" he asked.

I cleared my throat nervously. "Um . . . Brooklyn Heights."

"Oh."

"Yeah."

He cocked his head and looked at me. "So you *are* a rich girl."

I nodded. "Yup."

And then we both started laughing.

"Wow," said Jamal a minute later, wiping the tears from his eyes, "this is funny. This is really funny. I've never had a conversation like this with anyone. No tact. No tact whatsoever."

And that made us laugh even harder.

"Wait," I said, holding my aching sides. "What about your dad? I remember you said that he was gone. What does that mean?"

The smile seemed to literally fall off his face. "It means he's gone."

I wasn't sure how to respond to that. "Oh."

He rubbed his temples with his hands. "Sorry. That didn't make sense. Uh . . . he ran away when I was baby. So basically I never had a dad."

"Did you ever meet him?"

He smiled tensely. "Wow. Huh. Okay. Well, I guess I got myself into this, didn't I? I was the one who said I wanted to know everything."

"You don't have to talk about it," I reassured him. "It's okay. I don't need to—"

"No," he said. "It's good. It's probably good for me. I never talk about this stuff with anyone except my mom."

There was a pause.

"I grew up hating my dad," he said. "I mean, *hating* him. I'd never met him. All I knew was that he'd gotten my mom pregnant, and that the second he found out, he took off. Then when I was thirteen we got this postcard from him the mail. He was living somewhere in Queens and he wanted to meet me. The guy had been living in New York City and it had taken him thirteen years to get in contact with me! At first I refused to see him. Then I thought about how much I wanted to tell him off, in person. I wanted to tell him what a jerk he was, and how he'd left my mom penniless, and how she'd had to work three jobs until I was six. All of that stuff. I wanted him to, like, realize what he'd done."

I nodded. "That makes sense." Not only that, it reminded me of how I felt about R.

"So one afternoon I took the train all the way to Queens. I got off the train and I walked over to his apartment. Then the whole time I was walking up his stairs I was thinking about all the mean things I was going to say to him. Words were running through my mind. *Scumbag. Loser. Jerk.* My heart was beating so fast. And when he finally opened his door..." Jamal paused.

"What happened next?" I demanded.

"Look," he said, pointing out the window. "It's snowing."

Fine, glittery snow was shimmering down from the black sky and dusting the ground.

"Please, please finish," I said. For some reason I felt like my life depended on hearing the end of his story. *I really like this guy*, I thought to myself. *Actually, I like him so much it's terrifying.*

"Sorry. Okay. So he opens the door, then there's just this person standing in front of me. And that completely shocked me."

I stared at him. "Wait. I don't get it."

"I mean, I don't know what I was expecting. Some kind of powerful... demon or something? I don't know. Maybe I just was so scared and angry that I forgot he was a real person."

"Who cares?" I said. "He totally screwed you over."

Jamal pressed a finger to the fogged-up windowpane and began drawing something. "I guess my point is that he was pathetic. And sad. And I realized that I wouldn't want to know him or be him, not in a million years. I mean, being mad at someone gives them power. And this was the least powerful man I'd ever met." He took a deep breath in, then let it out. "Wow. I can't believe I just told you all of that."

I stared out at the falling snow. Something about his story made me want to cry. I bit my lip.

"Is everything okay, Alice?" he asked gently.

I nodded and turned to face him. "Jamal?" I asked.

"Yeah?" He reached out and touched my shoulder. I don't think I'd ever realized how many pleasurable nerve endings were in my shoulder before that moment.

"You're amazing," I said.

He smiled, and then, his hand still on my shoulder, he leaned toward me.

Suddenly I froze. This was what I'd been wanting for years. This was the person I'd been waiting years and years to meet. And yet when his face started coming closer and closer to mine, his eyes shut, his lips parted, I was overwhelmed by fear and anxiety.

"Wait!" I yelled.

Jamal's eyes flew open, and he backed away. "Oh, my God. I'm so sorry. I thought—"

"No, no!" I said, my cheeks aflame. "I just . . ."

He looked at me. I could see insecurity flooding across his face. Oh, no. I'd ruined it. I'd ruined everything. *Get it together, Alice,* I told myself. *Don't let your fears push this guy away.*

"Jamal," I managed to say, trying desperately to articulate

what I was feeling, "I really, really want to kiss you. But I've only kissed one other guy in my life, and I didn't . . ."

Oh, God. What was I admitting to?

"I didn't even like him," I finished. "So I'm scared. I wanted to let you know that I'm scared. Because . . . I really, really like you."

He grinned. "Me, too. I'm totally terrified."

I gaped at him. "You are?"

"Yeah. I'm, like, totally worried you're gonna think I'm a bad kisser, or annoying, or dumb, or—"

"No!" I said. "I would never!"

His grin got even bigger. "You know what?"

"What?"

"I think *you're* amazing, Alice Bingley-Beckerman."

And then, suddenly filled with a totally unfamiliar feeling of security and joy, I grabbed Jamal Chapman's cheeks with both hands, brought his face toward mine, and kissed him.

And he kissed me back.

His lips were soft. And warm. And strangely familiar and unfamiliar at the same time.

We kept kissing.

I'm not sure how much time passed.

Maybe an hour. Maybe two.

Eventually someone—was it Pradeep Paruchuri?—shouted, "Chapman!" from the other end of the hallway.

"Oh, God," Jamal muttered, his mouth against my neck.

"We should go," I whispered, "I think it's way past curfew."

He nodded. "See you tomorrow morning," he said in my ear. "I can't wait."

"Me neither."

He planted a small kiss on each of my eyelids, and then darted away into the darkness.

I sighed, my lips aching, my heart bursting with happiness, and gazed out the window at the huge, perfectly round moon.

It was at that moment that I finally saw what Jamal had written on the fogged-up pane with the tip of his finger:

J loves A
(helplessly)

FOUR

Reena

I slammed the door to our bedroom shut and stood there, panting and praying that no one had seen me leave the ball.

It was time to execute my Master Plan.

I ran over to my suitcase and started pawing through my clothes. I had to focus. Still, I kept picturing Jamal Chapman asking Alice to dance, and it distracted me from the task at hand. I wanted the best for Alice—I genuinely did—and yet there was something about the timing of her good luck that startled me. I was forced to stand there and watch her, without warning, cross from the land of childhood into the land of adulthood, and I wasn't prepared. One second the three of us were standing there in the corner, comrades in loneliness, and the next second she was off dancing with one of the cutest guys in school. Just some kind of warning would have been nice. Because right when she took Jamal's hand and stepped away from my side I got this sinking feeling that made me feel like I was a little kid getting left behind by my mother.

I took a deep breath. *Focus,* I told myself. Tonight was going to be a lucky night for me, too. Tonight I would move out of the world of fantasy and into the world of mature, adult romance.

Tonight I was going to kiss David Newman for the first time.

I unearthed a long, white satin nightgown that Katie had given me for my fifteenth birthday. I scrutinized it. Risky. But gorgeous. And Katie had always said that it made my skinny body look more curvaceous than it actually was.

I slipped out of my red party dress and into the nightgown. I unwound my bun and let my hair tumble down my shoulders. Then I stared at myself in the mirror.

I was disappointed by what I saw.

I looked pretty—there was no doubt about that—but I looked *young.* Younger than I imagined. Whenever I pictured myself kissing David Newman, I pictured a sophisticated, older version of myself, maybe with a throaty voice and reading glasses perched on the end of my nose.

The person in the mirror looked . . . well, she looked fifteen.

I sighed and threw back my shoulders. There was nothing I could do about it. I had to Keep My Eyes on the Prize. I had to Stay Goal Oriented. After all, things were already working out pretty well—I hadn't wanted Alice and Molly to know about my Master Plan (they would have laughed at me or given me a long, serious lecture about teacher-student relationships), and Jamal asking Alice to dance had been the perfect opportunity for me to make a getaway upstairs. And then there was the conversation I'd overheard earlier that day between David and one of the other teachers—I'd distinctly overheard him say that he was going to spend the evening correcting papers in his room instead of chaperoning the dance.

That only made me love him more. He hated dances, too!

I squirted a little jasmine perfume on the back of my neck, and smeared the black eyeliner I'd been wearing so it looked like I'd been taking a nap. (I had to have some kind of excuse for wearing a nightgown.)

I brushed my teeth three times in a row, and then I sat on the edge of my bed and maniacally sucked a cherry Jolly Rancher. After all, I wanted my breath to smell clean, but not too clean.

And then I was ready.

I hadn't realized how nervous I was until I quietly exited our room and started padding in my bare feet down the hallway toward the teachers' wing. At one point I was so overcome with fear that I considered just turning around. But I kept going. *Paruchuris do not give up,* I kept telling myself.

I reached his door. 422. I only knew it was David's because I'd snuck a peek over Agnes's shoulder while she was reading the room assignments out loud. I stood there for a while, breathless, listening to hear if there were any sounds coming from inside. At one point I thought I heard the creak of a chair. I leaned in a little closer and tried pressing my ear to the door. I thought that I could hear someone turning the page of a book.

And then the door flew open.

I gasped.

David Newman was standing in front of me, wearing a rumpled flannel shirt and sweatpants. He was holding *Zen Ventura* in one hand and the door handle in the other.

"Reena?" he asked disbelievingly, as if he couldn't quite believe I was standing there.

"I was going to knock!" I yelped.

He furrowed his brow. "What are you doing here?"

"Um . . ." I cleared my throat and smoothed out my night-gown with my hands. For some reason I wasn't been expecting that question. I thought that when David Newman saw me, and saw the smoldering Look in my eyes (although now I was so mortified I was staring at my bare feet), he would just fold me into his arms and . . .

"Why aren't you at the dance?" he asked. He actually sounded a little annoyed.

"I . . . um . . ." I finally looked up at him and made eye contact. I put my hands on my hips and attempted to appear confident. "I thought you might want to see me."

"Do you have a question about the final?"

I blinked. "What?"

"Do you have a question about the Humanities final?"

"Um . . . no."

There was a long pause.

"I just thought the two of us could hang out and get to know each other," I whispered. Although wasn't it obvious? I was standing in front of him in a white satin nightgown. Why wasn't he inviting me in, sitting me in front of the fire, and pouring me a glass of burgundy?

Now David was staring at me, his eyes filled with something that I can only describe as . . . pity.

It made me feel about two years old.

"Reena," he said softly, "what are you doing? And why are you wearing that nightgown?"

Why? *Why?* Because it was *sexy.*

"Um," I said. I couldn't stop saying "um." But maybe he still didn't understand? Maybe I needed to make things absolutely one-hundred-percent clear.

"I really like you," I added. "And you said that you're not, like, a get-off-the-couch type of person, and I thought maybe you wanted me to—"

He interrupted me. "*What? When did I say that?*"

"When we were talking about *Zen Ventura?* After class . . . ?" My voice was starting to falter.

David closed his eyes and began kneading the space between his eyes with his thumb and forefinger. "Oh, Reena."

The "Oh, Reena" did me in. It was like a death sentence. It was like the cherry on top of the worst year of my life. Even though I hadn't cried all semester at Putnam Mount McKinsey, my eyes started filling with tears for the second time that night.

"Reena," David said slowly, "I have no interest in you. You're fifteen. You're a great kid. But I . . . I have a girlfriend, and even if I didn't . . . you are way, way too young for—"

"My stepmother is twenty-eight years younger than my dad!" I yelled. Then I froze, shocked. I hadn't even been thinking about my dad and Shanti Shruti. But suddenly the words just flew out of my mouth.

David reached out and put a hand on my shoulder. The warmth from his palm coursed through my body. "I'm so sorry, Reena," he said. "I didn't know."

"And they're married," I finished feebly.

"I'm so sorry," he said again.

Then I couldn't stand it anymore. His pity, the comfort of his hand on my shoulder, his sad eyes, his rumpled shirt . . . all I wanted to do was crawl into his lap and scream and cry for hours. *I don't even want to kiss David Newman,* I slowly realized. *I just want him to hold me and tell me everything is okay.*

And since he couldn't, and since I'd just humiliated myself more totally and completely than I'd ever humiliated myself before, I covered my face with my hands and ran down the creaky wooden hallway, back to my empty room.

"Reena?"

Molly's voice sounded like it was coming from a great distance.

Probably because I was lying in a fetal position under one sleeping bag, three blankets, and an oversized pillow.

"All the lights are out," I heard her say. "Are you there? This is creeping me out...."

I made a small, moaning noise, just to let her know it was me, but it must have frightened her, because she screamed and flipped on the lights.

I lay still underneath my snowdrift of blankets. I heard Molly's feet tiptoe in my direction, and then a hand reached forward and ripped back the pile of bedding in one swift motion. I shivered and squinted in the cold, bright light.

"It is you!" Molly yelled. "You abandoned me, you jerk!"

I grabbed a piece of my tangled, sweaty hair and covered my face with it.

"Reena!"

"Please leave me alone," I croaked.

"No, I will not leave you alone! You totally betrayed me out there on the dance floor! You left me high and dry!"

I began to snuffle and sob again, still shivering. Then I lifted up the hem of my nightgown and blew my nose into it.

"Oh my God!" Molly shrieked. "Ew! You are disgusting!"

I didn't respond.

After an exasperated silence, I heard her unzip my suitcase and paw through my clothes.

"Here," I heard her say, "lift up your legs."

I lifted up my legs. She slid a pair of flannel pajama bottoms onto my body.

"And put this on." She tossed me a soft, worn-out Polartec vest. "It's mine. You can wear it. It's really warm."

I finally sat up and put on the vest. I tucked my hair behind my ears and stared at Molly through my gooey, tear-filled eyes.

"You look pretty," I whispered.

With a resounding thump, Molly collapsed next to me on my bed and smushed her face into the pile of blankets. "I want to die," she murmured.

I shook my head. "No. I want to die."

"No. Me."

"No, Mol. There is no way you possibly, possibly humiliated yourself as badly as I just did."

She shook her head, her face still muffled. "You're wrong."

I reached over and grabbed her shoulder, flipping her onto her back.

"Did you just appear at the door of your teacher's room in a skimpy nightgown because you thought he wanted you to make the first move?" I demanded.

Her eyes widened behind her thick glasses.

"That's right," I told her, "top that."

"Oh, Reena," Molly said, and covered her mouth with her hand.

"No. No. I don't ever want anyone to say 'Oh, Reena' ever again. Worst phrase in the English language."

Molly propped herself up on one elbow and gazed thoughtfully up at the ceiling. "Well, the name Reena isn't technically a *word* in the English language, so it can't really be a phrase or else you'd—"

I pushed her and she toppled back down again.

We lay on our backs and stared at the ceiling for a while.

"Reen?" asked Molly after a long pause.

"Yeah?"

"Can I tell you something?"

"Sure. Anything."

Another long pause.

"I'm in love with your brother," she said.

It took me a few seconds to absorb the information she'd just communicated to me. At first I was shocked. Then, strangely, I felt a little grossed out and offended. As if Molly had just told me that she'd been using my toothbrush for the past two months, or wearing my underwear. But a few seconds later I thought: *Of course she's in love with Pradeep.* And a few seconds after that, I thought (and I felt like my heart might break right after I thought it): *There's no way he's in love with her.*

"Do you hate me?" Molly whispered.

I turned on my side and looked at her. Her blue eyes were swimming around anxiously behind her glasses. I reached over and pushed a tendril of hair back from her forehead.

"Of course I don't hate you," I said. "But I have to warn you, Mol, Pradeep is very weird when it comes to—"

She shook her head. "You don't have to say anything. He's dancing with Kristen Diamond right now. I'm an idiot."

I stared at her. "Kristen?"

"Yep. She's wearing some kind of swan dress. I don't want to think about it."

I shook my head. The tragedy of it all—of existence—was really starting to get to me. I hadn't understood it when I was younger. Life was easy then. My parents were married, we all lived together in one big house, I'd known my friends for

226

years, school wasn't that hard yet . . . but now I was starting to get it. Life was about bad luck. Bad luck and mistakes. Other people mucked up things around you, and then you went and mucked up things once they were done.

Molly was clearly thinking similar thoughts, because after we lay there and stared at the ceiling for a while she announced: "Everyone is in love with the wrong person."

I nodded. "I guess so."

A second later we said in unison: "Except Alice."

"Except Alice," Molly repeated. "Gosh darn Alice. She must be doing something right."

We lay there for a while, brooding. Then—as if jolted by an electric shock—I leapt to my feet.

"Molly!" I shrieked. "What are we doing? We're being passive! We're not taking fate into our own hands!"

Still lying on her back, Molly cocked an eyebrow. "I don't know. You put on a satin nightgown and marched right up to fate's door. And look where it got you."

Slightly wounded by that remark, I plowed on anyway. "No. I'm not talking about romance. I'm talking about the Poison Apples. I mean, think about it. When did your life start going to pieces?"

Molly thought. "I guess . . . I guess when—"

"When Candy Lamb came into your life, right?"

"Yeah. I guess."

"And my life started going to pieces the day I met Shanti Shruti at that stupid yoga class."

"So what are you saying?"

"I'm saying our stepmothers are the root of the problem! That's why I formed the Poison Apples in the first place, right?"

Molly sat up on my bed and cupped her chin in her palm.

"Yeah. I have to say, though, Reen, I'm really glad David Newman didn't want to kiss you. No offense, but I think that would have been pretty creepy."

This remark also hurt my feelings, although now, in the harsh cold light of After the Fact, she kind of—*sort of*—had a point.

"Anyway," I continued, waving my hands in the air to dismiss that particular topic, "screw boys! We need to reclaim our lives!"

I was happy to see that Molly was nodding. Then she actually got to her feet and started pacing up and down the room.

"Okay," she muttered. "You're right. This is a war. But how do we win the war?"

"What do you mean, how do we win the war? We haven't even gone into battle yet!" My cheeks were flushed with excitement. I was starting to feel a little bit better.

"Okay, so . . . what? What do we do now?"

"We go to battle! We get revenge!"

"How?" She stopped pacing. "Seriously. How?"

I put my hands on my hips. "Um . . ."

Molly stroked her chin. "Well, okay. Let's think about it. Like what revolutionaries have done in the past. The Boston Tea Party, for instance. That was really effective."

I sat down on the bed, embarrassed. "Um. I kind of forget what the Boston Tea Party is."

"The Americans threw all the tea into the ocean. The tea that belonged to the British people."

I wasn't quite getting it. "Okay . . ."

"They took the thing that was most important to the British, and then they just . . . trashed it."

It was starting to make sense to me. Weird sense. But sense.

"So," Molly continued, "one way to wage war, or initiate war, or whatever, is to, like, take the thing that's most important to the person . . . and, like, throw it away."

We looked at each other.

"Molly Miller," I said. "I think you've got it."

"Get out some paper and pen," she instructed me, pushing up her glasses with her forefinger like she always did when she got excited, "and take notes."

Revenge—A Comprehensive Plan
(calligraphy by Mlle. Paruchuri)

The Enemies:
R. Klausenhook, actress/evil stepmother

Shanti Shruti, yoga instructor/evil stepmother

Candy Lamb, pregnant housewife/waitress/evil stepmother

The Heroines:
Alice Bingley-Beckerman, student/wronged stepdaughter

Reena Paruchuri, student/wronged stepdaughter

Molly Miller, student/wronged stepdaughter/lexicography expert

The Goal:
1. Destroy what is dearest to the enemy.
2. Get away with it.

The Time Frame:
Thanksgiving vacation.

Plan 1:
R. Klausenhook
What R. Klausenhook holds dearest: her acting career.

Instructions for A. Bingley-Beckerman: Destroy Acting
   Career.

Plan 2:
Shanti Shruti
What Shanti Shruti holds dearest: her penguin.

Instructions for R. Paruchuri: Destroy Penguin.

Plan 3:
Candy Lamb
What Candy Lamb holds dearest: her harmonious relationship
   with Spencer.

Instructions for M. Miller: Destroy the Relationship.

FIVE

Molly

"Destroy Spencer?" Alice gasped.

"No, no, not Spencer," Reena said. "The Poison Apples is a nonviolent organization. Destroy Candy Lamb's *relationship* with Spencer."

Alice drew a blanket around her shoulders and shivered. It was Sunday night and we'd just arrived back at Putnam Mount McKinsey, but Reena had insisted—on tiny slips of paper that had mysteriously made their way into our suitcases that morning—*Mandatory Poison Apples Meeting Tonight*—that we all meet on the roof of Middleton right after curfew. Reena had just unfurled the Revenge Plan and read it out loud to us.

"I don't get it," Alice said, shaking her head. "When did you guys come up with this plan? When did you make this list?"

Reena stood up, exasperated. She was wearing a bathrobe and slippers, and her hair was standing up in messy chunks. She actually looked kind of insane, with the stars and the night sky behind her and the full moon illuminating her profile. And she'd been acting a little insane, too. Almost as if to compensate for the great disappointment that turned out to be David Newman, she'd become maniacally focused on the Poison Apples and our Thanksgiving revenge plan.

"We made this list," barked Reena, "while you were making out on a bobsled with Jamal Chapman!"

Alice ducked her face behind her hair and waved her hands in the air. "Okay, okay."

"Show a little appreciation!"

"I appreciate it, I appreciate it. I'm just . . . I'm not quite sure how we're going to, um, *execute* the plan."

"That's up to each of us, individually. Thanksgiving is this coming Thursday. I'm going back to LA, you're going back to New York, and Mol is going back to . . . um . . . North Flywood."

"North Forest," I said.

"Right, right."

I shook my head. "Wow, Reena. You really do have zero interest in any place that isn't a major city."

Reena smiled. "That's correct."

"So let me get this straight," Alice said. "Before Thursday, I have to find a way to sabotage R.'s career, Molly has to find a way to, um, find a nonviolent way of ruining Candy's relationship with Spencer, and you have to . . . steal a penguin?"

Reena nodded. "Yup."

"And what will happen once we've completed these near-impossible tasks?"

"We'll have power," Reena said grandly. "Negotiating power."

"We'll be the ones holding the poison apple," I said, feeling poetic.

Reena looked at me, her eyes glinting. "Exactly," she said. "And they'll be the ones eating the poison."

This time no one was waiting for me when I got off the bus in North Forest. Not even Spencer. I shouldn't have been surprised—no one knew I was coming—and yet I still felt sad and lonely standing alone in the middle of the snow-covered parking lot next to the Savings Bank.

I don't belong here anymore, I thought.

But then I thought: *Did I ever really belong here?*

I trudged along Main Street, past the post office, past the American Legion, past the gas station, and, finally, past my mother's boarded-up hair salon. A light snow began to fall, and I stared at the streetlamps through the wet flakes that had landed on my lashes. The round yellow lights pulsed and beamed in all directions like stars.

I felt like a ghost. The town center was totally empty—it was the day before Thanksgiving—and the muffled silence of the falling snow made it feel like North Forest had been abandoned years and years ago. The sun had just set, and the sky was a deep indigo.

I was started to get cold. Really, really cold.

And I still hadn't figured out how to execute Revenge Plan 3.

Reena had made it explicitly clear: Spencer was my bargaining tool. But what did that mean? And what exactly was I trying to bargain for?

Maybe (and it was painful for me to realize it) I wanted

233

to be able to see my father again. To have dinner with him occasionally and still feel like I had a home. And I wanted to be able to do that without Candy threatening to pull me out of Putnam Mount McKinsey and make me her live-in maid.

I wanted North Forest to be a place I could go back to, and not the place where I lived.

Was that selfish of me?

I shook my head to clear my thoughts. ("No time for doubts!" Reena had instructed me. "No time for feeling guilty!") I continued walking down Main Street and then turned right, up the unplowed road that led to Candy's house. My old house—empty for over six months now—was on the other side of Main Street, and down a hill. I tried not to picture my bedroom, dark and cold and dusty. I tried not to picture the mice that were probably skittering over the floors, up and down the stairs—I always used to hear them moving inside the walls as I was lying in bed at night. Now they were probably having the time of their lives.

I continued up the side of the road, wading through the deep snow, shielding my face with my hand whenever a car swung its bright headlights around a bend. My boots were leaking, and my toes were starting to go numb.

Eventually I was standing in front of Candy's house. Or now, I reminded myself—my father and Spencer had been living there for more than six months, after all—it was my family's house.

Their car was in the driveway, and almost all the lights were on.

I stepped into the front yard. The top layer of the snow

had iced over, and my boots made a horrible crunching noise. I winced. I couldn't afford for anybody to see or hear me. I stepped behind a tree, then leaned out and peered through the dining room window.

They were all there.

Framed in the picture window, lit up by the yellow glow of a lamp. And—like a movie—they were all laughing. Even my dad, who almost never laughed. At one point Candy reached over and touched Spencer's hair. They were sitting around the table and passing around food and pouring drinks and they looked so . . . happy.

And instead of feeling angry, or left out, or abandoned— all the feelings I'd been having since the summer, all the feelings I'd ordinarily expect to have—I experienced a different sensation. At first I couldn't tell what it was, exactly. It was a slight stirring in my stomach, an impalpable feeling of longing. I didn't want to be inside with my father and Candy and Spencer and Sandie and Randie—I wasn't longing for *that*. After all, I wasn't part of that family.

And then I realized what the feeling was.

I missed my mother.

So then why was I standing by the side of the road, covered with slush, staring at them like some kind of crazy stalker, when my mother was sitting alone at Silverwood less than five miles away? So what if she was bonkers? She was my mother. And she needed me. Just like I needed her.

My heart surged with joy, and I stepped backward in the snow, away from the house. My boots made another loud cracking sound as they broke through the ice, and this time I saw Candy stop talking and turn toward the window.

She'd heard me.

Praying I wouldn't slip and fall, I turned and ran, sloshing through gray puddles of freezing slush.

I ran and ran and ran.

I stopped briefly just before I reached the highway, to catch my breath and take out my cell phone with cold, trembling hands. I quickly sent Reena a text message: *PLAN 3 ABORTED.*

Then I started running again.

When I reached the big wrought-iron gates of Silverwood, I bent over, put my head between my legs, and almost started hyperventilating. I couldn't feel my feet or my hands or my ears or my face, just the icy-cold air I kept gulping into my lungs. A minute later, my heart still pounding in my chest, I pulled open the heavy gates and started walking up the long driveway to the Silverwood's reception center.

"Oh my God," the woman at the desk said when she saw me.

I could barely see anything, because my glasses had steamed up the second I stepped inside the overheated building. I took them off to wipe them on my jacket, but then I realized that my jacket was soaking wet. Along with my shirt. And my pants. And my boots. And my hair.

"Hi," I said. My entire body was shaking.

The woman rose out of her chair and came out from behind the desk. She had a puffy gray halo of hair, and a pin shaped like a turkey affixed to her turtleneck sweater. "Are you okay?" she asked me.

I nodded, my teeth chattering. "Yeah," I said. "I'm okay."

"Do you need a change of clothes?"

"No. I'm . . . I'm okay. I'm actually here to see my mother."

She frowned. "Your mother? She's a patient here?"

I rubbed my hands together to try to get some feeling back in my fingers. "Yes. Patsy Miller. Is she still in Room 152? I'd like to visit her."

The woman suddenly took a step back, and her hand flew up, almost protectively, to touch her turkey pin. "Patsy Miller?"

"Yeah. I'm her daughter."

She closed her eyes, revealing a shaky blue line drawn across each of her eyelids. "Oh, dear."

There was a sharp, throbbing pain in my feet. "What . . . is something wrong?"

"Oh, dear," she repeated. "Oh, dear."

"Please just tell me what's going on," I said, trying to sound calm.

She took my elbow and led me over to one of the orange plastic chairs near the desk. "Have a seat first."

I sat. She stood in front of me, wringing her hands and moving her lips around, as if she were trying to find the right words.

"Patsy . . . ," she began, "your mother . . ."

"Yes?"

"She . . . no one told you?"

A cold drop of water ran down my cheek. The pile of snow that had collected on top of my head was starting to melt. "No one told me *what*?"

The woman folded her arms over her chest. "Your mother disappeared two weeks ago."

I stared at her.

"I'm sorry that I'm the one to tell you this. We told her husband—I'm sorry, ex-husband—and we assumed he'd let the rest of the family know."

I rose up out of my chair so fast that the woman backed away from me, her fingers still fluttering nervously.

"I don't understand," I told her. "I'm sorry. What does 'disappear' mean?"

The woman took another step backward. "It means that when the nurses showed up with her breakfast in the morning she was gone."

"I don't understand how that could happen."

"She was doing quite well, and we put her in a less closely watched wing of the building. We think she just . . . climbed out the window in the middle of the night."

There was a long pause.

"I'm so sorry," she whispered.

Melted snow dripped down my forehead onto my nose, and from my nose onto my chin. I didn't say anything.

"Let me get you some dry clothes," she said gently.

I shook my head, still speechless. She reached out to help me take off my jacket, and I jerked away from her.

"Are the police"—I couldn't even believe the words that were coming out of my mouth—"are the police looking for her?"

"Yes," she said. "Of course. But they haven't had much luck."

I nodded numbly, then turned around and started walking out the door.

"Wait!" she called out. "You can't go back out in this weather!"

I wrenched open the big glass doors, stepped out into the dark night, and started to make my way back down the long, slippery driveway.

It was snowing harder now, half sleeting, and the sky was

a mottled, churning shade of black and gray. The wind whipped against my face and I could feel my wet hair freezing into long icy strips.

I didn't care.

My mother was gone.

And it was all my fault.

This time there was no point running. After all, I didn't have anywhere to go. I took my cell phone out of my pocket and looked at it. Reena hadn't responded to my text message. Of course. She was probably furious with me. Now she and Alice were going to refuse to be my friend, due to my failure as a member of the Poison Apples.

I was alone in the universe.

I'd never known despair like this. It obliterated everything. It made the bleakness of the world around me—the storm, the night, the wind, the cars whizzing past me on the highway—seem insignificant. The hopelessness rising inside my stomach and taking hold of my heart was much, much scarier than any blizzard.

Walking along the edge of the road, I turned my face up to the sky and let the hail and snow pelt my cheeks and eyelids.

"I GIVE UP!" I screamed. "DO YOU HEAR ME? I GIVE UP TRYING TO CHANGE MY FATE! LUCK IS LUCK AND I'M JUST UNLUCKY!"

A car screeched to a stop next to me.

Now I was going to be murdered by an axe-wielding serial killer.

I wasn't even sure if I cared.

Someone rolled down the passenger-side window.

"Molly?" a voice asked.

I tried to squint into the car, but I could barely see through my soaked glasses and all the snow flying in front me.

"Oh, my God! It is you! Molly Miller, get in the car right now!"

The car door opened.

It was Candy.

Maybe the last person on the planet I wanted to see.

"No," I said. "I will not get in the car."

"I can't hear you! Get in the car!"

"No," I whispered.

I heard an exasperated sigh, and then a plump arm reached out of the car door and yanked me inside. A second later I was sitting silently in a puddle in the passenger seat, shivering and refusing to look up.

"What in God's name are you doing out here?" Candy shrieked.

I peered into the backseat. Spencer was sitting in the darkness, staring at me, her eyes wide with fear.

"I was trying to visit Mom," I muttered into my lap.

"Were you standing in our front yard an hour ago?" Candy demanded.

I nodded, sinking my head deeper into the neck of my soaking wet jacket.

"I thought so! We've been driving all over town looking for you! Why didn't you knock on the door?"

I shrugged. The misery inside my chest was deepening and thickening.

"Molly! Say something!"

I finally turned and looked at Candy. What I saw actually

surprised me. Her face looked pale and drawn. She looked . . . worried. And sad.

"Why didn't you tell me about Mom?" I asked her. My voice cracked.

She shook her head. "I . . . I can't believe this." The edges of her mouth started trembling. "I *told* your father that we owed you a phone call."

"Then why didn't you?" I asked, my voice getting louder and angrier. "Why didn't you?"

"He didn't think you wanted to talk to us. And he didn't want to hurt your schoolwork or disrupt your—"

"She's my mother!" I screamed. I couldn't tell whether it was melted snow or tears running down my cheeks. "For God's sake! She's my mother!"

"Oh, Molly." Candy held out her arms. "Come here."

I recoiled and threw myself against the car door, pressing my face into the window. "No!"

And then with the same surprising strength with which she'd yanked me into the car, Candy reached over, grabbed my shoulders, and pulled my body against hers. My freezing-cold face was smushed against her warm chest. Her round arms laced tightly around my back.

"Let go of me!" I said muffledly into her sweater, but I wasn't even sure if she could hear me.

"Molly Miller," she told me, "you are coming home with us."

I shook my head, still contained in her warm vise grip.

"Yes," she said. "You are."

I succeeded in wrenching my face far enough away from her bosom to make myself heard. "I don't want to have to leave Putnam Mount McKinsey," I bawled. "I like it there. You and dad are going to make me—"

"We won't make you do anything."

I stared at her. She stared back at me, her eyes still filled with that new, unfamiliar sadness.

"We won't make you do anything, okay?" she said again.

It was the strangest thing. I hadn't executed my revenge plan. I hadn't destroyed her relationship with Spencer. I hadn't done anything.

But the words I'd been wanting to hear all semester were coming out of Candy Lamb's mouth.

So even though I was still miserable, and full of despair, and terribly, terribly lonely, I pressed my face into the warmth of Candy's chest and cried. And she let me cry for what felt like a long time. Until Spencer piped up from the backseat: "Hey! When are we going home?"

I turned around in my seat. "Hey," I said, wiping my eyes, "Spencer."

"What?" she said, staring at me suspiciously.

"I'm sorry if I haven't been around that much this fall. I love you, you know. You're my sister."

She turned and gazed thoughtfully out the window. I was kind of expecting her to respond with *I love you, too, Mol*. Instead, after a long silence, she said: "Well, the twirling finals are next weekend. You can come see me then if you really want."

I smiled weakly. "Okay," I said, "that sounds great. Can I bring my friends Reena and Alice?"

She nodded.

"Awesome," I said. "I'll be there."

A small, almost imperceptible smile crossed my sister's face.

I sat back and fastened my seat belt. Candy cleared her throat, started the ignition, did a three-point turn in the middle of the empty highway, and started driving back to the center of North Forest.

Halfway home a small beeping noise came from the pocket of my jacket.

Reena had sent me a text message.

SIX

Alice

Port Authority Bus Terminal.

The embodiment of everything wonderful and horrible about New York City.

I stepped off the bus into the dimly lit building, and I breathed in a smell that I'd almost forgotten existed during my three months at Putnam Mount McKinsey.

That signature smell—the smell of midtown Manhattan and its seething bus and train stations—can be only described as a combination of car exhaust, urine, garbage, and roasting peanuts.

Strange to say, it is not entirely unpleasant.

I was so busy inhaling and exhaling, filling my nose with the scent of the city I'd missed so much, that I almost forgot about Jamal, standing next to me with his duffel bag, shifting nervously from foot to foot.

We'd taken the bus all the way from Massachusetts to Manhattan together, sharing a seat, holding hands, and listening to the same iPod (he got the right earpiece, I got the left).

Now it was time to say good-bye.

He had to take the A train to 175th Street in Washington Heights. I had to take the Number 2 train to R.'s apartment on the Upper West Side.

I threw my arms around his shoulder and buried my face in the nook behind his ear. That nook was my favorite thing about Jamal Chapman. Well, I had a lot of favorite things about Jamal Chapman. But the nook ranked pretty high. It was soft and tender and always smelled incredible.

He pulled away and looked me in the eyes. "Are you gonna be okay?"

I frowned. "What is that supposed to mean?"

"I don't know. Seeing your Dad and R. again. I don't want them . . ." He looked away, embarrassed. "I don't know what I'm talking about."

"Oh, Jamal." I reached out and touched his cheek. "It's okay. I'm okay. I mean . . . ," I trailed off. I'd just gone blank in the head. "Have a good vacation. That's what I mean."

He nodded, still looking worried, and then hoisted his duffel bag over his shoulders and trudged away under the flickering Port Authority lights.

"The Yankees suck!" I called after him.

"The Mets blow!" he yelled, not turning around.

And then he rounded a corner and was gone.

I sighed.

I had made a point of not telling Jamal about the Poison Apples' Revenge Plot, even though he'd asked me during the bus ride what my specific plans were for each day of vacation. And I'd told him about most of my plans: Thanksgiving dinner with my dad and R. on Thursday, the opening of R.'s new play (a highly anticipated revival of Chekhov's *The Cherry Orchard*) on Friday, and then a dentist appointment on Saturday morning.

Not only had I failed to mention the Revenge Plot, but I'd also failed—in the two weeks we'd been dating—to bring up the existence of Poison Apples at all.

Jamal knew that Reena and Molly were my best friends, and that we all had crazy stepmothers. He just didn't know anything about our clandestine meetings on the roof of Middleton. Or our plot to avenge and overthrow our respective stepmothers and reclaim our fates.

I'd like to say that I didn't mention the Poison Apples to Jamal because, as Reena had informed us that first night, the existence of the Poison Apples was Top Secret, Never To Be Mentioned to a Soul.

But the truth was, I secretly believed there was a chance Jamal would disapprove.

I lifted up my bag and started hauling it up the stairs towards the Number 2 train. *Jamal Chapman may be one of the best things that has ever happened to me*, I told myself, *but it won't do me any harm to forget about him for the next four days.*

After all, revenge plot aside, I had the world's craziest stepmother to deal with.

"THE TURKEY IS BURNING!"

R.'s voice pierced the air like a clarion call. I leapt up from the couch where I'd planned on just taking a minute to sit and flip through old issues of *The New Yorker*. Instead I'd dozed off.

I rushed into the kitchen and found R. standing in front of the stove, a potholder covering each hand, waving her arms in the air and fanning smoke.

"It's ruined!" she wailed. Then she turned to me, dagger-eyed. "How could you mess up the *one* thing you were in charge of?"

I sighed, yanked open the door to the oven, and, pulling my shirtsleeves down over my hands, took out the tray, and slammed it down on the counter. Huge billows of smoke rose up into my face. I started coughing.

"I can't breathe!" R. shrieked, and ran out of the room.

Alone in the kitchen, I surveyed the disaster that was going to be Thanksgiving dinner.

R. had announced to both me and my father the day before that she was going to cook the entire meal herself. From scratch.

"Really?" Dad had asked mildly as we all sat over breakfast. "I had assumed we were just going to order takeout."

R. had shook her head, her earrings a-jangle, her eyes shining. "I'm going to do it all."

"But opening night is the day after tomorrow," Dad reminded her. "Maybe we should all just hunker down and take it easy."

"Don't rain on my parade, Nelson!" she snapped at him, and then her eyes immediately slid in my direction, challenging me to speak up.

Now I'd ruined the whole thing. R. had instructed me to take the turkey out of the oven precisely at 5:00 PM, and now it was 5:30, and sitting in front of me on the counter was a . . . charred black mess. It didn't even look like a bird anymore.

R. stormed back into the kitchen, a silk handkerchief wrapped around her mouth like a bandit.

"Mmr dmmr in yer," she informed me through the cloth.

"I can't hear you," I said.

She lifted the handkerchief up for a second. "I am very disappointed in you," she announced, and then folded it back down.

I didn't answer. Instead I just gazed out the kitchen window. Our old kitchen window—the window in our Brooklyn house—looked out on a backyard, and the swaying leaves of a dogwood tree and a London plane would brush against the glass whenever there was a breeze. R.'s kitchen window faced the wall of another looming, gray, twenty-story apartment building and part of an air shaft.

I couldn't wrap my mind around why they wanted to live here.

By 7:00 PM, the three of us were sitting in a booth at Rick's Luncheonette, a dingy, fluorescent-lit diner around the corner from Dad and R.'s apartment.

I chewed morosely on a French fry while we all sat in silence.

R. had refused to order anything. Dad was eating some kind of horrible cole slaw.

"You know," Dad said after a while, "this isn't so bad. We could always be starving, you know. Or homeless."

I glanced at R. hopefully. But I think Dad's comment only made her angrier.

"What I was trying to do," she informed Dad coldly, "was cook a nice Thanksgiving meal for your daughter." Then she turned to me. "And you don't seem very thankful, young lady. You know, if you weren't here, your father and I would have made reservations at that great French restaurant across the

park weeks ago. But now it's too late. Now we're stuck with"—
she gestured around the diner in disgust—"*Rick's.*"

Don't freak out, I told myself.

"I would have been fine with a French restaurant," I said
quietly.

She slammed her glass of water down on the table. "Great,"
R. said. "That's really sweet, Alice. You know, it would be nice
if once in a while you tried to be a tiny bit less spoiled. But apparently that's impossible for you."

I gaped at her. A million retorts sprang to my lips. But I
stopped myself: *Wait. Don't ruin Revenge Plot Number One. By
tomorrow night, R. will have her comeuppance. Stay cool.*

A few hours later, I was lying on the air mattress Dad had
set up for me on the floor of R.'s study and staring at the ceiling, my head swimming with anger.

Any guilt or hesitation I'd had the day before about exe-
cuting Revenge Plot Number One was completely gone.

Screw Thanksgiving.

Screw my dad.

Screw Jamal and his Goody Two-Shoes view of the universe.

R. Klausenhook was going down.

I was going to take what was dearest to her and ruin it, ir-
revocably and forever.

I was supposed to meet Dad in front of the theater at 7:30,
and the curtains opened on *The Cherry Orchard* at 8:00. The
New York theater community had been anticipating this
night for months.

I couldn't have cared less.

And yet it was only 4:00 PM and I was skulking around outside the stage door, shivering in my thin winter coat.

Why?

Because I was going to infiltrate the production.

And then destroy R's career.

I'd been thinking for days about the best way to get inside the theater, and that morning it had struck me: of course. How obvious. How did everyone else in the production get in and out of the theater?

The stage door.

The cast and crew had keys, of course. But all I had to do was wait around, look unassuming, and then when someone entered or exited, just follow behind as if that was the most normal thing in the universe to do.

So I waited. And waited. I knew the actors—R. included—wouldn't be arriving until 6:00, so I had plenty of time. Still, it was cold outside. And the street I was standing on was pretty loud, with cars honking and garbage trucks coughing up coffee grinds and turkey carcasses.

Finally, at 4:30, a woman with a baseball cap and glasses hurried up to the stage door and unlocked it. This was my chance. I jumped forward just as she opened the door and tried to follow her inside.

The woman stopped, turned around, and squinted at me.

"Who are you?" she asked.

I wasn't expecting that.

"Um ... I'm ..." The truth—that I was R. Klausenhook's stepdaughter—would have probably gotten me in. But I didn't want to leave a recognizable trail. "I'm ... the assistant stage manager."

She glared at me. "That's impossible."

"Why?" I asked, trying to sound confident.

"Because *I'm* the assistant stage manager." Then she stepped all the way inside the building and, pointedly, slammed the door in my face.

Shoot.

I walked back over to my spot on the brick wall next to the theater and went back to waiting. This time, though, I was more nervous. What if I couldn't get inside? Or what if the woman caught me once I *was* in the theater and reported me? What if I was arrested? What if the police—

The door was opening.

But this time from the inside.

I darted forward and held it just as a sweaty, overweight man in overalls exited, pushing a cart full of two-by-fours.

He looked at me, surprised. "Thank you, miss."

I smiled. "No problem." Then the next sentence just popped out of my mouth. "Everyone in a production should help everyone else out, right?"

He looked confused. "You're in the production?"

I looked at him, temporarily flummoxed. Then something amazing happened. Without even deciding to, I became R. I lifted my chin. I flared my nostrils. I batted my lashes. I looked simultaneously contemptuous and sympathetic.

"Darling," I said to the man, "I'm the *star*."

He blinked. "Oh. Sorry."

I waved my hands in the air, picturing myself with long, purple fingernails. "No matter," I said airily.

Then I stepped inside the darkened theater.

The door slammed behind me.

I took a deep breath, taking in the smell of must and sawdust. Then I lowered my head and walked down the first hallway I saw.

I had to get to the dressing rooms without anyone noticing me.

Luckily, it seemed like almost no one was there. I could hear a few people moving around scenery onstage, but otherwise the theater was silent. I tiptoed down the hallway, checking the sign on every door: PROP ROOM. BOILER ROOM. COSTUME CLOSET.

That last one made me catch my breath. Reena would love me forever if I brought her back some kind of 1920s boa. And a pair of cool Victorian boots for Molly . . .

I made myself keep walking.

BATHROOM. TECHNICAL SUPPLIES. DRESSING ROOM.

I came to a halt.

DRESSING ROOM. Did all the actors share a single dressing room? It hadn't occurred to me. If that was true, my plan was in trouble. I took a few steps down the hallway just in case, and peeked at the sign on the next door:

DRESSING ROOM-KLAUSENHOOK.

Perfect. Of course R. would demand her own dressing room. How could I have expected anything less of her?

I pressed my ear to the door, and holding my breath, listened for any sounds inside.

Nothing.

I reached into my jacket and felt for the little pouch I'd been storing inside my pocket. That morning I'd gone to my old favorite toy store in Brooklyn Heights and walked straight back to the jokes-and-gags section. There it was, in its pink package with a cartoon on it of a man scratching himself wildly, his eyes bugging out in pain.

FRANKIE'S EXTRA-POWERFUL SUPER LONG-LASTING ITCHING POWDER.

I'd never bought it as a kid, just stared at it with curious longing. But now Frankie's itching powder was going to serve a real purpose in my life.

It was going to ruin R.'s career.

I was going to sneak into her dressing room and pour it in her shoes. In her dress. In her pantyhose. In the Russian shawl she'd been wearing around the house so as not to "break character."

There was no way that R. was going to be able to turn in the kind of awe-inspiring, life-changing, breathtaking performance that all the theater critics in all the New York newspapers had been anticipating. Not if her skin was on fire. That was the definition of breaking character. And—as she'd made a point of telling me and Dad five times over breakfast—everyone who was anyone was going to be at opening night. The reviews would come out the next morning.

I opened the door and stepped into the dressing room.

And there she was.

Sitting in front of the dressing room mirror on a stool. Hunched over, wrapped in her shawl.

Crying.

My jaw dropped. I stood there, trying to decide whether or not I should just run out of the room without offering an explanation.

R. slowly lifted her head up and stared at me, mascara streaks running down her face. "Alice?" she croaked.

I nodded.

"You came," she wept. "You came to see me. That's so nice."

She put her head in her hands and cried even harder.

I took a tiny step toward her. "What's—" I started to say.

"Your father called and told you?" she asked through her sobs.

"I . . ."

"I just . . . I can't imagine going on tonight. I can't do it. I can't go on." Her shoulders started shaking.

What was happening? I was living in some kind of alternate universe. One in which R. wanted to sabotage her own career.

"Why can't you go on?" I asked.

She looked at me indignantly, even more makeup started to drip off her eyelashes and eyelids. "Would you have been able to go onstage and play Ranevskaya right after your mother died?"

My mouth opened and then closed.

R.'s mother had died?

I'd seen R. at lunch and everything had seemed just fine.

"Um," I said. And then after a pause: "No. No, I wouldn't have."

R. flung herself onto the dressing room cabinet and moaned. Weirdly enough, she was actually reminding me of a real person for the first time in the entire year I'd known her.

"I'm so sorry," I said softly. "I know how awful it feels."

"They called twenty minutes ago," she sobbed. "A heart attack. She was perfectly . . . the last time I talked to her she seemed fine."

"Where does—where did she live?" I asked.

"Cleveland, Ohio."

I was shocked. "That's where you're from?"

She nodded. I'd had no idea. I had always just assumed

that R. was born and raised in Manhattan. Or at least Paris. Or London. Maybe—although it was a stretch—Madrid.

Definitely not Cleveland.

I pulled up a stool and sat down next to her. After a second, I reached out and touched her shoulder. She didn't pull away, so I started stroking it, making a small circle with the tips of my fingers. Just like my mom used to do when I was a kid.

She began breathing in big, heaving gulps.

Watching her, it was all coming back to me. The call from the hospital in the middle of the night. Dad and I had stayed there until midnight and then took a cab back to the house to get a few hours of sleep before we went back to visit Mom in the morning. And then the phone rang at 4:00 AM, and from my bed I had heard Dad let out a strange yell . . . a totally new and unfamiliar sound. . . .

Tears were starting to spring into my eyes. I tried to blink them back.

"Listen," I told R. firmly. "You have to go on tonight."

She shook her head. "I can't."

"Do you have an understudy?"

"No." She sniffed. "This show is all about my performance."

Of course.

"Just get through it," I said helplessly.

"I can't. I'm not in character. I feel . . ." She burst into a fresh round of choking sobs. "I feel like I'm five years old."

I kept rubbing her shoulder, unsure of what to say or do next. "I'm sorry, R. I understand what it's like, and it's horrible."

She nodded. "I know you do," she murmured.

I was shocked. There was no sarcasm in her tone, no irony. We'd just communicated for the first time.

"Oh, God," she bawled. "I'm going to ruin my career. I can't do it. I can't go on."

I sighed. "Listen. Two days after my mom died I had an English final. And I was sure I couldn't do it. I couldn't even get out of bed or speak to anyone. But I knew that if I missed the final, I'd have to make it up a week later. And I probably wasn't going to be feeling any better a week later. I was maybe gonna be feeling worse, because in a week my mom would still be dead, and the realization would just be sinking in even more. Then I realized that if I didn't take the test at all, I wouldn't be able to finish eighth grade."

She blinked at me through her tear-encrusted eyelashes. "What did you do?"

"I woke up the morning of the test and I thought: I can't do this. There is no way I can get out of bed and take a shower and put on my clothes and go to school. It is physically impossible."

R. stared at me, her mouth open, a small droplet of snot hanging from the tip of her nose. "And?"

"And then I got out of bed and put on my clothes and went to school and took the test." I started to giggle, remembering. "I refused to take a shower, though. I don't know why. Somehow taking a shower still seemed impossible."

R. cracked a tiny smile. "That makes sense."

We were silent for a while.

"I can't believe you did that," she said finally. "I can't believe you took an English test right after your mother died."

"I got a C-minus," I admitted.

She shook her head. "It doesn't matter. It's still a miracle."

I thought about it. "Well, you know what? I was just performing. That morning I was just pretending to be someone whose mother hadn't just died."

R. nodded. "You took your fate into your own hands."

I stared at her. Reclaiming your life. Taking your fate into your own hands. That was the goal of the Poison Apples.

But had I *already* reclaimed my own life without even realizing it?

R. stood up shakily and pulled the shawl around her shoulders. She faced the dressing mirror and slowly began wiping the makeup stains off her face. "I'll go to Cleveland on Monday," she said softly. "That's when we have the day off."

I stood up, too. "Good for you, R."

She turned and faced me. Her green eyes pierced into mine. "Thank you, Alice."

"You don't have to thank me."

She bit her lip. "Listen. I'm sorry if I . . ."

I held my breath. I'd never even heard the words *I'm sorry* come out of R.'s mouth before. What was she going to apologize for? Sending me off to boarding school? Selling the brownstone? Making me a flower girl instead of a bridesmaid? Screaming at me at least once an hour? Trying in every way possible to ruin my life?

After a long pause, she shook her head. "Never mind."

Then she turned back to the mirror and started pulling her hair back with her hands.

I tried to look like I didn't care. "Okay," I said, taking a step back toward the dressing room door, "I'm gonna go now."

She nodded, not taking her eyes off her own reflection. "I'll see you after the show."

"Cool."

I opened the door and was about to leave when she called after me: "Alice?"

I whirled around. Maybe the apology was coming after all.

She was looking at me curiously, her head tilted, her hands on her hips. "How did you get here ten minutes after I called your father and told him about my mother?"

I shrugged helplessly.

"The commute from the Upper West Side is at least twenty minutes," she said.

"Um . . ." I said.

We looked at each other.

"It was a Thanksgiving miracle," I blurted out. Then I turned and ran as fast as I could, down the hallway, out the stage door, and onto the crowded, smelly street.

SEVEN

Reena

It was our old house. Or at least it looked like our old house, from the outside. Same marble white mansion, same green lawn, same puny dying palm tree next the driveway that Pradeep had always refused to let us chop down. (He had a tendency to get attached to random nonhuman objects and attribute them with human traits. "That tree is a good tree!" he would scream at us. "It knows right from wrong!")

So when Dad pulled up to the house after picking us up from the airport in his brand-new red Audi, I was relieved to see that the tree (or "Palmy," as Pradeep was fond of calling it when he was younger) was still there. I wasn't sure how Pradeep would've reacted if they'd chopped it down.

And then we stepped inside.

It's hard to describe what we encountered in the foyer of what used to be our normal, all-American home. I guess it was the twenty-foot-tall wooden statue of Vishnu that caught my attention first. And I only found out it was Vishnu because I gasped and said, "What is *that*?"

"Vishnu," Shanti said, gliding out of the kitchen and smiling at us. "Don't you recognize Vishnu? He's one of the most famous Hindu gods."

I shook my head. "I don't know any Hindu gods."

Pradeep tugged at my sleeve and pointed. "Forget Vishnu. Look at that."

There was a huge golden fountain right next to the entrance to the living room, with a gigantic leaping golden fish spitting an arc of water out of its mouth.

I shook my head in disbelief.

"And *that*." Pradeep pointed to the right. There was a tapestry hanging on the wall next to the staircase. Set against a forest background, it was an intricately embroidered picture of a blue man intertwined with a red woman.

"Oh, my God!" Pradeep shouted. "Are they having sex?!"

Dad, who was standing behind us, placed his hands on our shoulders. "Okay, you two. Calm down. The house is decorated differently now. No reason to go crazy."

"I repeat the question," Pradeep said, not taking his eyes off the tapestry. "Are they having—"

"ENOUGH!" Dad boomed.

We fell silent.

I gazed around the foyer, then walked over and peeked into the living room. Then I opened the kitchen door, looked inside, swallowed a gasp, and walked back into the foyer.

"Wow," I said to Dad and Shanti. "It's very . . ."

"Different!" she said cheerfully.

I nodded. "Also . . . Indian. It's very Indian."

Dad shot me a warning glance.

"Yep," Pradeep piped up. "It's, like, more Indian than it was when four Indian people were living here."

"Pradeep...," Dad said.

"Which makes me think," Pradeep said thoughtfully, "is it actually Indian at all? Or is it just a white person's version of—"

"OKAY!" Dad yelled. "I'm taking your bags upstairs! Follow me!"

We followed him. Reluctantly.

"Rash!" Shanti called up after us. "Don't forget! The landscapers are coming this afternoon!"

We turned around at the landing and peered down at her.

"Why are the landscapers coming?" Pradeep asked suspiciously.

"Forget it," Dad said.

But Shanti didn't hear him. "To cut down that tree!" she yelled gaily up to us. "The horrible little one next to the driveway!"

I can't even really put into words the look that passed across my brother's face.

But I will never forget it.

"Why don't you come see me tonight?" My mother's voice was buzzing plaintively in my ear. Sort of like a mosquito.

I transferred my cell phone from one side of my face to the other and propped my legs up on the windowsill. I was sitting in my bedroom, which—it was hard to believe—looked pretty much the same as it did before.

Except for a tiny decal of a many-armed Hindu goddess stuck onto the windowpane.

But I was okay with that.

"I'll come visit you and Pria tomorrow, Mommy, okay?"

"I don't understand. I don't understand why your father and . . ." Her voice shook. ". . . and That Woman get to see you first."

I sighed. "You don't understand. I have something I have to do here tonight."

"What?"

"I can't tell you."

"Why?"

She sighed. "I sold the flat-screen TV. Did I already tell you that?"

"Yes." My mother had taken up the habit of calling me and telling me which luxury items she was being forced to sell, post-divorce. So far she'd mourned the loss of her Manolo Blahnik high heels, her television, her visits to her favorite five-hundred-dollar-an-hour hairdresser, and her jet skis. (There was no way she was giving up her Porsche or her personal trainer or her monthly visit to the Golden Door Spa. Or the lawyer she'd hired to sue my father within an inch of his life.)

"So what are you doing tonight? Are you doing something fun with That Woman?"

"No. They're not even home. They went to some kind of fund-raiser." The second I said it I realized it was a mistake.

My mother gasped in indignation. "You're choosing to be home alone tonight when your poor mother is—"

Without even thinking, I pressed End on my cell phone and snapped it shut.

Then I stared at it, horrified. I'd never hung up on my mother before.

She was going to kill me when she finally did see me on Thanksgiving. But I had no choice. This was the one night Dad and Shanti Shruti were guaranteed to be out of the house. And Pradeep was hanging out at a friend's house down the street.

I had a mission to accomplish.

And I had to do it all by myself.

I crept out of my bedroom and into the hallway.

"Hello?" I called out.

I wanted to make sure no one was home.

"HELLO?"

Still no answer.

I walked down the hallway, past some kind of wrathful wooden mask hanging on the wall, and then I descended the staircase.

I had to find the penguin.

Dad and Shanti Shruti had both pointedly avoided the subject when showing us around the house, and I didn't want to ask, in case they got suspicious.

But there was a million-dollar arctic terrarium somewhere inside the mansion. And I was going to find it.

First I walked around the kitchen. Besides the fifty new paintings hanging on the wall (illustrations from the great Indian epic, the *Ramayana*, Shanti had informed me), everything was the same. Then I walked around the living room. Then the dining room. Then the foyer. Then Dad's study (I almost puked when I saw the framed picture of Shanti in her pink sari on his desk). Then I ran back upstairs and, starting to get frustrated, checked everyone's bedroom.

Nothing.

Where was Ganesh the penguin?

I walked back inside my bedroom and, exhausted, collapsed on my bed and stared out the window. I'd always loved the view out my bedroom window. Our house was on top of a small hill, and my window faced the sloping green of the backyard. In the nighttime, everything was black except for a few twinkling lights in the distance that made up the small cluster of skyscrapers in downtown LA.

But this time there was something different.

A small white light was pulsing in the darkness of the backyard.

I sat up and stared at the source of it.

It looked like a little barn, with a single, brightly lit-up window.

I leapt out of bed, ran downstairs, through the kitchen, out the back door, and stood in front of the small building.

I reached out and opened the metal door in front of me. It made a suctioned slurp, like the sound of a refrigerator opening. Then a gust of freezing-cold air blasted my face.

Bingo.

I shielded my face, hugged my sweatshirt close to my body, and walked inside. The door shut behind me.

What I saw once I was in nearly took my breath away.

It was like I was back on top of Mount McKinsey. In the middle of Beverly Hills.

Snow crunched under my feet. Snowdrifts lay piled against the walls. A bright white light shone down from the ceiling, so it suddenly seemed like midday.

There was even a small blue pool of half-iced-over water in the center of the room.

And then I saw Ganesh himself. Paddling slowly through

the miniature lake. Leaping out of the water and skidding onto his stomach against the snow.

I yelped in delight and clapped my hands. "You are so cute!" I exclaimed.

He looked my way, terrified, and flapped away behind a snowdrift.

I tiptoed after him, crooning, "Good Ganesh, good Ganesh." I peeked around the snowdrift, and he angrily waddled away again.

If I could just pick him up—and then make sure he didn't squirm his wet little penguin body out of my grasp—I could get him out of his little habitat and then just...leave him somewhere. The side of a highway? Next to the ocean? No. That would be too cruel. I would take my old childhood bicycle out of the garage, put Ganesh in the basket, and then deposit him at the gates of the Los Angeles Zoo.

Then Shanti Shruti would learn her lesson.

"Ganeshy," I murmured. "Come here, Ganeshy."

He was standing by the pool again. I leapt forward, my arms outstretched. He jumped into the water. I groaned and watched as he swam in anxious little circles.

I reached into the water and winced. It was, as I should've expected, painfully cold. I trailed him in the water with my hands for a few seconds, and then, gritting my teeth, grabbed his slippery little body and lifted it out of the water.

He writhed and squawked and almost successfully slid of out of my grasp, but I held on tight.

"Shh," I said, and brought his soaking-wet penguin body to my chest. "Shh."

He was still squirming.

For some reason I was starting to feel miserable. I wasn't sure why. *Maybe,* a little voice inside me said, *it's because you're kidnapping a penguin. What could be more depressing and pathetic?*

I grunted and made my way toward the door while Ganesh attempted to launch himself out of my arms. I couldn't wait to get out of there and just get the deed over with. I put my free hand on the metal doorknob and turned it to the right.

Or tried to turn it to the right.

It didn't budge.

I turned it to the left.

Still nothing.

"Oh, no," I breathed. "Please, God, no."

I tried pulling the door. I tried pushing the door. Ganesh squealed feebly and then attempted to peck me through my sweatshirt.

"NO!" I yelled, kicking the door.

Still nothing.

In one final burst of strength, Ganesh kicked his little penguin feet and flapped his little penguin arms and pushed his way out of my arms. He landed on the ground with a thump and skidded away into the outer regions of the room.

"I don't care," I shouted after him. "We're screwed anyway!"

I tried pushing and turning the doorknob at the same time. I tried pulling and turning it at the same time.

It was hopeless. I was locked inside.

I slid down along the ice-covered wall and sat down in a pile of snow, shaking. I was too cold to even start crying.

I'd left my cell phone inside my bedroom.

I was going to freeze to death unless someone came home

in the next two hours and, seeing I was gone, thought to look for me in . . . Ganesh's terrarium.

That was *so* not going to happen.

Oh, my God, I realized. *I'm going to die. I'm going to die because of Revenge Plot Number Two. I'm going to die because I tried to steal a penguin to get some kind of control over my life. Instead I locked myself inside a freezer. Now I'm not even going to live to age sixteen.*

Thoughts of my life, my beautiful life, flashed through my mind. The chapel on top of the hill at Putnam Mount McKinsey. The times Alice and I stood at the window of our dorm room and watched the sun set across the highway. Molly lecturing us on word derivations at the lunch table. David Newman and his gorgeous flashing eyes. Pradeep and the way he could always make me laugh, even when I was feeling horrible. My mother and the way she loved me, fiercely, so I never felt like a little piece of her wasn't with me. My crazy aunt Pria. Why hadn't I gone to see them tonight? Regret started welling up in my stomach. Why didn't I appreciate everything while it had lasted? A great brother. A great mother. Best friends. And even though things were terrible with my dad, at least he was alive. After all, Alice only had one parent.

I had the urge to cry again, but my tear ducts were frozen. My body was beginning to convulse and shake uncontrollably. I held my hands out in front of me and looked at my fingers. They were starting to turn purple.

Please, I prayed to the fluorescent white lights on the ceiling, *someone rescue me. I promise to start appreciating everyone in my life. I will be nicer to my mother. I will be nicer to the Putnam Mount McKinsey cafeteria ladies. I will be nicer to the nerdy kids who hit each other with foam swords on the student union green.*

267

I'll even be nicer to the mean popular kids like Jamie Vanderheep and Rebecca Saperstein and Jules Squarebrigs-Farroway and, okay, even Kristen Diamond, I will be nicer to Kristen Diamond, and, okay . . . I will try to be nicer to Shanti Shruti. I will never attempt to steal her stupid penguin again. I will—

The door flew open.

"YOU ARE SUCH AN IDIOT, REEN," someone yelled.

I looked up. My older brother was standing in the doorway in a pair of basketball shorts, staring at me with utter disgust.

We looked at each other for a long time.

"Hi," I finally managed to whisper.

"I repeat," he said. "You. Are. Such. An. Idiot."

"How did you find me?" I asked in a small voice.

But before he could even answer, I'd already thrown my arms around his legs and was sobbing hysterically onto his stained Adidas sneakers.

Apparently my tear ducts weren't frozen after all.

EIGHT

Molly

We all sat in silence for a while, stunned.

"Kristen?" asked Alice. "It was *Kristen*?"

Reena nodded and passed me the thermos of hot cocoa. "Yup. She was taking her own personal revenge, I guess. I must have really hurt her feelings on top of Mount McKinsey."

"What I don't understand," I said, "is why she thought Pradeep would rat you out."

Reena shrugged. "I think the girl doesn't understand the concept of loyalty."

"So, she was hiding in the room the whole time while we were coming up with the Revenge Plan?"

"Yup."

I shivered. It was the last day of November, and we'd just gotten back from vacation. It had made sense to call a meeting immediately, but the roof of Middleton was *freezing*.

"That girl is truly pathetic," said Alice, shaking her head.

"You know what's even more pathetic?" I said. "The fact

that I have to spend all of Christmas vacation taking care of Sandie and Randie and Spencer all by myself. My dad and Candy are going to Aruba. Can you believe it?"

Reena's jaw dropped. "You're kidding me. When did they break the news to you?"

"The second I was back inside the house in dry clothes. And they're not paying me a cent for the whole three weeks. Apparently, Candy wants to go on one last vacation before it's too late in her pregnancy. And she started bringing up how much help she could use around the house again."

"Wow," said Alice. "So, Candy was nice to you for—"

"All of three minutes," I finished.

"Yeah. R. was nice to me for like three *seconds* that afternoon."

We sighed.

"So, I guess this is the end," Reena said quietly. "No more Poison Apples."

"That's it?" I asked. "We're disbanding?"

"Wait a second," said Alice. "Just because our revenge plots failed? That doesn't mean the Poison Apples have to disband."

"Yeah, but then what good are we?" asked Reena.

"I thought the point of the apple is that we want to reclaim it," Alice said. "I mean, why do the Poison Apples have to be about getting back at people?"

"Well, we are called the *Poison* Apples," I pointed out.

"Yeah, but it's the evil stepmother who gives Snow White the apple, not the other way around. Maybe we can just be about reinventing the apple. Making it ours. We don't have to be evil in return. After all, two wrongs don't make a—"

"DON'T SAY IT!" I shrieked.

She grinned. "Fine. Sorry."

Reena stared pensively out at the night sky. "Yeah, I guess we do have a lot to be thankful for," she said. "I mean, we live in this beautiful place. We have each other. We—"

"Have to spend all of Christmas vacation taking care of our stepsisters," I moaned.

Reena looked at me, confused. "*That's* what you're upset about? I thought you'd be . . ." Her voice trailed off uncertainly.

I lowered my head. I knew what she was going to say. The problem was, I was just in denial when it came to thinking about my mom. No one had heard anything from her. Occasionally, I wondered if she were dead. Then the thought was too much to take and I just forced myself to focus on other things.

Alice came up to me and put her arm around my shoulder. "I have an idea," she whispered in my ear. "I *definitely* don't want to stay with my dad and R. for Christmas. Why don't I come back to North Forest with you and help out?"

I looked at her, amazed. "You would do that for me? What about Jamal? Weren't you guys gonna hang out over Christmas?"

"Well, you're just as important to me as he is. And he can come visit us, anyway."

I buried her face in her shoulder. "You're the best, Bingley-Beckerman."

"Hey," Reena barked. "What about me?"

We looked at her.

"You," I said finally, "are the world's worst penguin-napper."

She started laughing. "Well," she admitted, "even if the door hadn't locked behind me, that little sucker was much, much tougher than I expected."

Alice stepped back and frowned. "Wait a second. I just

271

thought of something. If Kristen was listening to that whole conversation on top of Mount McKinsey, then doesn't she know that we meet on the—"

Suddenly, the little door that opened onto the roof flew open.

We all gasped.

A few seconds later, Agnes's pale, tired-looking face peeked over the edge.

"Unbelievable," she drawled monotonously.

"Please, Agnes," Reena begged, "don't report us to Headmaster Oates."

Agnes rolled her eyes. "Oh, please. You think I would do that? Then I would get in trouble for not knowing about this sooner."

"Thank you, Agnes," I said. "You're the best. You're—"

"Not so fast," she told me. "Don't think you guys are going to get off scot-free. All three of you are going to be doing my laundry for the next month."

We groaned.

"And," she added, grinning maliciously, "every night I expect someone to bring dinner up to my room."

"Oh, God," whispered Alice.

"Sweet dreams," Agnes said. "Be in your rooms in the next five minutes or I will personally murder you."

And she disappeared back down into stairwell.

"Well," said Reena finally. "Goes to show. There are evil stepmothers everywhere."

A few minutes later, I was tiptoeing through the darkness of my dorm room back to my bed. I groped around, then felt

272

something on my pillow, where Kristen usually left my mail (when I got any at all). I held it in my hands. It felt like some kind of card.

I reached under my covers and pulled out my little flashlight. I crawled under my covers, pulled them over my head, and turned the flashlight on, squinting until my eyes adjusted.

It was a postcard.

And the handwriting was unmistakable.

It was from my mother.

My dear Molly, she'd scrawled. *I'm writing to let you know I'm okay. Don't tell anyone you got this. I am finding a new life. You and I will see each other at some point. Much love, Mom*

On the front of the postcard was a picture of the Grand Canyon. The word *Arizona* was printed across it in big red letters.

At first I felt incredible relief. My mom was alive. She was okay.

But a few seconds later, I was infuriated. We would see each other at "some point"? Didn't I have anyone I could rely on?

And then I realized I did.

I had two best friends.

My life was definitely a mess. But I wasn't alone.

It was a funny thing. I'd fantasized about Putnam Mount McKinsey for years, but it was always somehow related to boys in pink shirts reading Emily Dickinson. I definitely hadn't met any of them in the past three months. (Except for Pradeep Paruchuri, who was about as interested in me as Candy Lamb was in dictionaries.)

What had I gotten from boarding school was entirely unexpected: a new family.

Feeling a kind of bittersweet contentment, I pulled my blanket over my head and tried to focus on falling asleep.

And that's when I heard Kristen crying.

At first I couldn't believe it. It actually seemed . . . impossible. But then I listened harder. There were definitely muffled sobs coming from her bed.

Good, I thought triumphantly. *Whatever she's crying about, she probably deserves it.*

But a few minutes later, I found myself whispering: "Kristen?"

The crying stopped for a few seconds, then continued.

"Kristen."

She barely choked out her reply. "What?"

"What's wrong?"

A huge, honking sniffle. "Why do *you* care?"

"Um . . ." Why *did* I care? "I'm curious, that's all. You don't have to tell me."

"You hate me," she cried.

"I don't hate you." That was true. I didn't like her, but I didn't hate her. She'd made my first month at PMM hell, but that was the least of my problems.

There was a long silence, and then, from underneath her covers, I could hear her, just barely audible: "My parents are getting divorced."

I shot up in bed. "You're kidding."

A fresh round of sobs. "No," she wailed. "I'm not."

"Oh, my God. Kristen. I'm so sorry."

I was stunned. If there was anyone who seemed like she had a perfect life, it was Kristen Diamond. The wall above her bed was covered in glossy pictures of her and her father and mother, all of them unbelievably good-looking, leaning

274

against Porsches and playing tennis and canoeing down rivers and waving from the windows of villas in Tuscany.

Her crying started to peter out. "I just can't believe it," she whispered. "They told me on Thanksgiving. On *Thanksgiving Day*. And my mom is . . . oh, God. My mom is already dating her *golf* instructor. And they're acting like they're in love or something. Can you believe that?"

"Yes," I said. "I can. Family dysfunction never fails to shock me with how dysfunctional it is."

I held my breath. After a long pause, Kristen giggled.

Thank God.

The two of us lay there in the dark. After a few seconds she asked, "Molly?"

"Yeah?"

"Um . . . I'm sorry."

I wasn't exactly sure what she was apologizing for. It could've been about a million different things.

"I've, um, had a really hard semester," Kristen said quietly.

"Yeah," I said. "Me, too."

"I know."

"Well," I said after a while, "thanks for apologizing."

She laughed, still sniffling a little. "You're welcome."

I pulled the covers over my head.

It was the weirdest thing.

Nobody was ever who she seemed to be. There was something very beautiful about that.

I pulled the covers off my head.

"Kristen," I said.

"Yeah?"

"Can I give you one piece of advice? For whatever happens with your parents during and after the divorce?"

"Sure."

"You are not them."

There was a long pause.

"I think I understand," she said.

"Just for the future," I said. "Remember it. It'll make you a lot happier. Your life is your life. Your fate is your fate."

"Okay," she said. "Thanks."

"You are not them," I repeated.

Then, a few minutes later, just as my eyes were starting to close, something occurred to me.

"Four apples instead of three," I muttered. "Would it work?"

"Did you say something?" asked Kristen.

And did evil *stepfathers* count? I would have to consult with Alice and Reena about that at the next meeting.

"Forget it, Kristen," I said. "I'll tell you later."

And I dropped off to sleep.

Acknowledgments

Many, many thanks to:

Jean Feiwel, who continues to surprise me with her intelligence, good humor, and uncanny knack for story and character.

Rich Deas, creative director/genius.

Melissa Flashman, phenomenal agent and dear friend.

RR, without whom my lifestyle is not bearable.

And B, my teammate and oldest friend. I hope we have meltdowns in front of each other for many, many years to come.